He was wounded in many ways, she thought

Sebastian had come back to Valley Ridge with visible scars. He definitely had more hurdles to overcome, and watching Hank decline would probably be the hardest thing he'd ever done. But Lily was sure he'd come out stronger on the other side.

She wished she felt as if she would.

What she wanted to say was *I'll be here for you as long as you'll let me.* But the truth of the matter was, she didn't know how to say those words.

Dear Reader,

Sebastian and Lily were part of Sophie and Colton's wedding party in *You Are Invited…* (Harlequin Superromance, April 2013). To say Sebastian and Lily didn't exactly hit it off would be an understatement. I couldn't wait to get to their story and see how it all worked out.

Sebastian is a prickly ex-marine. He's come home, although the worst of his injuries are the kind you can't see. He doesn't just want to find everything in Valley Ridge the same...he *needs* it to be. But life doesn't always happen that way and Sebastian has to adjust. Part of that adjustment is Lily, whose interference in Seb's family raises his ire at first, but then…

Families are made of love, not DNA. That's a theme that weaves through all the books in this A Valley Ridge Wedding trilogy. I believe every writer has themes she or he explores again and again. Family and friendship would certainly be two of mine. The wonderful thing about them is that there are so many ways to approach them, because neither is ever exactly the same. But there is one commonality...love. And love might just be what Lily finds with the cantankerous former marine Sebastian.

Happy reading,

Holly Jacobs

April Showers

HOLLY JACOBS

ISBN-13: 978-0-373-71852-8

APRIL SHOWERS

This edition published by arrangement with Harlequin Books S.A.

For questions and comments about the quality of this book, please contact us at CustomerService@Harlequin.com.

Printed in U.S.A.

ABOUT THE AUTHOR

In 2000, Holly Jacobs sold her first book to Harlequin Books. She's since sold more than twenty-five novels to the publisher. Her romances have won numerous awards and made the Waldenbooks bestseller list. In 2005, Holly won a prestigious Career Achievement Award from *RT Book Reviews.* In her nonwriting life, Holly is married to a police captain, and together they have four children. Visit Holly at www.hollyjacobs.com, or you can snail-mail her at P.O. Box 11102, Erie, PA 16514-1102.

Books by Holly Jacobs

HARLEQUIN SUPERROMANCE

1511—SAME TIME NEXT SUMMER
1601—UNEXPECTED GIFTS
1615—A ONE-OF-A-KIND FAMILY
1677—HOMECOMING DAY
1733—A FATHER'S NAME
1846—YOU ARE INVITED...*

HARLEQUIN AMERICAN ROMANCE

1232—ONCE UPON A THANKSGIVING
1238—ONCE UPON A CHRISTMAS
1247—ONCE UPON A VALENTINE'S

HARLEQUIN EVERLASTING

THE HOUSE ON BRIAR HILL ROAD

*A Valley Ridge Wedding

Other titles by this author available in ebook format.

To Marge. It might be hard to describe our May–December friendship to others, but we don't need an explanation. I hope you know I treasure it.

And to the entire Milliron family, who had the best swings ever!

CHAPTER ONE

SEBASTIAN BENNINGTON was home.

He waited for a wave of nostalgic happiness to sweep over him as he turned off I-90 and headed toward his hometown—toward Valley Ridge, New York.

The wave never came.

No warm glow telling him that all was right in the world again because he was here. No feeling that he should never have left. No feeling that it was good that he was coming back.

No feeling at all. Nothing. Nada.

That pretty much summed up his emotions since he'd received his separation orders from the marines. Hearing that he was unfit for service hurt, but after that, it was as if everything froze and became a blank grayness.

He reached over and turned up the volume of the car's stereo, thinking maybe the music would inspire some feeling. "This is 93.9, The Wolf," a female DJ's voice announced. Sebastian flinched when his left hand tried to grip the wheel, as Lady Antebellum's plaintive song soon filled the car. Sebastian had always loved country music, and this song seemed nice enough, but it was new and evoked no particular emotion or memory.

Gray.

Sebastian had planned on driving immediately to his grandfather's diner once he arrived in town. He'd talked to Hank often on the phone, glossing over why he was delayed. He didn't share anything about the surgeries, or much at all about the injury. He'd simply said that he hurt his hand and was having trouble getting leave. He'd explain the discharge in person.

But instead of taking Park Street to the Valley Ridge Diner, where his grandfather would be this time of day, Sebastian went north toward the lake. Without thinking about it, he found himself standing at the edge of a rocky cliff, looking out over Lake Erie.

He breathed deeply and took comfort in the expanse of gray-blue water below.

When they were young, Sebastian and his best friends, Finn and Colton, came here often. There was a small path that led to the spit of rocky beach sandwiched between the lake and the cliff wall. His grandfather had hollered when he'd found out the boys had gone down there, but Sebastian only grinned as Hank lectured him about the dangers of that stretch of shore. Back then, he'd thought he was invincible. Back then, he'd thought that there was nothing he couldn't do if he tried. There was no cliff he couldn't scale, no situation he couldn't get out of.

Sebastian Bennington knew better than that now.

He knew that even if he wanted to climb down that cliff today, he probably couldn't.

He flexed his damned-near-useless left hand and winced at the sharp stab of pain. April in Western New York was still chilly, especially at the lakeshore. However, he wasn't wearing a jacket because he was particularly cold. He wore it because he was home and he'd be seeing his grandfather and friends soon. His jacket's pocket was a great place to disguise how damaged his hand was.

You should be thankful you're right-handed, a therapist had joked.

You should be thankful you're alive, his doctor had informed him.

Maybe he should be thankful to be alive, to be right-handed, to be back in Valley Ridge, New York.

But thankfulness was an emotion he couldn't manage.

Sebastian knew he should get back in his car and drive into town now. Instead, he continued to stand on the cliff's edge. He didn't ponder anything special. He didn't think any great thoughts. He just stared at the lake, his thoughts and emotions as flat and monotone as the water.

"Sebastian Bennington?" a woman asked, pulling him from his indistinct mental foray.

Sebastian turned and saw a dark-haired woman he couldn't place. He searched her features, waiting for the click of recognition, but still nothing. Valley Ridge was filled with friends and acquaintances. It was a small enough town that even if he didn't know someone, they at least looked familiar. But the woman didn't.

A stranger.

She had to be because she had the kind of look that a man would never forget. She had on some kind of flowy skirt, with a blousy top and big, chunky jewelry around her neck and wrists. And she had on dangling earrings that brushed her shoulders. But it was her hair that got him. Dark brown on the border of being black. It was long—way longer than most women wore their hair—and hanging down her back in soft waves that hinted at curls.

"Sebastian?" she repeated, staring at him with very

blue eyes. Those eyes were even more memorable than her hair.

He realized he'd been staring and nodded. "Yes? Do we know each other?"

"No, not exactly, although I know you in a way I've known very few people."

He must have looked puzzled because she laughed. The expression seemed at home on her face, as if that upturned curve of her lips and the crinkling of her eyes were their default positions.

"Sorry, how do you know me?"

She struck a pose similar to that statue his grandfather liked, *The Thinker.* Her hand was under her chin and she was serious for a split second, then smiled again, as if whatever thought she'd had was a pleasant one. "Well, I know that your grandfather served you brussels sprouts when you were young and you dropped them on the floor in hopes your dog would eat them for you. Problem was, Chance didn't like brussels sprouts, either. Of course, I've had Hank's brussels sprouts and there's really nothing to recommend the vegetable the way he prepares them. I mean, he's a good cook, but he's never really had to perfect vegetables at the diner, has he?" She punctuated each item with more laughter and he was sure he was right—this was a woman who laughed a lot.

"Who are you?" Sebastian asked.

This didn't invoke any laughter, but her smile lingered. The crinkling around her very blue eyes wasn't quite as pronounced, though it was still there. Laugh lines. He'd never understood why they were called that until this minute. They weren't a sign of aging, as he'd always imagined, at least, not on this woman. On her, they were a sign of a happy disposition.

He wished he could work his way up to feeling happy…to feeling something.

On the back of that thought came the awareness that if he mentioned those laugh lines, the woman wouldn't thank him for it. Not that he would mention it. He might not know a lot about the female gender, but he was pretty sure most women didn't want to hear they had lines of any type.

The woman extended her hand. There was a zing of awareness as they touched, and he realized it had been a long time since he'd been this attracted to a woman. And that little zing sent a ripple through the blandness he'd been living with for a long time.

"Sorry," she said as she shook his hand. "I'm Lily. Lily Paul. Hank's tenant and—"

He pulled his hand away, disregarding any attraction that he imagined he'd felt. He knew who this was, and he was absolutely not attracted to her. As a matter of fact, he felt an immediate surge of another emotion. Annoyance. Not that he'd thank her for that, either.

"You're her," he said.

"I am." She didn't seem to notice that he was less than thrilled to be meeting her, just as she didn't seem to notice he wouldn't appreciate a stranger calling him and reading him the riot act on how he treated his grandfather. Telling him he needed to get home. Telling him that Hank needed him.

"What are you doing out here?" he asked.

He knew he'd meet this Lily eventually, but he wouldn't have guessed that she'd be the first person he'd see upon his return to Valley Ridge.

"We're having Sophie's shower at the Nieses' cottage. I spotted you and figured I should come over and introduce myself."

"How?" he asked.

She looked confused now, although not unhappy. "*How* what?"

"How did you know some stranger on the cliffs was me—Hank's grandson?"

"Oh, that *how.* That's easy. Hank has a wall of your photos. I've seen you almost every day since I moved here. I'm especially fond of the one of you in your dress blues. Sophie says you're going to wear them for the wedding. I can't wait to see you in them in person."

He flinched as she mentioned the uniform he'd given up. He didn't want to wear it to the wedding, but he wasn't sure how to tell Colton that, so he was probably stuck, even though he'd feel like a fraud putting it on. She couldn't have known that she'd induced yet another feeling. Sebastian found himself wishing for the grayness that had been his norm.

The woman continued, "But I think I'd have recognized you even if I hadn't seen the pictures. Hank loves you and has missed you, so he's talked—"

The woman—Lily—was making Sebastian feel uncomfortable. He didn't like the thought of Hank sharing stories about him with a stranger. He didn't like that this woman was looking at him as if she could see to his very core.

All that time he'd been in the hospital, he'd dealt with a shrink regularly. He hadn't liked the man analyzing him. And he'd only shared the things he wanted to share. He had control over what information was disseminated. He wasn't convinced that it had helped any, but he had the situation in hand. With this woman, however, he didn't have control at all over what she knew about him or what things Hank had revealed.

"Speaking of Hank, I'm on my way to see him. I only stopped here—" Wait. He didn't owe this woman an explanation for being here.

When he abruptly became silent, she continued, "I'm so glad you're home. I need your help with Hank. He had a doctor's appointment scheduled the other day, but he skipped it. He claimed he forgot, but this time there was none of the confusion I mentioned over the phone. He doesn't want to hear a doctor's official diagnosis. I've rescheduled the appointment, but unfortunately, it's not for another three weeks and—"

"No." Sebastian didn't have to know this woman to know what she was talking about. She'd talked to him already. And she was wrong.

Hank had always been scatterbrained, but that didn't mean he had Alzheimer's or dementia like this woman claimed he did. Forgetting a few things only meant Hank was who Hank had always been, multiplied by a few more years. And right now, Sebastian found the thought of that comforting.

"If my grandfather, who is in his eighties, by the way, doesn't want to go to the doctor's, if he doesn't think he needs one, then that's that. You weren't asked to schedule appointments for him or make a diagnosis." He realized he was talking with his hands in motion, an old habit he was trying to break, and until lately, his left hand had been in so much pain he hadn't slipped. But maybe it was a sign he was getting better, or it was a sign this woman was annoying him more than anything, because he caught himself using his left hand.

And he saw that Lily had noticed it. She took a step backward. He didn't blame her. The hand was a mass of angry scars. The doctor said they'd fade in time and no one would pay attention to them, but that time hadn't come yet.

"But he does need to see a doctor," she insisted quietly. "When you're with him—"

"Ma'am, I want to be clear. I know that you're my grandfather's tenant, and I know he seems to like you." That was an understatement. When he talked to Hank, he was all Lily-this and Lily-that. "But Hank's a grown man. I won't *make* him do anything."

Hell, he'd spent the past few months feeling boxed in, forced into places and situations he didn't want to be in. Forced into surgeries. Forced into talking with shrinks and working with physical therapists. Now he'd been forced to separate from the marines. He'd been forced to leave the job he'd worked for, the career he loved. He'd been forced to watch his unit leave for battle without him.

No, he would never subject anyone else to that kind of treatment, especially not Hank.

He would never make Hank feel as frustrated as he'd felt.

Suddenly, it occurred to him that maybe he needed his homecoming to be without too much emotion or drama. Feeling numb was preferable to feeling as frustrated as he'd felt in the hospital.

And it was damned better than the frustration this wrinkly-eyed woman was making him feel now.

Yeah, Miss Laugh Lines here didn't seem to understand the term *even keel.* She'd gone from laughing and smiling to hair-pulling aggravation in the blink of an eye.

"But he needs—" she started again.

Sebastian interrupted her. "My grandfather is an adult. I'm sure he knows what he needs better than some nosy, pushy stranger who rents a room from him." That was all this Lily Paul was—a tenant. She hadn't even lived in Valley Ridge for a full year. She didn't know what she was talking about.

"It's more than that," she said softly. "Hank and I are business partners."

That stopped him. "Business partners?"

"I bought a share in the diner. The accounts were a mess, and that's part of the reason I suspect—"

Sebastian felt something else now, but this went beyond aggravation. "So you've not only moved into my grandfather's house, but now you're buying his diner. You're pushing your way into his business and messing with his books?"

"I didn't push anything. I bought a share. A small share. Hank was behind in paying suppliers and I offered him a loan, but he wouldn't borrow money from me. He couldn't pay the bills himself. I don't think you understand the situation." She stopped, met his stare with her blue eyes unblinking and crossed her arms over her chest, setting her baubles to clinking. "Don't look at me like that. This was his idea. So I—"

Sebastian shook his head. "You can be sure I'll be looking into that. I've heard about people who prey on the elderly."

"You were telling me that Hank's an adult and doesn't need looking out for. Now you're accusing me of taking advantage of his mental infirmity. You can't have it both ways, Seb."

Sebastian bristled at the childhood nickname. This woman didn't have any right to use it. "It's Sebastian. And Hank is an adult. I'll thank you to remember that. But I'm not some grasping person out to… Well, I have no clue what you're out to do. But I'm his grandson and I love him."

"Yeah? You couldn't prove it by me. He's been saying you were on your way home for weeks, and rather than go see him at the diner, you're here? Hank needs you."

Sebastian clenched his fist in his pocket. Truth was, his hand barely made a fist, and what little there was of it sent spasms shuddering down his lower arm that served as a reminder of so many things he didn't want to deal with. This woman was one of them.

Well, he couldn't escape his injury, but there was nothing to say he had to stand here and allow himself to be browbeaten by an utter stranger.

"Now, if you'll excuse me, I need to go find my grandfather." He stalked away from this woman who looked like a gypsy, all wild and free, but sounded like a house-bound shrew.

He'd been waiting to feel some sense of homecoming—to feel any emotion—about coming back to Valley Ridge. And now he did. Annoyance and suspicion about this woman who'd wormed her way into his grandfather's home and business.

Well, he was here now, and he'd take care of things.

"'Now, if you'll excuse me, I need to go find my grandfather,'" Lily muttered as she stormed over to Sophie's shower. She wasn't much of a stormer by nature, but for Sebastian Bennington, she'd make an effort.

All tall, dark-haired Lieutenant Bennington, eyeing her with suspicion. *Pretty is as pretty does.* She wasn't sure where she'd heard that saying. Though in this case, the lieutenant might present himself in a handsome package—she'd developed quite the crush on him as she'd looked at all his photos and listened to the stories of the irrepressible rogue he'd been as a kid—after talking to him for a few minutes, she didn't find him attractive in the least.

She'd felt a momentary spurt of sympathy when she'd seen his scarred hand, but that totally evaporated quickly enough.

Lily's friend and fellow bridesmaid—maid of honor, to be precise—Mattie Keith, appeared at her shoulder when she finally walked up to the Nieses' cottage.

"You okay?" Mattie asked.

"Sure, I'm fine," Lily assured her, but she wasn't. She was angry, and since she wasn't someone prone to anger, it made her a bit sick to her stomach. She didn't like it. She prided herself on being upbeat and happy in the face of difficult circumstances. It was a skill she'd honed for years.

Even when she didn't feel like being cheerful, she found that if she faked it long enough, she'd eventually fake her way out of whatever funk she was in.

Right now, she was anything but happy or upbeat, and she doubted any amount of faking would improve upon that.

She glanced at the bridal-shower decorations, which had made her smile only a half hour ago, and hoped they would jolly her out of her Seb—pardon her, *Sebas-*

tian—Sebastian-inspired funk. She'd had to explain to Mattie that such events were always decorated in pastels. Mattie had seemed flummoxed, which made Lily wonder why that was true. She'd finally decided that it was true because pastel colors were bright and cheery, and everything about Sophie Johnston's wedding to Colton McCray should be bright and cheery. They were the most perfect couple Lily had ever seen.

Lily could look at Sophie and Colton and believe that true, everlasting love did exist.

"Who was that you were—" Mattie hesitated "—talking to?"

Lily resisted the urge to growl her response, took a long, deep breath and said, "That was Sebastian I'm-sure-Hank's-all-right Bennington."

"He's home!" Mattie looked pleased at the thought.

Well, that made one of them.

"It doesn't appear that you two hit it off," Mattie continued with what had to be the biggest understatement of all time.

Lily had been looking forward to having Hank's grandson around. She thought she'd have an ally, but instead, she had Sebastian. Hit it off? She was pretty sure her snort was audible as she said, "No. I don't think we did. In fact, no, I'm sure we absolutely did not."

"Anything I can do?" Mattie asked.

"No." She paused. "I take that back, yes. If he asks, would you assure Mr. Sebastian Bennington that I didn't come to Valley Ridge with some nefarious plan to steal his inheritance?"

"What?"

Mattie's shocked expression mollified Lily slightly. "He's mad that I bought into the diner. I tried to reassure him that I'm simply a silent minority partner." Lily sighed. "Hank needed help, and I've been pitching in when I have time. But it's taken more and more time." *And money,* she thought but didn't mention.

Hank had let so many of his bills lapse that his suppliers were threatening to stop his deliveries. She'd used her small savings to pay them all off and infuse the diner's account with what money she had left. It was enough to keep things going for a while. And yes, she'd taken a one-third ownership of the diner in exchange. But she would have been as content with loaning Hank the money. "He was forgetting to place orders and pay bills. I've taken over most of that."

"That's a lot, on top of your home visits," Mattie said.

"I work at Hank's mainly in the evenings." And frankly, her patients didn't keep her nearly busy enough to pay all her bills. Investing in the diner meant a small but steady revenue stream that she could rely on as she built her home-health-care business here in Valley Ridge.

It was more than a financial mess at the diner, though. There was the morning she found Hank sitting at the backyard picnic table wearing his pajamas and bathrobe. It was March then, and there was still snow on the ground. When she'd asked him what he was doing, he seemed to come out of his fog and tried to laugh it off, but she didn't buy it.

There was the time he'd left a pan on the stove and it had burned dry. The fire alarm had gone off and he'd been confused, unsure what to do.

And sometimes, he called her Betty. It wasn't a slip. Lily knew it was more.

She told Mattie how he was refusing to see a doctor

and how, as she wasn't related, she had no way to make him see one. Sebastian had been her last hope to get Hank some help, and now even that was gone.

The Seb stories she'd heard from Hank had painted the image of a rapscallion. Someone who frequently found himself in trouble, but due to a sense of mischief rather than any real badness. The man she'd met today hadn't been that. No aura of mischief, only a dark cloud of anger that seemed to pulsate around him. This man wasn't going to lift a finger to help her get Hank to the doctor's.

In all honesty, there could be a number of reasons for Hank's problems. Some could be fixed, some managed and for some there was nothing that could be done, but at least if he visited a doctor they'd know. Hank would have some time to make whatever arrangements he needed to. He could take control of what would happen. Having that control—that mattered. She knew that more than most.

No, she couldn't make Hank do anything, but Sebastian could. If only she could convince him.

Maybe Sebastian would see the problem when he caught up with his grandfather today?

Maybe.

But even if he did, she wondered if he'd be willing to admit his grandfather needed help.

Mattie seemed to sense Lily's thoughts and offered reassurance. Lily looked at the short blonde woman who'd become her friend. Lily was grateful to have had Mattie 24/7 when she was looking after Bridget Wallace Langley—Finn's sister and Mattie's best friend—until her passing.

Mattie hugged her, which was a surprise, but a nice

one. She tried to assure her that Sebastian would come around to what Lily was saying, and until then, it was his loss that he didn't realize the good person she was. Mattie was so kind.

"We should tidy up the place and go." Sophie's bridal shower had been a hit. Up until she'd had her run-in with Sebastian, she'd been enjoying the talking, the eating and particularly the traditional bridal-shower games. She'd felt lucky to be counted as a friend by Mattie and Sophie, and accepted as part of the community by the other women who'd attended.

"Yes, we should finish cleaning up," Mattie agreed. "But it would be a shame to waste this view."

And that was why, despite knowing each other a bit less than a year, they were friends. Mattie had sensed that Lily needed a moment to collect herself, to tamp down her anger.

Lily could do many things, but she didn't do anger well. She worked hard to avoid that emotion.

She sat next to Mattie on the picnic table, looking out at Lake Erie. The Great Lake was vast. So huge it was easy to forget it was merely a lake and not the ocean. The waves crashed into the shore, one after another. There was a fierceness to the water on this early-spring day, as if the lake was beginning to wake up from its long winter's nap.

Sometimes that was how Lily felt. She'd left home. Not simply left. She'd turned her back on it and tried to forget it. She'd gone to school and then landed a job in Buffalo. Thinking about it now, it all felt as if she'd been sleepwalking. It wasn't until she arrived in Valley Ridge, New York, to care for Bridget Langley that she started to wake up.

Bridget's brother, Finn Wallace, was a doctor she'd worked with at a hospital in Buffalo. He'd paid her to move here and care for his dying sister and had expected her to return to the hospital after Bridget died. But Lily hadn't returned.

She wouldn't return.

Here, in the small farming community beside the lake in Western New York, she'd found her true home. A sense of acceptance and freedom had settled over her here. She was working with Dr. Neil Marshall and taking care of some of his patients in their homes. Her patient roster, and thus her income, fluctuated week to week.

And yet, she was happier here in Valley Ridge than she'd ever been.

Sebastian Bennington might not believe her, but now that he was home, he'd have to believe what was happening with his grandfather, and when he did, he'd agree that Hank had to visit a doctor. She'd have an ally.

Eventually.

Until then, she was going to be upbeat and understanding, even if it killed her.

She helped Mattie finish cleaning up the cottage, then headed home, ready to charm Sebastian. He was going to like her before he knew what hit him.

CHAPTER TWO

It was almost six o'clock that evening when Sebastian actually entered Valley Ridge. Not that the town was much to speak of. There were essentially four blocks that made up the town center. Heading from the west side of town to the east, the first block had a park on one side, city hall and the volunteer fire department on the other.

The next two blocks had various businesses like his grandfather's diner, MarVee's Quarters, Park Perks Coffee Shop, Burnam's Pharmacy, the grocery store. The final block had the high school on one side of Park Street and the grade school on the other, then there was a small bridge that he'd always felt marked the end of town, though the library and a church sat on the eastern side of it. Frankly, he'd never had much to do with either of those places when he was growing up, which might color his view, he admitted to himself.

During the holidays, the town strung those four main blocks with lighted garland. The festive strands stretched between the lampposts, each sporting a giant wreath. MarVee's did up their huge front display case with a train system that old Mr. Mento spent weeks building each year. His nephew Chris had taken to assisting him the past few years, according to Hank. Sebastian remembered Chris as a small, bubblegum-chomping redhead who'd once broken the window at the diner with a stone. He'd spent a few weeks working off his debt. Now he was in high school, according to Hank.

It was a reminder that despite the fact the town looked the same, things had changed. Time had marched on while he was gone.

The parking meters that lined Park Street hadn't been updated since Sebastian was a kid. They still charged a dime an hour, with a four-hour maximum. To the best of his knowledge, no one had ever gotten ticketed if they went over a bit.

He had to park a block away from Hank's. The evening dinner crowd had taken all the closest meters and filled the tiny lot behind the building. He walked down the block and stopped in front of the huge plate-glass window that read Valley Ridge Diner. He looked inside and everything was the same. The red vinyl seats and Formica tabletops. Booths lined the walls, tables settled in the center of the floor. The jukebox in the corner. The long counter that many of the locals preferred.

Then he spotted Hank, coffeepot in hand, working his way from one end of the counter to the other, smiling and chatting as he went. Looking the same as he always looked.

He'd like to grab that crazy nurse who'd practically taken over his grandfather's life and shake her shoulders and scream, *See. See, he's fine.*

Nurse Lily with her wrinkly blue eyes, her wild clothes and wilder hair thought she and Hank were close, but she'd been in Valley Ridge less than a year. Sebastian had lived with Hank for as long as he could remember, and Hank never changed. In his mind's eye, he'd always been like this. Thinning gray hair, enough wrinkles on his face to make a shar-pei jealous.

Hank had always walked with a brisk step and a slight bow to his spine. And he'd never been a type A personality. Hell, he'd never been a B or C, either. Hank had always felt that things would get done in their own time, which was why Sebastian learned to do laundry in grade school. It seemed *its own time* didn't always match up to the number of underpants he'd owned.

Taking a deep breath, and making sure his stupid left hand was secure in his jacket pocket, Sebastian opened the door and was greeted by the smell of home.

Some people might say the diner smelled of French fries and burgers, but for Sebastian it was more home than Hank's house was.

"Hank," he called.

His grandfather glanced up and set the coffeepot down with an audible thud, then hurried over to Sebastian. "Good to see you, boy."

"Good to see you, too, old man."

Pleasantries exchanged, Hank gave him a hefty thwack on the shoulder. "You look well."

"And you do, too." He paused, then added, "For an old guy."

His grandfather burst out laughing. "I've missed you, boy. Of course, I had a carbuncle once, and I missed that, too, when the doctor finally got rid of it."

Sebastian and his grandfather weren't the type to get all sappy with each other. Sniping was more their thing. And Sebastian knew that being compared to a carbuncle was his grandfather's way of saying *I love you.*

Hank pushed him onto a stool at the counter. "So what'll you have for your welcome-home dinner?"

"What else?" Sebastian asked.

"Hey, Tony, we need a double cheeseburger, extra cheese. Some pub fries. And because I'm a firm believer in good nutrition, throw a few pickles on the burger." Hank looked at Sebastian and grinned. "Vegetables, you know."

Maize, who was as much a fixture at the diner as the Formica tabletops and the jukebox in the corner, walked over and kissed Seb's cheek. "Welcome home, kid. Can I get you something to drink?"

Sebastian didn't have a chance to answer. His grandfather said, "Maize, how about a chocolate shake? And you probably should make the rounds with the coffeepot."

"Sure, boss." She turned to Sebastian and grinned, her whiter-than-white teeth glowing beneath her largely styled hair and overdone makeup. But on Maize, the over-the-top look worked. "How's my favorite marine?"

"Doing fine."

Her grin slipped a notch and she asked, "How's the arm?"

"Still there," he assured her, though he didn't pull his hand out of his pocket.

She laughed. "Seb, we've missed you."

"Sebastian," he corrected.

She stopped and winked. "Sebastian it is. I'll have that shake to you in a minute." She leaned down and kissed his cheek again.

Sebastian waited until she'd moved to the floor before he wiped the cheek, pretty sure that she'd left a lipstick mark in the kiss's wake.

"So, boy, you here for a while?" his grandfather asked.

"Till Colton's wedding."

For a split second, Sebastian thought he saw a hint of confusion, but it was over so quickly he couldn't be sure. Hank nodded and said, "Weddings are a big deal."

"They are. Me and Finn have to throw him a bachelor party."

"Of course, you do. I remember my bachelor party. Me and the boys went into Buffalo. Betty said, 'Hank, don't you be doing anything you can't tell me about afterward.' That's it. That was my only rule. Finding my Betty was the best piece of luck I ever had. She's an amazing—"

"Hank, there's a message from Jerilu's Produce on the machine. They—" Lily stopped short when she spotted him, and frowned. "I figured you'd get here eventually."

"I dropped my stuff at the house before I came over." He should have come directly from the lake to here. Hell, he should have come here before the lake. He couldn't explain his hesitation.

Okay, so he knew why. He didn't want anyone noticing his problem with his arm and being sympathetic. He'd hoped that Hank would be home before the dinner rush. When he wasn't, Sebastian had given up and come here.

"I'm sure that was a priority," the formerly smiling woman snapped without a smile in sight.

"You two have met?" Hank asked.

Lily smiled at his grandfather, like she had at him… at first. "Yes, we met," she told Hank. "Your grandson stopped at the lake on his way into town."

"Oh, that boy and his friends, they've always run the lakeshore like they owned it. Betty's always scared one of them will go tumbling down the cliff and end up in the water, but I've watched them scramble up and down it enough times to know that's not likely."

"I think the proximity to Lake Erie is one of Valley Ridge's greatest assets," Lily assured him. She shot Sebastian a look.

Yes, he'd noticed his grandfather speaking about his grandmother in the present tense, as if she were still here. "Before she passed, Grandma spent a great deal of her life worrying about me."

There was a clear see-what-I-mean look in Lily's eyes. Sebastian gave the merest shake of his head. He wasn't buying there was a problem because of such a small matter.

Lily sighed, shifting her attention to Hank. "There was a message from Jerilu's about a bill for produce. I can't find it. Do you have any clue?"

"I've been putting them all in your file."

She nodded. "I'll call on Monday and get the total. You two enjoy your dinner."

"Lil, honey, come join us," Hank called. "I want my two favorite people to get to know each other."

"Maybe next time, Hank. I wanted to finish up here before visiting Mrs. Burns."

"You work too hard, Lily," Hank scolded.

"Well, somebody's got to work around here," she said, his grandfather joining in partway.

That had always been his grandfather's saying. It was their special joke. *Somebody's got to work around here.* He and Hank tossed the line back and forth. Hank would come in and see that Sebastian had done the dishes and thank him, and Sebastian would respond, *Well, somebody's got to work around here.*

He'd come home and find that Hank had finally done some laundry and when he commented, Hank would respond, *Well, somebody's got to work around here.*

That saying was theirs. It had always belonged to him and Hank. A private thing between them. A phrase that was guaranteed to provoke a smile.

Lily obviously had heard it more than once and adopted it.

Sebastian felt… Hell, he couldn't be jealous, could he?

Jealous of a woman who'd helped his grandfather when he hadn't been here? A woman who'd been around enough to know some of Hank's sayings and quirks? A woman who'd known who he was because she'd seen Hank's pictures and listened to his stories?

Sebastian had come to town feeling nothing…a solid block of nothing.

But then he'd met Lily and felt a wild swing of emotions. Anger, suspicion…and now jealousy.

He wished he could go back to feeling nothing, but as she bustled away, he suspected that Lily wasn't the sort of woman to inspire calm grayness.

And he didn't think he liked that.

LILY MANAGED TO AVOID Sebastian for two whole days. Sunday, she hibernated in her apartment with a good book that was due back to Maeve at the library next week. She knew that Sebastian was around to look after Hank, and she didn't have to work. She should have enjoyed the day.

Yet, instead of relaxing, she found herself staring at the common wall she shared with the main house and wondering what Sebastian and Hank were doing.

It was a relief to leave the house on Monday. She'd been running her start-up home-health-care business through Dr. Neil Marshall's practice. Not only did he refer patients to her, he was her physician backup. When his office wound up unexpectedly understaffed, she'd agreed to work there on Mondays.

A lot of her patients were short-term. Intravenous therapies and wound care made up the bulk of her visits. But there was always something different. Miss Helen was her one long-term patient. She lived about ten miles outside of Valley Ridge, and Lily visited her every Friday to fill her MedMinder and do a checkup on a stubborn sore on her leg.

Being at Neil's office every Monday meant another steady source of income, and his putting her on the practice's insurance was huge. But her house calls added to the medical practice one day a week and evenings at the diner meant she hardly had time to catch her breath. Tuesday, she had three house calls to make, and in the evening she went into the diner, hoping that Sebastian had found something to keep him busy.

But her luck had run out. When she walked into the diner, juggling her bag, a box and a shopping bag, there he was…sitting at the counter. She'd talked about making him like her, but she couldn't seem to muster any enthusiasm for the mission, so she gave him a curt nod and hurried toward the kitchen door.

"Hey, Lily," someone called. She turned and saw Colton, then a moment later, Sophie following him into the diner.

"Hang on a second and let me set this stuff down." She reached the small office behind the kitchen and deposited everything on the desk. Hank was busy plating a burger for Red, one of their cooks. "Hi, Hank, Red," she called.

Hank looked surprised to see her. "Lily, is it that time already?"

"Close enough," she replied. "I'm running out front for a few minutes to talk to Sophie, then I'll go through the invoices."

"It'll keep until you're done," he told her as she strode into the dining room and found her friends sitting at a booth.

With Sebastian.

With no way to avoid him any longer, she decided to try to ignore him. "How are you guys doing?"

Colton answered, "Just talking with Seb—"

"Sebastian," Sebastian corrected.

"Sebastian," Colton agreed. "About the stag. Told him I'm not sure what I want."

"You don't need me for that, and I have work to do in the office—" Lily tried.

"Can you spare a minute?" Sophie asked. "I know you've been busy, what with also being at Dr. Marshall's office."

"How did you know?" Lily asked as she sat on the bench next to Sebastian, who thankfully slid over toward the window, putting as much distance as possible between them.

Her friend smiled. "This is Valley Ridge. Everybody knows everything about everyone. The news spreads faster here than it does on Facebook or Twitter."

"Oh." Lily knew that. The sense of community, of having people know who you were, was part of what had attracted her to Valley Ridge. The fact that they frequently knew more than you liked wasn't nearly as much of an attraction.

"Marilee was in for a checkup and saw you there, remember?" Sophie asked.

Marilee and Vivienne owned MarVee's Quarters, the old five-and-dime on Park Street.

"If Valley Ridge's information network had a hub, it would be Marilee and Vivienne's," Sophie confirmed.

Lily grinned. "You're right."

"With all the jobs you do, you could be a farmer," the normally quiet Colton said.

"Pardon?" Lily asked.

"I never do the same job two days in a row. There's always something different that needs my attention. Fields to till. Crops to plant or harvest. Vines to sucker. No day is ever exactly like the last."

"That is a very good point," Lily agreed. "I'm only working for Dr. Marshall on Mondays. Trish wanted to cut back on her hours, so it was a good fit for both of us." Trish Millrose had a baby a year ago and had wanted to spend more time with her.

"There's nothing wrong with being a jack-of-all-trades," Colton assured her.

"'You chould be a farmer' is Colton's idea of the biggest compliment he can give," Sophie teased.

"I took it as such." Lily had grown to adore Sophie's fiancé. She'd read the phrase *salt of the earth* over the years and realized it described Colton perfectly. "But much as I'd like to stay and hang out, this jack-of-all-trades has a stack of invoices calling her name. Unless you needed me for something."

Colton said, "I stopped to see if Seb here—"

"Se—" was as far as Sebastian got.

Colton caught himself and said, "If Sebastian here would like to ride into Erie with me tomorrow. I've got some things to take care of, and I could use the company."

"I'll let you gentlemen figure out the details. Sophie, maybe we can have lunch one day this week?"

"I'll call you," Sophie promised. "And I wanted to tell you again, the shower was beautiful."

It sounded wrong to say so, but Lily thought the shower had been beautiful, too. "I'm so glad you liked it." She rose. "Can I get you all anything before I leave?"

"I can manage that," Sebastian said.

Lily nodded at him as she walked away. Normally, she'd have stayed with Colton and Sophie. Maybe even ordered dinner. It was always nice to have someone to share a meal with.

But not with Seb—no, pardon her, *Sebastian*—sitting next to her. They hadn't touched, but that didn't mean Lily wasn't aware of him sitting next to her. There was a constant awareness radiating off him. And when he shifted in his seat and his elbow came perilously close to brushing against her, she'd sensed it without seeing it and had moved out of the way.

Everything about Sebastian seemed to trigger a response in her. Mainly a negative one.

"Hey, Lily, how were your patients today?" Hank asked from the doorway to the office.

"I only had a few house calls, so it was easy. Do you need any help with anything?"

"No. Maize has gone home, but Megan, that high-school girl we hired, is coming in soon." Megan wasn't a new hire, and normally, Lily would have pointed it out in hopes of reorienting Hank. But right now, she was too exhausted to fight the battle that Sebastian claimed didn't exist.

"Call me if you need me." Hank shut the door to the office, and Lily slumped into the nearby desk chair.

What on earth was it about monosyllabic Sebastian Bennington that upset her equilibrium so much? She didn't know, nor did she like it.

She should have said something to Hank. Dementia wasn't her area of expertise, but she'd talked to a friend from Buffalo. A doctor who specialized in geriatric care. He'd said as long as Hank didn't get upset, giving him cues to keep him focused didn't hurt. When things got worse and the reminders upset him, it would be time to stop.

But it wasn't time yet.

Feeling reenergized, she took one long breath. She couldn't believe it was already the end of April. This year was going by fast.

Maybe it had to do with her being busy, or maybe it was a sign that she was getting older. She read a lot of Regency novels, and she knew by those standards being in her late twenties would have qualified her as an old maid. A spinster. The word always left her with the impression of a dried-up husk of an old woman.

She'd bought a new calendar, flipped it to April and hung it up on the bulletin board where Hank had always posted everyone's work schedule. She'd taken over the scheduling for the most part, too.

The work schedule was a week-by-week list, but the new calendar showed the entire month in very large blocks with an oversize font that called attention to them. As if to say, *Here, this is the date.*

She picked up the marker and x-ed out the first twenty-five days of the month.

At the hospital, they'd kept calendars beneath the clocks in all the patient rooms because it was easy to get disoriented when you were sick or on medication. She thought having the calendar in the diner might help Hank more than simply a list would.

And on that note, she'd made another purchase. She opened the large cardboard box she'd brought and took out a big wall clock that was framed in shiny red plastic. She thought it would look perfect in the dining room, given that the seats were upholstered in red vinyl. She put batteries into the clock and set the time and date. She opened the bottom-left drawer of the desk, where Hank stored a few basic tools. Hammer and fastener in hand, she grabbed the step stool out of the storage closet and went out into the front. Sebastian was at the counter, which meant Colton and Sophie must have left. The rush was over, and only two tables were occupied.

She juggled the ladder and hammer in her hands and walked to the far wall. The space above the window would be the perfect spot for the clock. Hank could see it from the counter as he served or visited his customers.

She put the clock down on an empty table and tilted the tall step stool over the booth as if it were a ladder.

"What are you doing?" came a male voice that she easily identified.

Lily checked behind her and, as she'd suspected, found Sebastian. And even if she wasn't surprised it was Sebastian, she wasn't sure why he was glowering at her. No, she wasn't sure why, but that part didn't surprise her, either. He seemed to spend a lot of time giving her less than cordial looks.

"What am I doing?" she repeated, then in a slow voice she answered, making sure she punctuated each word. "I. Am. Setting. Up. A. Ladder."

He took a deep breath, which she suspected was to help calm himself, then asked, "To be accurate, you're setting up a step stool, but incorrectly." He took the stool and opened it so the two halves formed an A against the wall. "My question is, why?"

Lily tried to be happy and easygoing. But something about Sebastian drove away all that hard work. She should feel bad about that, but she didn't. Sebastian Bennington grated on her.

"I am setting up the ladder—step stool—because that's a necessary first step if I want to climb it." It might be childish, but she knew the response would annoy him right back.

She saw from his expression that it had.

This time, Sebastian didn't bother to take a cleansing breath. Instead, he made a small growling noise in the back of his throat, then asked, "Again, why?"

"Because I want to pound this nail through the hook—" she reached into her pocket and produced them "—into the wall." She gestured to the wall the ladder was set up next to.

He frowned. "Is there a stud there?"

The fun of teasing him evaporated. He'd stumped her. "I don't know," she admitted.

"I'm going to take a guess that you were planning on hanging that clock—" he pointed with his good hand "—from the nail and hook that you're so proudly displaying. And I'm also going to guess that you weren't planning on seeing if there was a stud there, and so you wouldn't know if there wasn't, which leads me to believe you hadn't thought about what would happen if you drove a nail into drywall with no anchor."

"Uh." Darn. No fun at all.

"The weight of the clock could pull the nail out, which means the fastener would come out, and the clock would fall. And it would land on?" he prompted.

She knew what he was saying. The oversize clock could easily land on a patron. "Fine. I'll get an anchor." She wasn't sure exactly what an anchor was, but she could call Mattie. Mattie had worked at dozens of jobs. If anyone knew what an anchor was in this case, it was her friend Mathilda Keith.

Mattie was the first to explain that for many years she hadn't stayed in one place for long ever since graduating high school, but she'd thrown her footloose lifestyle aside to come back to Valley Ridge and care for her childhood friend Bridget when she'd become ill.

And it was through Bridget that Lily, Mattie and Sophie had also become friends.

When Bridget passed away, Mattie had remained in Valley Ridge to raise Bridget's children. And Lily had stayed because she'd grown to love the town and the people in it.

"First see if there's a stud."

She didn't have a clue how to check for that.

He sighed. "I'll do it."

"I don't need your help."

"But you're going to get it." His expression said he was no longer annoyed—he was feeling as if he'd won this. Whatever *this* was.

"Fine." Lily knew that was a less than gracious response and she was being childish, but there was something about Sebastian Bennington that evoked a strong response from her. That first time she'd met him at the lake, her initial response had been attraction. Now…

Sebastian extended his good hand, and she handed over the hammer and nail. He carefully placed them on the top of the ladder and climbed up with his injured hand still in his pocket.

Lily had noticed that he kept the hand hidden away. She'd recognized the surgical scars that covered his hand and moved up past his wrist, presumably up his arm. They had that red, raised look that said they were fairly recent. If he asked her professional opinion, she'd tell him that the scars would fade over time. Her cursory glance said they were made by someone who knew what they were doing. But he didn't ask, and she couldn't think of any way to toss that into a conversation.

She looked up at Sebastian as he thumped around the wall with the hammer. Even from where she was, she could hear the difference between the solid and the hollow thumps.

"The stud?" she asked.

"Yes." He held still. "Will that work for the clock?"

She took a step back, studied the spot and nodded. "Yeah, it looks fairly centered."

He faced the wall and finally pulled his injured hand from its hideaway in his jacket pocket. He studied the hammer and nail a moment. Lily could have kicked herself. There was no way he was going to be able to hold the nail in his damaged left hand while he hammered with the right one.

Lily knew he'd rebuff her offer if she said she'd get up there and do it, so she climbed on a chair next to the ladder. "Why don't you let me position the nail? That way I can get the clock where I want it."

"Fine." The word was almost a grunt.

He set down the hammer, passed her the nail, then picked the hammer up again. She held the nail as high as she could reach and hoped it was high enough. She also prayed that he didn't smash her fingers as he tried to pound the nail in.

A couple sharp thwacks with the hammer, and her fingers were still intact.

Sebastian said, "You can let go now."

She did and he finished pounding the nail into the wall. He finished with the hammer and she handed him the clock. He gripped the edge with his good hand and supported it with his damaged left hand more than holding it. It was an awkward way to hold the thing, but Sebastian managed to get the clock on the nail and climb down the step stool.

"There," he said triumphantly.

Lily took a few steps back and admired it. "That's great."

"Now, can you tell me why we needed a clock here?"

They hadn't talked about Hank since that first day, so Lily wasn't sure how Sebastian felt about the matter now. "I've found that having clocks and calendars around can give confused patients a touchstone. A way to recognize *when* they are."

"We're back to that?" he muttered.

"You've spent time with Hank, and you're going to tell me that you haven't noticed any problems?"

SEBASTIAN WANTED TO TELL this woman no. No, he hadn't noticed anything off about Hank. But that would be a lie. There were moments when Hank seemed…lost. That was the only word to describe it. Hank would be talking and suddenly drift off course, then sputter to a halt and go quiet.

When Sebastian had come out for breakfast this morning, Hank had seemed surprised to see him. And when Hank had walked into the room and found Sebastian picking up peas and dropping them into the glass bottle he kept them in, Hank had seemed surprised by the scarring on his hand, as if he had never heard about his injury and surgeries.

Yeah, he'd noticed some difficulties, but rather than admitting them, he said, "A little confusion isn't unusual when you get older."

Lily shot him a disappointed look. "I thought that marines were known for facing things head-on. That when a marine sees a problem, he addresses it—he doesn't hide from it."

"I do address it," he defended.

She nodded. "Then let's not stand here arguing about whether there's a problem. Hank's appointment is on May 18 at one. Help me get him there, please? Once Hank's there, the doctor can answer all our questions."

"Fine," he agreed.

Lily sighed. "A reluctant ally is better than no ally. Thank you."

He was about to counter that they weren't allies, but he was saved from sounding peevish when Hank joined them, coffeepot in hand, and asked, "What are you two arguing about?"

Whenever Sebastian thought about his grandfather, this was the image he had. Hank wearing his ever-present flannel shirt and holding a pot of coffee. When he saw Hank like this, he could believe there was nothing wrong.

And though he couldn't explain it to himself, much less explain it to Lily, he desperately needed Hank to be all right.

"We're not fighting," Lily assured his grandfather. "Sebastian hung the new clock up. Isn't it great? I got it on eBay for a steal. It looks like it was made for the diner."

"It does." Hank studied the clock a moment. "You make sure you take the money for it out of our funds."

"It's a gift, Hank," she scolded. "You don't pay for gifts."

He turned to Sebastian. "This girl is always like that. Doing things for everyone else and not taking anything back for herself." Hank addressed her. "Miss Helen was here the other day and told me about how you took care of that sore on her leg and stayed to get her clothes out of the dryer. And that you made her lunch while you waited. That's not part of your job, is it?"

"When I took care of Bridget—" her voice hitched as she said the name "—I discovered I liked that I could take care of all her needs, not only the medical ones. It's the same thing for Miss Helen. Yes, she needs me to dress her wound. It's taking a long time to heal and has to be seen to regularly. But she also needs someone to share a lunch with. And those stairs are hard on her."

Sebastian could feel her pain when she mentioned Bridget. He'd wanted to come home for her funeral. He knew Finn would need all the support he could get. But he'd had the last of his surgeries the day he got the news, and he couldn't convince the doctors to let him go.

Hank laughed. "I rest my case. Take the money for the clock, Lily. I know things have been tight for you." The bell above the door jingled, and a man took a seat at the counter. "Seems like I'm on," Hank said and walked over to the new customer.

Sebastian should have said something sympathetic. It was obvious that Lily had gotten close to Finn's sister. He had no trouble imagining why. Bridget Wallace Langley had been one of those rare individuals people gravitated to. Losing her had cut at Finn and Mattie Keith, who'd always been underfoot along with Bridget. Those two were like salt and pepper shakers. Very different, but always together.

Yes, he could imagine that Lily had gotten close to Bridget and felt her loss keenly. He should have offered her his condolences, but instead he asked, "What is your angle?"

Lily visibly bristled. Her laugh lines around her blue eyes were all but hidden now. "Making sure Hank keeps the appointment, Sebastian. That's my angle. Hank says I help people, and I do, I guess. But he's spent his life helping the community. I've seen it time after time. Sure, people come here for a meal, but it's more than that. They come here for Hank. More than one person has mentioned his occasional confusion. He needs to be checked out. It could be something addressed with a simple fix."

"And it could be nothing," he felt a perverse need to point out.

"It could," she allowed, though her expression said she didn't believe it.

This woman wore her feelings right there on her face for everyone to see. Happiness, annoyance, pain.

Sebastian purposely masked his feeling of terror that she could be right. "I'll see to it that he goes."

"Thank you." Before he could respond, she said, "I

hate that we got off on the wrong foot. I know you're not happy I bought a share of the diner. When Hank and I put together the deal, we left provisions for him to buy me out at any point. You're welcome to go over the books. We're doing better. Bills are being paid on time. If you want to use your own personal money, or if you want to wait until Hank can afford to buy me out, I'm willing…either way. But if that is what you want, you'll have to start overseeing the finances."

"I'm not staying."

"Then Hank will need to hire someone to take care of the bills because if I hadn't stepped in, this place would have gone under."

She didn't say anything about the fact he was planning to leave town as soon as Colton's wedding was over. She could have laid on quite the guilt-trip.

"He never was very good at keeping the books," Sebastian admitted as he scrutinized Lily. Tonight, she had on a pair of jeans and a loose top, with bangles on both wrists. Her dark hair was down again, and the rich color highlighted her blue eyes. As he looked in them, he saw no scheming. He saw concern for his grandfather. A very real concern.

"I'm an ass," he said more to himself than to her.

Lily grinned, those laugh lines coming back out and enjoying where they belonged. "I didn't say it, but since I'm offering a truce, I won't agree too vehemently."

Despite himself, Sebastian chuckled. Even to his ears, it was a rusty sound, but she still stood there grinning, and he couldn't help it. "Then we're agreed that I'm an ass, and we have a truce."

"We are agreed on both issues," she said. "And since we've got a truce, do you mind if I come over for breakfast in the morning? Hank and I had a routine, but I…" She left the sentence hanging.

"But you didn't want to intrude while I was home," he supplied.

She nodded.

"I'll see you at…?"

"Six. And I didn't mean you had to get up to have breakfast with us. I know that sometimes Hank forgets to eat before work. But I wasn't saying you're not invited." She spoke hastily, as if she was worried he'd be insulted.

"I'll be up."

"I'll see you then." She folded up the step stool and made her way toward the kitchen.

Every fiber of Sebastian's being wanted to offer to help her, but he'd already proven how useless his hand was with that whole hammer-and-nail incident. He didn't want a repeat.

He went back to the counter and took up his seat. A very young girl in blue jeans, a T-shirt and a baseball cap that proclaimed VR Diner came in. "I'm here, Hank."

"Megan," Hank greeted. "This is my grandson, Sebastian. Seb, this is Megan, our new waitress."

"Not all that new, Hank." She smiled warmly at Sebastian. "I've been working here since my sophomore year. But when you're as old as Hank, a year and a half is short, I guess." She laughed, obviously friends enough with Hank to be comfortable teasing him. But Sebastian saw the momentary confusion in his grandfather's eyes. It was soon gone, replaced by Hank's laughter. The moment was so quick that if Sebastian hadn't been watching his grandfather closely, he might have missed it. But he was watching Hank and it had been there.

Sebastian clenched his mangled left hand, which immediately obliged him by cramping. He needed Hank to be okay. And he had a sinking feeling that Lily was right that his grandfather was anything but okay.

CHAPTER THREE

SEBASTIAN WOKE UP to the sound of…singing. Not good singing by any means, but singing nonetheless. He crawled out of bed and reached for his sweats with his left hand and swore as he grasped them.

Sometimes he forgot. The pain was especially bad first thing in the morning because in his dreams, his hand was fine. His best dreams were set here in Valley Ridge when he was a kid, running around with Finn and Colton. His worst dreams…

No, he wouldn't start his day thinking about that. Sebastian forced his left hand to join his right and grip the waistband of his pants. He pulled them in place, then tossed a T-shirt on and went out to investigate this pseudo-singing.

Hank was standing at the top of the stairs, smiling. "She's back for breakfast, so that means you two settled whatever was bothering you?"

"We didn't—" Sebastian started to deny there was anything to settle, but Hank's expression stopped him dead in his tracks. "Yeah, we're fine."

"I'm glad. She's a good girl. She's got a heart of gold. But the more pure gold is, the easier it's damaged, Seb."

He wanted to correct his grandfather but resisted. Hank could call him whatever he wanted. To be honest, Hank calling him anything other than Seb would feel wrong.

"Tread lightly with her," his grandfather admonished.

Miss Wrinkly Blue Eyes seemed fine as far as he could see.

"What is that she's singing?" he asked. "If you can call that singing."

"Oh, it's singing. 'Course, she couldn't hit a note to save her life, but if she's singing, she's back to herself. She hasn't been since you got home." It was a statement without any blame, but still, Sebastian recognized the truth of it. He'd seen Lily Paul's true nature in those laugh-lined eyes, and he knew he was the one who'd caused her to be less than herself.

"Let's go find out what the song is." Hank started down the stairs and Sebastian followed.

"Good morning, Hank," Lily called out when she saw Hank. As Sebastian stepped into the room, her happy smile became a bit more guarded. "Sebastian."

"What's for breakfast?" Hank asked. To Sebastian he observed, "She worries I don't eat right. I tell her I work around food all day. I always eat."

"But there's eating, then there's eating *right,*" Lily said in such a way that Sebastian knew this was a topic the two of them had hashed out before. "You don't want me to get Mattie over here to lecture you on nutrition, do you?"

"No, not Mattie." Hank whispered to Sebastian, "She's even worse about healthy food than our Lily."

Hank almost argued that Lily wasn't his, but thought better of it. As if she'd read his mind, she gave him a questioning look, and when he didn't voice the thought, she nodded and said to Hank, "To answer your question, today's breakfast is Irish oatmeal and fresh blueberries. Rumor has it that it's Sebastian's favorite."

Sebastian didn't like being reminded that Lily knew so many things about him. If Hank had gone to the trouble of sharing he liked oatmeal, what else had he told Lily?

"That boy." Hank chuckled. "He wouldn't touch regular oatmeal. I bought instant oats once and you'd have thought I tried to feed him poison."

"So I've heard," Lily set a bowl down in front of Hank. "Well, he might have bed head, but he's got good taste in oatmeal. Sit down." Lily went back to the stove, and Sebastian ran a hand over his hair, trying to smooth it out. He hadn't gotten it cut since he'd been back stateside.

Lily turned and caught him midsmooth and laughed. Sebastian couldn't help but laugh, as well.

"Vain much?" she asked.

"I'm not used to having to worry about my hair first thing in the morning." Okay, that sounded defensive.

Lily didn't seem to mind. "Me, either," she said and shook her head, making her heavy ponytail bob one way and then the other.

"Your hair always looks good," Sebastian said.

"Yes, it does," Hank agreed. "And so does breakfast."

Lily served Sebastian oatmeal, got her own bowl, then set the coffee carafe on the table. She picked up the newspaper. She handed Hank the sports section, took the entertainment section for herself and handed the rest of it to Sebastian. "Hank and I called our sections. You can have the national news, or local news."

They sat in amicable silence, eating their breakfasts

and reading the paper together. As if they'd done it so many times it had become a comfortable routine. And even though Sebastian ate his oatmeal and read the national news, he didn't really feel part of the routine.

It's Sebastian's favorite.

Who was this woman who knew so much about him? She was his grandfather's business partner and obviously at home in his kitchen.

He stole surreptitious looks at her as he ate.

His grandfather finished his section first; a few moments later, Lily finished hers, and without asking, they exchanged sections. "Doesn't anyone read the actual news?"

They both started laughing. "Lily says that the news is almost always doom and gloom and no one should start their day with that."

"And yet, those were my options," Sebastian groused.

"You don't read about sports. You play them," Lily said. "Professional sports don't interest you. You're the kind of man who wants to be in on the action, not watching it. And even though I have a wonderful imagination, I can't make it stretch far enough to picture you reading an advice column."

Hank chuckled. "She's got you pegged, boy."

Sebastian now asked the question that had been on his mind since he'd first meet Lily on the banks of Lake Erie. "Hank, how much did you tell Lily about me?"

"Just enough to scare her," his grandfather teased.

"I'm not scared of anything," she countered. And though she smiled as she said it, as if she were simply joining in Hank's teasing, those laugh lines at the corners of her eyes didn't fall into their default pattern. They were strained, as if she were forcing the smile.

And Sebastian thought her expression was telling, though he wasn't sure exactly what it was telling him.

He surprised himself by saying, "You owe me something."

"Something?" she asked.

"You know so much about me—tell me something about you to even things up."

"I wouldn't know where to begin."

Again, her smile wasn't quite right, as if she didn't want to share anything about herself. Sebastian wanted to push. He wanted to understand this strange woman his grandfather thought so highly of. But that something in her eyes told him to leave it, and so he asked, "What was that song you were…*singing* this morning?"

And just like that, the *something* in her eyes disappeared and her natural laugh lines reappeared. "Oh, I know, I slaughtered it. Miss Helen has been teaching me folk songs."

"You're taking singing lessons?" Sebastian asked. If that was her voice after lessons, he hated to think what she'd sounded like before.

"No, Helen's one of Lily's patients." Hank ignored the look she sent him and continued, "Lil, you didn't say anything, so you can't get in trouble." He turned to Sebastian. "Helen gets all these sores. Lily goes to see her a lot."

"Ah, so it's not formal lessons."

"No. Changing her dressings can be painful. Before she retired, she taught music at the grade school for years, and sharing songs she loves with me distracts her. That was 'The Parting Glass.' It's an old Irish pub song."

"Well, next time you're in a pub, you'll be set," he teased.

"Yeah, I figure that in a pub surrounded by people who are drinking, my singing might sound okay."

Sebastian took a sip of coffee in order to give a quiet pause before he said, "I don't know if I'd go *that* far."

She looked at him as if she wasn't sure if he was teasing, so he smiled to let her know he was. He could read that she was surprised that he'd teased her, and Sebastian felt surprised as well, but they both laughed, and Hank joined in, and for a moment, for a simple moment, Sebastian felt…good.

The rest of the meal was amicable. Lily took off for a home visit, and Sebastian strolled over to the diner with his grandfather. He couldn't help but think about what his grandfather had said. Lily did seem to have a heart of gold. She'd come to Valley Ridge to care for Finn's sister, Bridget.

Lily had stepped in to get his grandfather out of a jam, and despite Sebastian's early suspicions, he couldn't find anything questionable in her cooking breakfast, or even putting her own money into the business. His friends thought highly of her—she was a bridesmaid in Colton and Sophie's wedding party. And she let retired teachers impart their knowledge in order to feel useful and distract them from painful procedures.

He also remembered his grandfather's warning. The finer the gold, the more easily it was damaged. Maybe, but though she might have a heart of gold, Lily Paul seemed strong enough to him.

WEDNESDAY SPED BY for Lily, and Thursday was just as crazy.

When she had worked at the hospital, she had a steady paycheck and a set schedule. Her new life in

Valley Ridge was more piecemeal. Even with her connection to Dr. Marshall, Valley Ridge's only general practitioner, she was basically working for herself.

She was hurrying out of Miss Helen's house when her cell phone rang.

She dug it out of her purse and saw Mattie Keith's name. "Hi, Mattie. What's up?"

"I picked up Abbey from school. She's not feeling well and is running a temperature. I wanted to check what to do and Finn's in surgery."

Mattie was new to caring for Bridget Langley's children. She and their uncle Finn had been pulling together since Bridget's passing. He was a surgeon in Buffalo, but had been home weekends lately.

Lily ran through the fever basics, then offered, "Why don't I pick up Zoe and Mickey?"

"Really, that's not why I called."

"I know. I offered." She might not have known Mattie long, but she'd worked side by side with her while Bridget was sick. Things like that brought people together. So she knew that taking help wasn't Mattie's strong suit, so she said, "Sometimes it's okay to say yes and let friends help you out, Mattie."

She heard Mattie's sigh over the phone line and was pleased when her friend said, "Yes."

"Great. I'll see you after school."

She hung up and glanced at the time. She could pick up the kids, then make her last home visit before heading into the diner.

Piecemeal might be questionable on the wallet, but it allowed her to tailor her schedule as needed, and right now, she was happy she could help Mattie out. It would be good to see the kids—she missed seeing them every day.

It might have made her day a bit busier, but busy was a good thing.

That was a lesson she'd learned years ago.

SEBASTIAN'S HAND WAS THROBBING. Actually, his entire left arm was throbbing.

He'd been pretending to sleep for the past hour, trying to convince himself he wasn't in pain. Turned out he couldn't avoid the facts forever.

He glanced at the clock. One-ten in the morning.

Well, it was officially Friday. That was something. He wasn't sure what late-night television was like at one o'clock, but odds were there would be something on that would occupy him. He'd thought about getting a TV for his room, but it didn't make sense. He was only here until the wedding. Just eight short weeks.

Of course, he had no idea where he'd be going after that or what he'd be doing then. Fact was, he didn't have a clue.

He tiptoed down the stairs. He didn't want to wake Hank. He went to the kitchen for a drink and was about to flip on the light when he heard something outside. Squeaking. He couldn't figure out what it was and walked through the still-darkened kitchen to peer into the backyard. The moon was bright enough that he could see someone sitting in the glider that had been in the side yard as long as he could remember. Two bench seats that faced each other, hanging from a wooden frame.

He went to unlock the door and realized that it hadn't been locked. Hank had said he'd done it. Well, no harm done.

He ignored the sinking feeling in the pit of his stomach. The fact that Hank was mistaken didn't mean that Lily was right and something was wrong with his grandfather. Everyone forgot things on occasion.

He walked quietly toward the glider. The seat facing him was empty. Someone was sitting on the other side of the glider, her back to him. It took a split second for him to realize it was Lily.

Right after that, he realized she was crying.

"Lily, what's wrong?"

She jerked at the sound of his voice and turned around. "Sebastian. What are you doing up?" She wiped at her eyes.

"I heard a noise. The glider squeaks." He took the seat across from her on the ancient wooden glider. When he was younger, it was his favorite place to sit and think.

"Be careful. There are a few boards that are rotten," she warned midsniffle.

"So what's wrong?" was his only response.

"I was sitting here thinking," she said.

"Not happy thoughts from the sound of it."

She sniffled. "No. I took Mattie's kids home from school today. Well, Bridget's kids, Finn's nieces and nephew, but it's Mattie who has custody now that Bridget…" She let the sentence trail off, as if she didn't want to say the words *Bridget died.* He understood that. To him, Bridget was still Finn's younger sister who'd made their childhood challenging as she and her best friend, Mattie, tagged after them. Mattie Keith. Waltzing Mathilda, her brothers had called her. She'd stopped *waltzing* and had come home to take care of Bridget when she was sick, and then stayed to take care of the kids.

He wasn't exactly sure why she had custody and not Finn. "How's she doing?"

"Not good. I collected the older two kids after school because Abbey, the youngest, was sick. Mattie thought it was a flu or cold. She mentioned that Abbey had a fever, and I told her to give her acetaminophen. Kids run fevers all the time. They're the body's way of fighting infection, so normally they're a good thing, if you think about it." She sniffled again.

"But not this time?" he asked gently.

"No, not this time. Abbey had a febrile convulsion."

All he got was the word *convulsion.* "What?"

"A seizure brought on by a high fever. As a nurse, I know that there's no way to predict when a child will have one. Not every fever or every sudden spike in a fever brings one on. The great percentage of fevers don't. I know that Mattie did everything she could do. If I'd been there, I couldn't have done anything more. But still, I feel guilty. I dropped the kids off and asked if she wanted me to come in and look at Abbey, but I was busy. I was going to run late for an appointment, so when she said no, I was relieved."

Sebastian understood feeling helpless. Wanting to help, but not being able.

"Lily..." Sebastian wasn't sure what to say. He didn't know how to make her feel better. So he moved over to her side of the glider and it tilted back as he put his arm around her. His bad arm. It seemed that although there was a lot it didn't do well anymore, it could do this. It could hold someone and offer comfort.

"Shh," he said. "Will she have more?"

"Usually, kids have just one and never have another, some have more. Most of the time there are no long-term effects."

"Then you're right, there's nothing you could do, and

odds are Abbey will be fine." He felt her give a little shake, as if she were holding back more tears. He tightened his hand around her shoulder.

She seemed to accept his attempts at comfort. He felt her take a deep breath. "I know all that. Really, I do. And telling you reminds me that I know. In my head, I know it. But in my heart, I can't help but think if I'd have gone in, if I hadn't rushed off, I could have..."

"Lily, I've known you less than a week, and I already know that you're busy."

"Yes, but—"

"And in the midst of all that and the other stuff you do, you stopped at the school and picked up the kids and took them home for Mattie?"

"Yes. It wasn't a big deal. I was between calls."

"I'm betting it was a big deal to Mattie. I bet it was a big deal to Finn, too. And, Lily, take it from someone who knows—things happen. Sometimes awful things. Sometimes you can run interference and stop them. Sometimes, try as you might, you can't. You've just got to accept that."

She sighed. "I know. I've had a lot of experience with it. There have been so many times that I know I couldn't do anything to make a situation better, but I've still felt guilty. Knowing and feeling are two different things." She was silent a moment. Softly she added, "I guess it doesn't help that my mother called today."

"Is something wrong with her?" he asked. Here was something about Lily he didn't know. Something he doubted anyone else knew.

"No, nothing's wrong with her, at least, no more than usual. It made me think that no matter how hard I try to help, I can't save everyone."

Her response didn't really tell him anything but there was a finality in it, as if he'd gotten all he was going to get. "But Abbey's okay?"

"Yes. Finn came in from Buffalo, so Mattie has someone with her."

"Then maybe the best thing you can do is go to bed, get some rest so that you're ready when they do need you."

"Thanks, Seb—" Before he could correct her, she corrected herself. "Sebastian. Beneath your outer distrust and annoying veneer, there is a human being."

"Compliments?" he asked.

She shook her head. "Don't let it go to your head. I'm sure you'll annoy me again tomorrow."

"Go to bed, Lily."

She got out of the glider gingerly. And he immediately felt the loss. His arm had been throbbing all night, but while he was holding Lily, he'd forgotten.

She stood there a minute, then said, "Good night, Sebastian."

"Night, Lily. I'll see you at breakfast."

She walked toward the very back of the driveway and the small efficiency apartment. She turned at the door and waved at him. Sebastian got up and flexed his hand. Yes, it actually felt better. Maybe it was simply the heat of Lily's shoulder that helped ease the muscles.

Maybe.

A WEEK LATER, Lily had just ended a breathing treatment with Mrs. Burns. She'd been visiting her for a while now. At first, a few times a day, now just once.

The older woman pointed to the tea service on the table. "Do you have time for a cup?"

To be honest, Lily didn't. Mrs. Burns was her second-last call of the day. The very long day where none of her patients lived in proximity to each other. She'd spent the bulk of her time driving. But this was why she'd chosen this career. She could have a cup of tea or help a patient with something nonmedical. "I'd love a quick cup."

"I made the cookies. Pecan sandies. There's a bag of them on the table. I hope you'll take them to Hank. They're his favorite."

"I know you know Hank—everyone in Valley Ridge does. But you know him well enough to know his favorite cookie?"

"His Betty was my best friend. It's one of those things that friends know. And now that she's not here to bake him cookies, I like to take him a treat now and then."

"That's very sweet, Mrs. Burns," she told the older woman.

"I'd take it myself and check on the old coot, but I'm not feeling up to snuff. I'm so glad you're here and have saved me the trip into town."

She leaned over and patted Mrs. Burns's hand. "I'm happy to do it."

Mrs. Burns took a sip of her tea. She put the cup down on the saucer with a small clink and asked, "You're still renting the apartment from Hank?"

"Yes." Lily took a sip, too.

"So how is he?"

Lily wasn't sure how to answer that. He seemed more with it. He followed conversations smoothly and was more willing to interact.

"The same as ever," she told the older lady, which was the truth. Just a couple more weeks until his appointment, she'd reminded herself over and over. Until then, she was going to keep an eye on him and hope she was wrong.

"And that grandson of his? Oh, that boy gave poor Hank the runaround, but I think he saved Hank, too. The man was dying of a broken heart—missing his Betty and mourning Leanne. That girl was wild from the word *go.*"

"Rumor has it so was Sebastian," Lily said.

"No. He was rambunctious. And he was full of mischief, but he didn't run crazed like his mother. And then he went into the marines after college. He came home once, dressed in his blues. If I were twenty years younger, I would have swooned."

"Well, he's fine. Settling back into civilian life, I think." She finished her tea. "I really need to get going, but I'll be back tomorrow."

"Oh, I know you will. You and Dr. Neil are quite the pair."

She leaned down and kissed the elderly woman's cheek. "We both care."

"Thanks, sweetie. I'm making my next appointment with him on a Monday so I'll get to see you there. Then I may head over to the diner and check on Hank myself."

"That sounds lovely." Lily said goodbye and headed back to Valley Ridge. She'd planned on going straight to the diner, but it occurred to her that she'd left the most recent receipts from Hank on the counter at breakfast. She unlocked the kitchen door and was about to call out in case Sebastian was home when she heard a crash.

"Sebastian?" she called as she walked through the house. Glass and what looked to be dried beans littered the living-room floor. "Are you okay?"

He looked up at her and waves of anger seemed to radiate from him. “Am I okay? Why, sure, Lily, I’m great. I’m a grown man who’s sitting here trying to pick up dried beans from the table and drop them in a stupid jug like some toddler with a Tinkertoy.”

She stepped over the mess and reached out to him, placing her hand lightly on his shoulder. “Seb—”

He knocked her hand away. “*Sebastian.* It’s Sebastian. Why is it so hard for everyone in this damned town to accept that I’ve outgrown my childhood nickname?”

Fear. It might freeze some people in their place, but with Lily it caused her to jump back, out of striking distance, without even thinking. She felt a wave of nausea. She wanted nothing more than to bolt from Seb—Sebastian—and his anger and his mess. He wasn’t her problem. She didn’t need to put herself in harm’s way and be a target for his temper.

But Lily had long ago learned to face her fear, so she didn’t run. In fact, she drew a deep breath and forced herself to move back toward Sebastian. “That was uncalled for. I know how frustrating it must be—”

“Really? You know? You understand? Let me tell you, Little Miss Lily Sunshine, who goes around with a perpetual smile and an inner certainty that life is good, you don’t know anything about it. You don’t know what it’s like to see the career you planned, the life you planned, evaporate. I was a marine. Now I’ve got a crippled hand, my buddies are heading back to fight a fight I can no longer participate in, and I don’t know what the hell I am.”

Sebastian’s anger gave way to self-pity. Lily knew he’d deny it if she said so, but there it was. And she knew from personal experience that self-pity was a soul-killing emotion.

"Come on," she said, indicating he should take her hand. She didn't have time to spare, but she'd make this work.

He didn't take it; instead he asked, "Where?"

"You'll see. I mean, unless you're scared." She didn't wait any longer. She grabbed his good hand and pulled him along in her wake.

He followed. She would have pulled harder if he'd tried to break away.

"I'm not scared of anything," he assured her.

Lily had an idea. She'd used it once with one of her patients in the hospital. He'd been feeling sorry for himself, like Sebastian. "Come on and trust me."

Sebastian snorted but followed her.

Lily's momentary fear was forgotten. This was what she was good at.

She had the beginnings of a plan.

CHAPTER FOUR

LILY COULD ALMOST SEE Sebastian puff up when she made the challenge.

Scared? Of Lily?

Yeah, sometimes people underestimated her. It was as if they thought that happy people couldn't be tough.

Well, she'd dealt with injured patients for many years, and she was able to recognize when they needed something more than traditional nursing care. Sebastian had reached his limit of frustration. Time to burn off some of his energy, and hopefully some of his anger.

She was relieved that Sebastian got in his car and followed her as she drove the few blocks to the high school. He parked next to her in the lot and got out as she opened the car and took out a basketball and a piece of rope…the thin white kind that people used as a clothesline.

"What are you doing?"

"You'll see," she said. "Come on."

At the basketball court, she dropped the ball and made a slipknot in the rope, which she put over her left wrist and the other end around her waist, basically pinning her arm behind her back. "One-on-one."

She'd immobilized her hand in order to play basketball with him.

"What do you think this is going to prove?"

Oh, yeah, there was anger there in his voice. Anger brought on by the frustration of someone who'd always been healthy and suddenly wasn't. She wanted to ask about his accident. Hank told her so many things about Sebastian, but the things he talked about were in the past. More recent things, like Sebastian's accident or where he'd served, weren't in Hank's repertoire.

If they were friends, she'd ask. Whatever he told her couldn't be as bad as what she imagined. She might avoid the national news in the morning, but she kept up with current events. She knew there were marines stationed all over the world, in any number of dangerous situations. What she didn't know—and no one in town seemed to know, or at least talk about—was how Sebastian got hurt. Where he got hurt.

She wouldn't think about that now. Facing him, she replied, "I'm going to prove that I can whip your butt at basketball with one hand literally tied behind my back."

Lily wasn't sure Sebastian would accept her challenge. She wasn't even sure after witnessing his outburst that it was a good idea. But as a nurse she'd learned that the best way to help people who had profound injuries heal was to show them they were capable. Pushing them if necessary.

She couldn't give Sebastian back his career, and no one could help him discover where to turn next, but she could show him what he could do. Hank had told her that Sebastian had played basketball in high school. She knew he loved the game. She could show him that even if his left hand was impaired, he could still indulge in a favorite pastime.

"Chicken?" she asked, upping the ante.

He pulled off his ever-present jacket and tossed it onto the pavement. “You’re so losing this.”

“Keep dreaming, Bennington.”

Fifteen minutes in, Lily was losing and losing badly. Well, losing the game. The moment Sebastian had laughed, she was winning as far as she was concerned.

A couple of teenage boys came over. She recognized one of them, the son of an ex-patient. “Hi, Lily.”

“Hey, Joey. What’s up?”

“Want some help?” Joey nodded in Sebastian’s direction. “Looks like the big guy is beating you.”

“I’ll take all the help I can get.” She turned to Sebastian. “Are you up for a team game?”

“I’m still going to win,” he teased with a grin. “You don’t need to tie your hand back. With as bad as you play, I think even with a bum hand I’m still ahead of the game.”

Lily untied her arm and flexed it, working out the kinks. Joey and one of his friends teamed up with her, the other two with Seb. And the game began again.

Half an hour later, Joey called out, “Hey, I’ve got to pick up my sisters. They get worried if I’m late.”

Lily knew how much Joey helped his dad with his younger siblings. He sounded so much older than a boy in his teens. “Send Allie and Mica my love. I’ll stop in and see them soon. I think we’re about done anyway.” Lily nodded at Sebastian and his teammates. “You guys smoked us, but I suspect it was mainly my fault. Sorry, guys,” she said to her teammates.

“Hey, you did good for a girl,” Joey said.

Lily shot him a mock frown. “I think your sisters would get you for saying something like that.”

Joey laughed. “Yeah, but I can still handle them.”

"One day soon, maybe not so much."

Joey laughed as if he was positive that day would never come. He took off across the street to the middle school, his friends on his heels, all of them hollering goodbyes. Lily admired Joey Williams so much. He was barely in his teens and had faced such family heartache, but he could still laugh.

She glanced at Sebastian. "I won," he proclaimed, grinning.

"Yep. I guess you're not totally ready to be put out to pasture." She started walking back to the parking lot.

Sebastian was right behind her. "You're not going to let me feel sorry for myself?"

Lily shrugged. "I guess I can't stop you from self-pity."

"But you're not going to indulge me," he checked.

"No, I'm not going to indulge you," she agreed. "Everyone has things they have to overcome. Your injury is apparent. Even when you tuck that hand in a jacket pocket, the scars are there. Some other people's injuries aren't as visible, but don't assume they don't have their own hurdles."

"There's my Pollyanna. So will you share what sort of hurdles you've had? I'm certain you climbed on your sunshiny rainbow and sailed right over them."

Lily refused to comment on how ridiculous a *sunshiny rainbow* sounded. "Sorry. I'll have to leave you guessing. Besides, I don't have time. I need to get back home, catch a shower, go on one more call, then be at the diner. I had actually stopped home only to pick up some paperwork."

"Do you ever slow down?" he asked.

She thought about it a moment and then shook her

head. “No, because somebody’s got to work around here. See you later, Sebastian.”

Sunshiny rainbow?

Sebastian Bennington didn’t know a thing about her past.

And as far as she was concerned, he never would.

FORTY-FIVE MINUTES LATER, Sebastian heard the door slam of the small apartment tucked into the back of his grandfather’s house. Which meant Lily was leaving. He looked out the window and watched her disappear on foot down the street. Her house call must be in town.

He thought about going to the diner but decided to stay home and clean up his mess in the living room. He felt embarrassed that she’d seen him throwing a…well, *temper tantrum* was probably the most apt description.

He flexed his hand and almost relished the pain.

When he’d joined the marines, Hank had asked only one thing—don’t die.

And he hadn’t. With that thought came a sense of guilt. He was here, but his friends were still serving.

He knew he was lucky. Still, as Lily had said, knowing it and feeling it…those were two very different things.

He thought about getting something to eat. Sebastian opened the pantry door…and saw the milk container inside. It had to be from this morning when Hank had volunteered to clean up after breakfast.

Seb ignored the sinking feeling in the pit of his stomach. After all, anyone could make a mistake and put something where it didn’t belong. Milk in a pantry wasn’t so bad. Why, he’d put the peanut butter in the fridge more than once.

It didn't mean a thing.

He tried to believe that, but there was more than a good chance that Lily was right about Hank needing to see a doctor.

He dumped the now-warm milk down the sink and rinsed the plastic container before tossing it in the recycling bin.

He decided to go to the diner for dinner after all. He'd stop to pick up milk before coming home.

He thought about grabbing his jacket, but didn't. It was balmy for an early May evening. His hand felt awkward just hanging at his side, so he tucked his fingers into his jeans pocket. It by no means hid the scars, but he felt better for it.

Hank's house was a small Victorian. Farther down the block was JoAnn Rose's home, another Victorian that was much bigger than Hank's. It was a bed-and-breakfast these days. Mrs. Rose had lived there for as long as he could remember. She'd seemed old when he was a kid. He'd seen her a few days ago and she'd still seemed old, but not older. He couldn't decide if she was aging extremely well or if his perspective had changed over the intervening years.

So much about Valley Ridge seemed the same. The houses on the tree-lined streets. There were flowers in so many of the yards. It brought to mind the old saying "April showers bring May flowers." Well, there were flowers galore. Sebastian couldn't name them, but the bright yellow ones reminded him of Lily. Sunny. Cheerful.

What had she meant when she'd told him she had her own hurdles, and alluded to injuries that couldn't be seen?

The thought of his dark-haired Pollyanna ever being hurt bothered Sebastian, and he wasn't sure why. It wasn't that he wanted to see anyone hurt. It was that he'd learned a long time ago that pain was a part of living. He knew everyone suffered some kind of trauma, but still, he didn't like thinking that of Lily.

He liked his initial impression of her entire life being populated with sunshiny rainbows. Light and carefree. Her face punctuated with laugh lines that fell into place with ease and spoke of regular use.

He flexed his bad hand, and the spasm tore his mind away from worrying about Lily's past. If she had her own pain, she'd certainly learned to cope with it better than he was dealing with his.

He spotted Mrs. Dedionisio down the block with two large bags in her hands. She lived a couple of blocks over, and he didn't see how she'd carried the bags and her cane that far.

"May I?" He reached for the bags.

She did a double take. "Seb Bennington, I heard you were back in town."

He would normally correct someone who called him Seb, but somehow his scolding died on his lips. "I am. How about you let me grab one of those?"

"I am perfectly capable of carrying my own bags."

"You are. And I'm perfectly capable of helping… despite my injury." Oh, it was blatant, he knew it, but he thrust his damaged hand out and watched her expression turn from insulted to sympathetic.

"Heard you got knocked around, but your grandfather was mum about where and how."

"No big secret. Nothing really to speak of. It was a simple accident. A fluke. My hand's still not quite what it was. And I'll confess, I feel a bit useless now and then. If you don't let me help you, I'll feel totally emasculated."

She chuckled. "Oh, that was dirty fighting, young man."

"Did it work?" He grinned and felt his eyes tighten at the corners, and he wondered if he had lines, too. They wouldn't be laugh lines. He hadn't done much laughing since the accident. But maybe they were smile lines. He didn't mind relearning how to make them fit his face.

"Yes it worked, you rascal." She thrust the bags at him. "You may walk me home and carry the bags. Of course, this acting like a gentleman won't convince me you're not up to trouble, like you were in the old days."

He juggled the bags in his right arm and used his left hand for support. "I'm wounded, Mrs. D."

She nodded at his arm. "Yes, you are."

Sebastian realized that his injury had a few uses after all, and he smiled, thinking that Lily's optimism was wearing off on him.

After he dropped Mrs. Dedionisio's bags on her counter and was rewarded with a smile and her thanks, he decided to go to the diner. He was surprised at how quickly he could see the diner's plate-glass window. He went inside, and the bell on the door chimed merrily. Hank was at the counter, ever-present coffeepot in hand.

Hank chuckled. "You here to eat?"

He nodded.

"So what do you want for dinner?"

Sebastian checked the board and saw meat loaf was the day's special. "Special will do. And a cup of coffee. Do you have time to eat with me?"

His grandfather smiled. "The dinner rush is over.

I can take a break. There are a few perks to being the owner."

Sebastian got them a booth and watched as his grandfather called their order into the kitchen, then came back, drinks in hand. "Your favorite," he said as he slid a cola toward him. "Of course, you're going to rot your teeth with all that sugar," he warned.

"Hank, do you mind if I trade this in for a coffee?" he asked.

"Boys shouldn't…" For a moment, there was confusion in his eyes. "Sure. That's what you asked for, isn't it? I thought for old times' sake you might like a cola." Before Sebastian could respond, Hank took the cola and dumped it into the sink at the counter. He brought Sebastian a cup of coffee.

"Hank, are you okay?" Sebastian asked, wanting—no, needing—to hear his grandfather say he was all right.

When his mother left that last time, Hank had patted him on the shoulder and told him it was fine. They'd be fine.

He repeated the reassurance again all these years later. "I'm fine, boy. I'm the same as ever. But what about you? Are you okay?"

"I'm fine," Sebastian echoed. "I've been out helping Colton on the farm, and I've got your yard totally pruned and manicured. I was thinking that maybe, while I was home, you'd let me pull a few shifts here? I know it's been a long time, but I bet I can still flip a good burger or bus a mean table." Growing up, he'd worked pretty much every job there was at the diner.

"I'd like to work with you, Seb. You were gone too long." Hank reached across the table and patted Sebastian's hand. "You should ask Lily about getting on the schedule. She's been doing most of the paperwork."

Lily again. He seemed to waffle somewhere between being intrigued by her and being annoyed by her. Sometimes, like today, he was even slightly charmed by her.

"I'll do that," he promised his grandfather.

The bell above the door rang and a voice called out, "Hi, Hank. Is Lily in the back?"

He turned and saw Sophie.

Her smile increased by a kilowatt. "Seb, it's so good to see you," she bubbled over.

He'd thought that Lily and those damned laugh lines of hers were over-the-top happy, but compared to Sophie, Lily seemed almost grumpy. He wanted to correct Colton's perky little fiancée. He wanted to tell her to call him Sebastian, not his childhood nickname. If it had been Lily, he would have snapped at her. But snapping at Sophie would feel like kicking a puppy. Kicking a cute, wiggly puppy who couldn't defend herself.

Despite her optimism, Lily didn't have any aura of defenselessness to her. There was a sense of wildness—a feeling that you could never truly know everything about her. Maybe today had colored his impression of her, but he suspected no one knew anything more about Lily than she wanted them to know.

Tall, with startling blue eyes, Lily's long, dark hair and her weird bohemian clothes stood in stark contrast to Sophie's cotton-candy looks. Colton's fiancée had white-blond hair that fell into short curls and gave her an air of gentleness. Lily dared him to not find a bright side to a situation. *Look, Sebastian, your hand might be wrecked, but you can still play basketball.* Sophie oozed bright happiness and dragged you to the bright side despite yourself.

"I wanted to see you, too," Sophie insisted. "And you, Hank." She leaned over and gave his grandfather a kiss on the cheek, as if it were second nature to her. "We're having a party on Sunday around lunchtime. Colton has some wonderful news and wants to share it with all his friends at once. And now that Seb's home, it's a great opportunity for everyone to get together. It's a bring-a-dish sort of thing. Colton's got burgers and hot dogs for the grill." She chuckled with amusement. "That man does love his grill. I think if he had to choose, there's a chance he'd pick it over me."

Sebastian remembered Colton going on and on about his new stainless-steel grill. "I know he likes the thing, but I think he likes you more."

"Well, thank you." She shot him another dazzling smile as a reward. "So can you both come?"

"We'll be there," Hank assured her.

She beamed her happiness so brightly he almost needed sunglasses. "That's great. Now, I'm going to run back and see Miss Works All The Time. I've got to invite her to the party and tell her that our dresses are in. I need to find a day when we can all go for a group fitting. It's going to be so much fun." She hurried through the dining room toward the kitchen.

"I thought Lily was the cheeriest person I've ever met, but Sophie is all bubbly like soda. She sort of fizzes over with happiness."

"Like champagne," Hank added with a grin. "After all, Colton's got that winery. Sophie's champagne, and Lily's like a nice Riesling, slightly sweet, with a bit of a bite and very refreshing."

Sebastian laughed, some of his earlier fears disappearing. If Hank could compare Sophie and Lily to wines, he had to be okay. Milk in the pantry? That was no worse than peanut butter in the fridge. Cola instead of coffee? That was simply a caretaker who found it hard to remember his charge had grown up.

A young girl arrived at the booth carrying their plates. “Hi, Seb,” she said. “Saw you the other night, but we didn’t really talk. I’m Megan. I’ve heard all about you.”

He tried to hide his irritation at the childhood name. “I’m Sebastian these days,” he corrected much more gently than he’d corrected Lily. “And it’s nice to meet you officially. I was asking Hank if he’d find a few shifts for me, so maybe we’ll work together.”

“I’d like that,” she said. “You take your time with dinner, Hank. I’ve got the floor under control.” She sped off.

“Nice girl,” Hank said. “She’s young, but she’s good.”

“Speaking of young, how about Mattie? What kind of wine would she be?” He couldn’t avoid thinking of her as still a little girl, hanging out at Finn’s house with Bridget. Finn’s kid sister and Mattie had spent a huge chunk of their childhood making him, Finn and Colton miserable. They were forever hiding in closets and under beds, trying to discover whatever secrets young girls thought older boys kept.

Mattie had been the instigator. She’d been the one who taunted him about his friendship with Maeve Buchanan, doing that singsongy chant about sitting in trees and kissing, even though Maeve had only ever been a buddy.

Sebastian recalled Mattie in her early teens and

how she'd had a crush on Finn. Everything in him had wanted to throw that in her face, but he hadn't.

"Now, that girl's an earthy red," Hank said.

"An earthy red wine, huh?"

Hank nodded. "Mattie wandered the country. No one ever thought she'd come home, much less settle down. But when things got rough for Bridget, she came home to take care of her friend. And she's stayed. Everyone in this town, including her own brothers, thought she'd leave, but Waltzing Mathilda, she's put down roots here. She's good with Bridget's kids. A good earthy red… solid and dependable."

Sebastian had a hard time reconciling his memories of Mattie with the picture Hank was painting, but he did offer, "I'm not sure that you should share your analogies with the women in question."

"I might be old, but I'm not that stupid," Hank told him.

Something settled in Sebastian. For this moment, he could believe that everything was all right here in Valley Ridge and, more importantly, with his grandfather.

"KNOCK, KNOCK." Lily glanced up from the ledger and found Sophie grinning at her from the open office doorway.

"Come in and save me from figures. I dreamed I was a calculator last night." That wasn't exactly what she'd dreamed. She'd had the old nightmare again.

Sometimes she thought she'd outgrown it. That she'd finally put her past behind her, but then she'd slip right back into it.

Even now, in the light of day, remembering the dream made her shudder.

Dreaming she was a calculator was preferable.

Sophie came into the room and slumped onto Hank's old couch. "I'll save you from your calculator dreams if you save me from my nightmares. I dreamed that I was in front of the church, wearing my pajamas. Colton was wearing his cowboy hat and said, 'I can't marry a woman like you,' then he turned into a horse, but was still wearing his hat, and he galloped down the aisle."

Lily got up to sit next to her friend on the couch. "Uh, Sophie, that's nuts."

"That's kind of the calculator calling the cowboy-hat-wearing-horse woman weird, isn't it?" Sophie joked.

Lily could see that she was really shaken by the dream. "No, Sophie. The fact you dreamed your fiancé became a horse wasn't the nutty part, even though it is more than a bit odd. I'm talking about your dreaming Colton would ever walk away from you—"

Sophie interrupted, correcting her, "He galloped away because he was a horse."

"In either case," Lily said in her most reassuring tone, "he'd never walk away or gallop. You two are perfect together. Absolutely perfect."

Sophie shook her head. "I'm not perfect. I'm well aware of how not-perfect I am. But Colton pretty much is."

Lily cajoled, "You're the Mary Poppins of perfect."

Sophie looked confused. "Pardon?"

"Don't you know your Disney films?" She hummed the chorus of "A Spoonful of Sugar."

Sophie's blond curls bounced as she shook her head. "No. There was no time for fun movies at my house. I don't think I've ever seen a Disney movie."

Suddenly, Lily felt guilty of making assumptions,

which was what she'd accused Sebastian of. She had a mental vision of Sophie's life—assuming that it was a rosy one—but she looked at her never-seen-a-Disney-movie friend and realized that she didn't know what sort of family Sophie came from.

In the past year, she'd become close with Mattie and Sophie. She knew she could call them for anything. But there were times, like this one, when it occurred to her that they were all still filling in the blanks about their pasts and who they were.

"Really, this is an odd conversation."

"Okay, watch this conversational segue," Sophie said. "Speaking of odd, what's this I hear about you at the school?'

Lily laughed. "That was good. You're talking about me playing basketball with the kids?"

Sophie shook her head. "I'm talking about you playing basketball with Seb. Everyone's saying—"

"Sebastian," Lily corrected. "He doesn't like being called Seb."

"Seb's what Colton calls him."

Lily shrugged. She wasn't sure why he didn't like it, but he'd made his opinion of the nickname pretty clear.

Sophie accepted Lily's lack of an explanation and carried on. "I heard you were playing basketball with Sebastian and that you had one arm tied behind your back."

She should have known that if she played basketball on a town's main road, people would see. "How on earth did you hear that already?"

"The joy of the small-town gossip mill," Sophie explained to her. "So what was up with that?"

"I was proving a point. So is this a casual visit, or did you need something?"

"Yes, I did have a purpose. I came to personally invite you to a party on Sunday afternoon. Colton's got an announcement and he wants to share it with friends first."

"Before the town gossips get wind of it?" Lily asked.

Sophie nodded. "Exactly."

Lily loved living in Valley Ridge. She loved being part of a community. But there were aspects of small-town life that she'd forgotten. She wasn't sure how. When she was growing up, everyone had known what went on in her family. Not that anyone had talked about it or offered to help, but they'd all been aware of it. She'd seen it in their furtive looks.

A familiar bitterness roiled in her stomach, but she ignored it and smiled at Sophie. Here was a friend who would help if Lily needed it. And all she wanted in return was for Lily to show up at a party? That was easy. "I'll be there."

"And I got a call from Harper at Wedding or Knot... the dresses are in." Sophie seemed excited enough to burst. "I mean, they're here. My wedding dress. Your bridesmaid dress, along with Mattie's. And the wedding is right around the corner. It's getting so real. There's only weeks to go, not months. Weeks."

Lily noted that whatever nervousness had prompted Sophie's fiancé-galloping-away dream hadn't lasted, because all she saw before her was a woman enthralled about starting her life with her perfect man. "Do we have a fitting?"

"I was hoping some time next week all three of us could go. What's your schedule like?"

"Other than Mondays, I can juggle most days."

"Great. Let me talk to Mattie and then I'll set it up." Sophie's expression became more serious. "About Abbey. Is she really okay? I don't think Mattie or Finn would survive it if something happened to one of the kids."

Lily put on her well-practiced, reassuring nurse's demeanor. "Febrile convulsions are common in kids. It's over. Abbey's really and truly going to be fine."

Sophie sighed a breath of relief. "Good. I should go. I was going to stop at Mattie's, then I need to head over to Ripley. There's a concert at a winery out that way, and I want some pictures for the website."

Sophie's job involved promoting a loosely formed group of area wineries. Lily wasn't exactly sure what all that entailed, but Sophie didn't seem to ever be short on cash. She'd insisted on buying Lily's and Mattie's bridesmaid dresses. She'd said that as long as they were doing her the honor of standing up for her, the least she could do was handle their expenses.

When they'd still protested, she'd laughed and threatened to bring them a letter from her bank, telling them that the cost of the dresses didn't put a dent in her savings and investments.

They'd continued to argue, but eventually Sophie won. It was clear that Sophie had considerable money, but she'd never lived as if she did. Once, Lily might have felt that the financial divide was too wide to cross. She'd grown up on the poorer side of middle-class, and while she'd never gone hungry, she'd never had money to spare.

She earned a good living as a nurse, but since coming to Valley Ridge, she'd relearned old economies as she tried to get her home-health-care business off the ground as well as investing in the diner.

"I'll try to have a time and day for the fitting for you on Sunday at the party," Sophie said as she got up.

"That'll be great."

"Oh, and it's bring a dish," Sophie said. "Colton's grilling. And if you think of it, you can ooh and aah over his grill. If it were alive, I might be jealous."

Lily got up and hugged Sophie. Hugging friends—people in general—was not something that came naturally to her. She didn't like being touched, for the most part. But as a nurse, touching was part of the job description, and over the years she'd gotten better at it. "I don't think you ever need to be jealous where Colton's concerned. He loves you. Anyone can see it. As for a dish, I'll think of something."

"Think about something sweet and decadent. Mattie will bring something healthy. Good, but healthy. I don't want to be too good." She gave her best wicked grin.

Lily laughed as Sophie left. No, her friend might not want to be too good, but she couldn't help it. She reminded Lily of someone.... She sat for a minute trying to put her finger on who. "Glinda."

"What was that?" Sebastian stood in the doorway. "Glinda?"

"I was thinking that Sophie reminded me of someone. I couldn't think of who, then I got it."

A lightbulb turned on. "Oh, Glinda."

"Yeah. If Sophie's ever met a bad mood, she probably didn't recognize it."

"That's sort of the pot calling the kettle black."

"No, there's a definite difference between us. Sophie seems to naturally give off sunshine. She's happy. Me,

I work at it." Rather like she'd had to work at learning to touch and hug people without pulling back.

"What do you mean?" Sebastian was still in the doorway, lurking, as if he wasn't sure he wanted to enter the room.

She waved him in and he took a step inside.

Lily sighed. "What do I mean? It's hard to explain to someone else." The difference to her felt like night and day. "When I feel myself getting overrun with negativity, I force myself to think of something good. I look for that, oh, what did you call it? That sunshiny rainbow. I find it and embrace it. I choose to be happy. Sophie simply *is* happy. It's not the same thing." But even as she said the words, she couldn't help but remember that there had been a fleeting glimpse of something when Sophie talked about never having seen a Disney movie…something that said maybe she didn't grow up under a sunshiny rainbow.

"I think that's a fine line," Sebastian said. "You choose to be happy. She simply is. Either way, you two are—"

"All sunshiny rainbows?" she teased. "Well, you're wrong. There's a vast ocean of difference between working at it and simply being it."

He looked ready to run at the slightest provocation.

"You could sit down," she offered.

He shook his head. "I wanted to see if you're going on Sunday."

"Sophie's my friend. I wouldn't miss it."

"Hank and I are going, too."

"I figured." He stood in the same spot, and the silence grew to an uncomfortable level. She broke it by asking, "Did you need something else?"

"Hank asked me to check with you about getting

put on the schedule. I figured as long as I'm here until the wedding, I'd help out. I don't want to take anyone's hours, but if you have some holes, I can fill them for you."

"Really?" She was surprised that he'd offer to work at the diner. Given his frustrations with his hand, it seemed like a recipe for more outbursts. Things he'd done before would need to be done differently. "You're sure?"

He shrugged. "I don't have anything else I need to do. I've gone out to Colton's and helped him with spring chores. I've pretty much fixed everything there is to be fixed at Hank's. I've even pulled the weeds from the flower gardens. I don't know what to do with myself, so I hope I can be useful here. I might not be as fast as I once was, but I think I can manage it."

"Yeah, great. I'm sure we can find some holes in the schedule. Are there any time conflicts I should be aware of?"

"No, no time conflicts. I'll probably still go give Colton a hand, but I can work around that. And I've done every job there is at the diner, so you can put me wherever you need me."

Lily had a sudden image of where she needed Sebastian…in her bedroom.

More specifically, in her bed.

He was smiling at her, his arms open, inviting her to join him.

And—

Lily shook her head. She might try to be someone who was open to possibilities. She'd never say there couldn't be aliens or Sasquatch. She wouldn't even deny the idea of multiple dimensions. But no matter how open she was to the idea that strange things might be possible, the idea of Sebastian Bennington ever being in her bed and calling her to his side…

Well, some things could never happen.

That was one of them.

CHAPTER FIVE

LILY DROVE HERSELF to Colton's farm on Sunday afternoon. She wanted to have her own car in case any of her patients called.

A get-together with friends was exactly what she needed. She'd had another nightmare last night. She'd woken up scared and alone.

She wanted nothing more than to see Sophie smile and know that it was only a dream. Or sit and visit with Mattie. Even play with the kids. Anything to blot out the memories.

Colton's farm was north of Five, which in local parlance meant on the lake side of the busy Route Five. As she reached the top of one of the rises, she could make out Lake Erie. It was a deep blue today, echoing the color of the sky, which was a bright springtime blue and cloudless as far as the eye could see.

It was one of those lovely late-spring days that made you happy to be alive. And it helped ease the anxiety of last night's nightmare.

Lily forced a smile as she drove by a large patch of daffodils that were growing in merry clumps along with other spring flowers she couldn't identify. Everything was in bloom.

The tension eased even more.

It was spring. She was in Valley Ridge. She was

going to spend the day with friends. Mattie would be there with the kids. Despite her illness, Abbey was back to her normal self, or so Lily had been told. And Sophie would be there, excited that her wedding was getting ever closer. Lily would be at that wedding and witness a perfect marriage begin firsthand.

By the time she approached Colton's, she'd erased all but the faintest memory of last night's dream.

Colton's farm sat on a hill. She turned off the road and onto the long gravel driveway. The barn was to the left of the drive, the big white clapboard farmhouse to the right. She hadn't been here since Colton and Sophie's engagement party at the end of March. It had been colder then, but they'd held the event in the barn. It seemed most of Valley Ridge had come out that night.

What she remembered most about that party was how happy Colton and Sophie had seemed as they welcomed their friends and danced the night away. And for whatever reason, Lily could remember the song they'd danced to. "When You Say Nothing at All." She loved the song, and the idea that sometimes not saying something could be more profound than putting it into words.

She parked near a string of cars next to the barn. "Hi, Lily," six-year-old Abbey cried as she ran to the barn, her eight-year-old brother, Mickey, hot on her heels.

Though she'd known Abbey was fine, she loved seeing the evidence that the little girl had fully recovered.

Lily's heart felt even lighter as she continued toward the cluster of her friends. She hummed a few bars of "When You Say Nothing at All."

The tune died on her lips when she spotted Sebastian.

A second later, she was almost mowed over by Mattie and the kids' new dog, Bear.

She stepped out of the careening puppy's way in the nick of time and smiled at Sebastian. There was no smile in return. Like the song, he didn't need words to convey the message that she was back in the…well, doghouse.

"What's wrong now?" she asked as she approached him.

"Did I say anything?" he countered defensively.

Things had been easier for them since the impromptu basketball game, and now here they were back at odds. Lily wouldn't mind it but she didn't know why it was so.

"Sebastian, what is it now?"

"It's Hank. I found some misplaced items in the kitchen. I'm trying to tell myself that it could happen to anyone. I mean, how often do you misplace keys or the like, but milk? I found it in the cupboard on Thursday and almost convinced myself it was only a slip, but today, I found the butter in the dishwasher."

"And you blame me? Like maybe I snuck in and hid things to convince you there's a problem?" She forced herself to stand her ground and not back up in the face of Sebastian's palpable anger. She'd spent too many years cowering to fall into that pattern. But that sick feeling from last night's nightmare came back with a vengeance.

"No, damn it. I'm pissed in general. I worked that shift at the diner last night and I watched him. Hank seemed fine, except…"

"Except?" she pressed.

He took another deep breath and his anger ratcheted down a notch. "He didn't use anyone's name. That was one of the things about Hank and the diner. He knows everyone in town. He welcomed everyone by name."

Lily was at the diner on a regular basis, but she was in the office more often than not. She went to work on the books, or the bills, or her new goal of cleaning out the files. "Hank was still using names a month or so back, but he was mixing them up. He called Mattie Juliet."

"My cousin," Sebastian confirmed.

"Yeah, I know. He did it more than once and she worried."

"I'm worried, too," Sebastian admitted.

"I know you were mad when I pushed for this doctor's appointment, but, Sebastian, it could be something we can treat. Some medications can cause confusion. Sometimes a combination of meds leads to an unintended mental side effect."

"And sometimes? Sometimes it gets worse and worse until Hank's lost. I've done some reading. He could be having TAI—"

"TIAs," she corrected. "Mini strokes."

He nodded. "But I know we're both thinking that it's Alzheimer's. And if it is, he would eventually disappear in the disease. I can't lose my grandfather, Lily."

"Seb—"

She was interrupted when Colton and Sophie got up on the front porch, along with Mattie's brother. Colton seemed ready to make his big announcement. Evidently, he and Rich were partnering up on his winery, and Rich was considering taking on a partner in the coffee shop. Rich looked at Mattie in such a way that no one was left with any doubt who that partner would be.

Mattie and Finn were leaning together, talking quietly as Colton and Rich waxed enthusiastic about their plans. But it was Sophie who drew Lily's attention. She looked at Colton with a soft smile playing on her lips, as if he were the only one here at the farm.

Then Colton looked over at Sophie. The zing that passed between them was tangible. It spoke of love and a connection between two people that Lily had never witnessed before.

Sophie and Colton were so obviously in love. Lily didn't think anything could ever tear them apart. She couldn't imagine Colton ever speaking to Sophie in anything less that soft, loving tones.

Her observations were quickly replaced when Abbey screamed for her aunt Mattie. Their dog rampaged out of the barn, a saddle dragging behind him as he charged around like an enraged bull. Lily caught a glimpse of Mattie planting a hasty kiss on Finn's cheek, then saying something to him before they both took off after Bear.

Total pandemonium ensued as children and adults chased the dog.

Mattie had said something after that quick kiss.

Lily was no lip reader, but she'd have bet money Mattie had said *I love you.* Maybe it was because of the look Mattie and Finn had exchanged. It was the same look that Lily had noted passing between Colton and Sophie.

The thoughts and impressions were pretty much instantaneous. Lily joined in with the other adults as they tried to save Bear, but she knew there was more than a shared love of three kids that passed between Finn and Mattie.

They loved each other.

Mattie snagged the giant puppy, who didn't slow down until Mattie tumbled over him and landed next to the dog. Everyone laughed, Mattie included. She sat in the dirt next to Bear, who was licking the grime from her cheeks and leaving them streaked with mud. An errant piece of straw stuck out of her friend's blond hair.

Mattie looked one more time in Finn's direction, and there was no room for doubt in Lily's mind.

Mattie loved Finn. And as Lily glanced at her friend, Dr. Finn Wallace—who, to the best of Lily's knowledge, never let anyone get too close—looked at Mattie with such raw emotion there in his expression that she knew he loved Mattie.

Sophie stood beside Colton at the edge of the crowd, as if pulled next to him by some form of gravity.

Lily sighed.

Here were two couples who defined what love should be.

When she saw them together, she believed that love—a gentle, lasting kind of love—did exist.

She'd hold on to that belief.

Not that she held on to it for herself. She might refuse to live in fear, but she also acknowledged that she didn't think she could ever trust a man as fully as Sophie trusted Colton and Mattie obviously trusted Finn. She didn't have it in her. Sure, she enjoyed dating, but she'd never tie herself down. Once, she'd thought she could get beyond her past and give someone that kind of commitment, but she'd learned the hard way that she couldn't. She'd hurt herself—worse, she'd hurt someone else, as well.

She'd decided then and there not to even try for love.

When she'd moved here, she hadn't given much thought to the fact that there was such a limited pool of eligible bachelors.

That lack hadn't bothered her, until now.

And looking at Finn and Mattie, as well as Colton and Sophie, it suddenly bothered her very much.

She drifted away from Sebastian and turned the corner of the house, wanting to put a bit of space between herself and everyone else. She needed a minute to regroup.

She smiled when she saw the old swing that was strung on a huge log suspended between two trees.

The ropes that held the swing looked a bit too old to be trusted, but everything in Lily wanted to sit down on that swing and see how high she could make it go. She gave it a tentative push.

"I wouldn't try it."

She looked behind her and saw that Sebastian had followed. She said, "I can see it's not quite trustworthy."

"You like swings." It was a statement. As if he'd learned something about her.

She realized he was right. For her, a swing was a symbol of safety, of comfort. She couldn't count how many times while she was growing up she'd found refuge on the swings behind her house.

When she didn't answer, he said, "The other night, when you were upset about Abbey, you were on the glider, which frankly isn't in much better shape than this swing."

"It's only a swing," she said. "I—"

"There you are," Sophie gushed. "Oh, don't you sit on that swing. I've been after Colton to either put up new ropes or take the whole thing down. I don't want someone to swing on it and have it fall apart. Sebastian, could you loop it over a branch or something? Let's get it out of the kids' reach."

"Sure thing. I'm not sure Mattie or Finn would survive another trip to the emergency room with one of the kids." Sebastian heaved the swing over a branch with his right arm. His left steadied it, but even that was a lot and he grunted from the exertion, or maybe from the pain.

Lily wanted to ask if he was okay but knew he wouldn't thank her for it, especially not in front of a witness.

"And you," Sophie said, grabbing Lily by the hand and tugging her back toward the party. "Come on. We need to find Mattie so we can discuss our group fitting. We have the appointment on Wednesday, if that still works. Mattie has the coffee shop covered. I thought we'd make a day of it..."

Lily glanced back at Sebastian, who was rubbing his left hand with his right one while he grimaced.

It had definitely been pain.

She wondered if he had a script for pain medication or if he was medicating himself with over-the-counter analgesics.

She'd really like to ask, but she was learning. He'd seemed so much better with her since their basketball game. Not as suspicious and certainly not as...well, mad.

She didn't want to rock the boat.

SEBASTIAN RUBBED HIS lower left arm as he watched Sophie drag Lily back toward the crowd. He glanced up to where he'd tossed the swing over one of the maple's lower branches. He was pretty sure it was high enough to be out of the way of the kids.

He stared at the giant trees that shaded this side of the house. There used to be two swings side by side, but only this one remained. Sebastian wasn't surprised that Colton left it up when he'd bought this farm from his grandfather.

When they were young, he used to come out here in the summer with Finn and Colton supposedly to help out. But helping out generally turned into playing within short order. The two swings hung from a log that stretched between the two maples, the wooden planks suspended from thick ropes.

They'd twist the swings until the ropes groaned from the tension, then one of them would climb on and they'd let it go.

Around and around they'd spin.

Not a care in the world.

Somewhere in the copse of trees behind the house there were probably the remains of their old clubhouse. They'd built it from old pallets and other scraps of wood. It sat on a hill by the creek that ran down to the lake. As an adult, it seemed logical to him that the creek feed into Lake Erie. But as a kid, he'd been curious. He wanted to know where the creek led. He'd talked Finn and Colton into following it with him. It couldn't have been more than a mile, but for three young boys, it was a sublime and epic adventure.

They'd packed a knapsack with supplies. Thermoses, snacks and sandwiches. They hadn't even gone a quarter of a mile before he'd fallen into a water hole, soaking their sandwiches and snacks. But they'd made it to the lake. They'd all gone skinny-dipping, then trudged back home along the creek's path.

They'd returned to the clubhouse, three hungry, muddy messes, but none of the adults had ever found out what they'd done that day.

Looking back, Sebastian realized what a great childhood he'd had. His grandfather had taken Sebastian away from his mom and kept him here in Valley Ridge. Hank had given him the opportunity to be a kid.

Sebastian was back to thinking about his grandfather's problems. Lily was right about Hank. Sebastian felt guilty for lashing out at her because there was something wrong with Hank.

That thought weighed heavily on his mind as he returned to the party. He scanned the yard, looking for his grandfather, then spotted Hank down by the barn listening earnestly to something Mickey was saying.

Finn came up and clapped Sebastian on his good shoulder. "Your grandfather's still great with the kids."

"He is, isn't he?" Something might be wrong, but maybe it wasn't permanent. Lily was right. It could be medications or something else entirely. Just because Hank was confused a time or two didn't mean he had Alzheimer's.

Finn jerked his head in the direction of a vacant makeshift picnic table that consisted of a couple sawhorses with boards on top, surrounded by lawn chairs.

Sebastian understood the invitation and followed him over to it. They each grabbed a chair and Finn said, "So we need to talk about what we're going to do for Colton's bachelor party."

Sebastian had known he and Finn needed to plan something, but he couldn't help but groan. "I am so past the age where a wild night of drinking is my idea of fun."

"So am I," Colton said as he came up behind them, then pulled up another chair and joined them. "I know traditionally the groomsmen plan the night, but if I'm not stepping on any toes, I have a suggestion."

"It's your wedding…your stag. We're all ears," Finn said.

"I have a friend from Erie. Well, not from Erie anymore. He moved outside town to Whedon," Colton said. "Anyway, Tyler got married a couple years ago and he didn't have a stag. He had a Stag and Drag. It was basically a big party for male and female friends of the couple. No crazy-drinking night. No strippers. They rented out a room at a bar and hung out. I don't think there'd be enough of us to need a room, but we could get a reservation someplace fun and go out for a night on the town."

"That's what you want? You're sure?" Sebastian asked.

Colton nodded. "Sophie and I talked about it and we thought that rather than a stag or bachelorette party, we'd all head into Buffalo. Like I said, someplace fun. Not a ton of people. The bridal party, maybe Mattie's brother, since he's now my partner, and probably Ray, too. I know Maeve and Dylan might want to come, as well."

"What's Maeve doing these days?" Sebastian asked. He couldn't even count the times he'd been in the principal's office and seen her there. No one ever knew what she'd done. Rumors swirled, and more than once, he knew he was blamed for dragging Maeve into trouble. But he'd never dated her, much less gone out with her. They'd been friendly, that was all.

Maeve Buchanan had been a mystery then.

"She works in Ripley at a winery and has single-handedly reopened the library," Colton explained.

It might strike some people as odd that the town's bad girl was now a librarian, but in addition to spending a lot of time in the principal's office, his keenest memory of her involved her nose in a book.

"And Dylan?" That name didn't sound familiar.

"Valley Ridge's new cop. One of three for the county," Colton answered. "I'm not sure why, but everyone refers to him as The Sheriff."

"Hmm, Mr. Cowboy Hat, let's guess who started that?" Sebastian mused.

Finn said, "I seem to recall when we were young you were always the cowboy. Do you remember when you roped Mrs. Stevenson's goat?"

Colton took the ribbing with good humor. "That goat was in the garden, so I was performing a public service. As for the hat—" he took it off and tipped it "—I'm out in the field all day and needed something. It was either this or one of those wide-brimmed Amish hats that a couple of the shops have. The cowboy hat won out."

"You couldn't have gone with a baseball cap?" Sebastian asked.

Colton put the hat back on his head. "No. The back of my neck would still have taken a beating."

"Yeah, it's all about the back of your neck and not that you've always had a thing for cowboys," Finn teased. "Remember when he was a kid that cowboy sleeping bag he got one year?"

Sebastian nodded. "I'm surprised he's running a vineyard and not a cattle ranch. Do farmers in Valley Ridge ever need to rope their herds?"

"Doesn't matter," Finn assured him. "Colton would show those cows who's boss."

"You know, I'm sitting here, hat on head, ignoring your japes and asking what you think about the Stag and Drag. I don't want to deprive you both of a traditional guy's night if that's what you want."

Sebastian looked at Finn and they both nodded. "Stag and Drag it is."

"We could head into Buffalo to The Anchor Bar for wings," Finn suggested. "I'm sure I can get us a reservation."

Sebastian watched his boyhood friends as they talked about the night out in Buffalo and challenged each other to a wing-off.

For a moment, it was hard to believe he'd ever left Valley Ridge.

For a moment, it was almost as if everything was still the same.

Maeve Buchanan was still here, still reading books, even if she wasn't getting called to the principal's anymore. He'd seen the former mayor, Stanley Tuznik, as a crossing guard near the school the other day. JoAnn still lived down the street in a house that looked like Hank's but was bigger. The Five and Dime was still where everyone shopped, despite the chain stores in close proximity.

Finn and Colton continued to snipe and tease.

Things changed, but they stayed the same.

Maeve didn't only read books; she ran the library now. Mattie's brother was the mayor. JoAnn's big house was now a B and B. The Five and Dime was now Quarters, due to inflation was Marilee and Vivienne's quip.

And Colton was getting married, while Finn was a surgeon in Buffalo.

The same, but different.

Sebastian glanced around Colton's yard, admiring it and his family and friends. He spotted Hank walking by one of the fields with Finn's nephew, Mickey, and felt a spurt of nervousness. The worry he felt for his grandfather reminded him that things were not the same with Hank. They'd changed and not for the better.

Lily was talking to Mattie and Sophie, but she gave him a look and a slight nod toward the field, and he knew she'd seen Hank, too, and that she was worried.

"Where do you think they're going?" he asked the guys.

Colton followed where Sebastian was pointing. "Oh, I bet Mickey's showing Hank my surprise for Sophie out beyond the fields. There's not anything Mickey can get into…or Hank." He laughed, not realizing that Hank getting into trouble was exactly what Sebastian had been concerned about.

Sebastian gave Lily a slight nod to let her know it was okay.

And he realized that things had indeed changed, but he was lucky. Lily was one of the changes, and despite the hard time he'd given her initially, she was a good addition to Valley Ridge.

"SO WILL THAT WORK for you, Lily?" Sophie asked.

Lily had been so caught up with worrying about Hank that she'd lost track of the conversation. She struggled to remember where they were….

"Sure. I'll do some juggling with appointments and should be fine. That's one of the bonuses of working for myself." She smiled as if she didn't really mind the juggling. She only had a couple patients who had to be seen on Wednesday, but she'd simply see them after the dress fitting. Miss Helen was particularly fond of wedding plans. She'd love being the first to hear how beautiful Sophie looked in her dress.

Lily didn't need to wait until Wednesday to know that Sophie would be stunning.

"Great. Call me if you have to reschedule for a weekend when Finn's around to help with the kids." Sophie seemed about to explode with happiness. "I can't believe it's almost here. Me and Colton. Getting married. I never thought I'd be doing this. I never thought I'd be a bride. A bride who practically oozes her brideishness all over her friends. I will probably squeal and cry a bit when I put on the dress. I know, you both will be shocked when I do." She gave a little prequel squeal, as if she wanted to be sure she was prepared.

"Sophie, I don't think you've ever met an emotion you didn't embrace wholeheartedly," Mattie said, smiling indulgently at their friend.

Lily had to agree. But suddenly Sophie's bubbles of excitement popped and she got more serious than Lily had ever seen her. "When I was younger, I wasn't permitted to do either. *Proper young ladies* didn't giggle. They certainly didn't cry in public or dance with glee. I was a good daughter and tried to obey all my parents' rules, but they..." Sophie let the sentence fade, but it was easy to see that whatever her parents had done had deeply hurt her.

Lily understood that no matter how hard you tried to walk away from your past, it could haunt you.

But the moment passed and Sophie smiled, though it was an expression that didn't quite reach her eyes, as if the pain, once remembered, took some time to forget. "I vowed when I got older and could do what I wanted to that I'd never be a *proper young lady.* Thankfully, a certain farmer who's fond of cowboy hats doesn't mind that this is the result." And just as quickly as the bubbles popped, they were back as she bowed with a flourish. It was as if thinking about Colton wiped away whatever pain she still carried.

"So let's talk about Wednesday," Sophie said. "I think we should go to the fitting first. That way I won't be tempted to pass up dessert in order to fit into my dress. I so hope it fits. That it looks the way I thought it would look. I know getting married here at Colton's doesn't require a Cinderella gown. The one you two helped me pick out is simple and it..."

Sophie talked about dresses and lunch. Her excitement and joy were overflowing, and Lily felt...happy.

Lily knew that Sebastian mocked the fact that she looked for the bright side—that she concentrated on sunshiny rainbows. To be honest, sometimes finding that silver lining was hard.

She'd seen her friend struggle to let go of her past and regain her bubbly side.

Well, Lily might not wear every emotion she had on her sleeve, but she could ignore her past and embrace glasses half-full and clouds with silver linings.

Maybe, someday, she'd be able to get Sebastian to look at the bright side again.

CHAPTER SIX

ON MONDAY SEBASTIAN picked up his first official shift at the diner—it was only a four-hour one. Lily had scheduled him for washing dishes, which included busing tables. Washing the dishes wasn't so bad after he worked out a trick. He put a rubber mat in the sink. It held the dishes in place with very little input from his left hand while his right hand scrubbed them.

And when he bused the tables, he propped the handle of the bus pan against his left forearm, using that, more than his hand, to carry it. His hand still hurt, and it was awkward, but it worked.

"How'd it go?" Lily had asked with a smile, as if she was sure it had gone swimmingly.

Well, Sebastian guessed it could be counted as a success if he ignored the fact that his hand was aching.

"Pretty good" was all he'd said.

"Still looking to pitch in, or did we break you today?"

She was teasing, he knew it, but he couldn't help but bristle because he felt more than slightly broken. "Sure, I'll help," he said with more enthusiasm than he felt.

"Great. Red wants tomorrow night off, and none of the other cooks can work it. It's been a while since you've handled the cooking, but this would only be a four-hour shift."

"Are you scheduling me for half shifts because you

don't think I can manage a whole one?" The words came out a lot harsher than he'd intended.

Lily didn't pull back, as he noticed she so often did when he was testy. She stood her ground and forced a smile. He knew it was forced because those wrinkles around her blue eyes didn't fall into their normal places.

"I'm scheduling," she said slowly, as if she wanted to be sure he understood her, "your hours around the hours people can spare. Most of our employees live paycheck to paycheck and simply can't take a full shift off because you want the hours. Red has a new girlfriend, who complains he works too many evening hours and misses things. Her parents have an anniversary party, and he wanted to surprise her and go. It wasn't a reflection on you or your capabilities."

He'd felt like a heel for complaining. He should have understood that there were only so many hours available at the diner. Obviously not enough to keep him busy.

The next night, he quickly discovered that the rhythm of short-order cooking didn't come back as quickly as busing a table or washing a plate. There was an element of timing involved. Making sure all the dishes on an order were done at the same time.

And he'd lost that ability over the years.

His first two orders were not well-timed, but after the first couple hours, he felt his old skills coming back to him. He tossed three burgers on the grill and listened to the hiss as the grease splattered.

"How's it going?" Lily asked as she came through the kitchen, walking toward the office.

"Well, it might take me a while, but I'm getting back into the swing of things." He pressed the burgers with his spatula.

"Good."

"What are you doing tonight?" He tossed the hamburger rolls onto the grill next to the burgers.

"More of the files. I think it'll take me at least another week to go through all of them."

He plated the rolls and flipped the burgers again. More grease spattered. "I'd much rather cook a burger than do paperwork."

"That's how Hank feels, if those files are any indication." She paused. "What did you do to your hand?"

He glanced down and saw the massive blister on the back of his left hand.

"Must have burned it. Probably some grease from the burgers." He hadn't felt a thing.

She was all nurse as she examined it and said, "We should treat it."

His reaction to her wasn't medical at all. For one second, he wanted to take that hand and caress her cheek. Simply run his finger down along it and see if he could erase her worried look. Normally, he bristled when someone displayed any sympathy, and he wasn't sure why he wasn't bristling with Lily this time.

"I'll put a bandage on it when I pull these," he promised. He quickly put the window dressing on the buns.

"Didn't it hurt?" Lily asked.

"Nerve damage. There are sections of my hand and arm where I can't feel much," he explained. "The doctor said that some, if not all, will come back. But in the meantime, I guess that's a bonus."

"Bonus?"

"Grease burns hurt, and I don't feel a thing," he teased.

"Why, Sebastian Bennington, was that you looking

at a silver lining?" she teased, and her laugh lines fell back to their normal position.

He chuckled. "I suppose it was. You don't think you're rubbing off on me?"

"Oh, there's a possibility. Soon you'll be sitting on a rainbow, surveying life with a smile."

He snorted and plated the burgers.

By eight o'clock, he felt as if he'd never left. He'd put a bandage over the blister and was more cautious with his left hand. The small window between the kitchen and the dining area gave him a unique view of Hank.

He watched his grandfather on the other side of it, passing out greetings and coffee in turn. But not once did Hank call anyone by name. Not one person. Not even Jack Rooney, one of Hank's oldest friends. Between orders, Sebastian blatantly listened to the conversations and noticed Hank's contributions were mainly reactive. His grandfather didn't instigate topics of discussion; he only responded. And those responses were generic to the point of being interchangeable.

What do you think about the weather? Better than last month, not as good as next, he'd offered.

Hear you went fishing a couple weeks ago. Catch anything? Didn't catch a cold or the flu.

Hear Seb helped out Mrs. Dedionisio. That boy's a peach.

Of all Hank's responses, this one concerned Sebastian most of all. Back when he was growing up, Hank heard about…well, everything through the town grapevine, which seemed to begin and end at the diner.

Hank had known when Sebastian stepped over the line, out of line and when he occasionally toed the line. Hank had heard it all, and he'd mined every detail before he discussed every incident, good and bad, with Sebastian.

But he hadn't had one question about what Sebastian had done for Mrs. Dedionisio. It was a small thing, but Hank knew how fiercely independent Mrs. Dedionisio was, which meant he knew she wasn't prone to accepting help.

Hank had asked nothing—he'd said nothing.

At nine o'clock, Hank came into the kitchen and said, "I'm walking Megan home, if you'll close up."

"Sure, Hank."

His grandfather turned to leave, and Sebastian called him back. "Hank, I need your keys to the diner."

"Where are yours? Did you lose them again?"

"Hank, I haven't had keys since I left for college years ago."

Hank's expression was momentarily blank, as if he didn't understand what Sebastian was talking about. Then it cleared, and he quickly fished in his pocket and handed Sebastian his keys. "There you go. I'm taking Megan home. A gentleman should never let a woman walk home alone at night," he lectured.

"Okay, Hank."

Sebastian watched via the pass-through as Hank and Megan left. He finished cleaning the grill and prepped the kitchen for the next day. The office light was on, though he didn't need it to know Lily was still back there. He'd checked in on her a few times, and she'd been focused on whatever paperwork she was doing.

He went in and found her studying a sheet of paper from where she sat on the floor surrounded by stacks of files.

"What do you have there?" he asked.

She looked up as if surprised to discover him. "What time is it?" She didn't wait for him to answer, but looked at the clock, her surprise registering on her face. "Wow, I can't believe it's so late. Did you know your grandfather kept everything? I mean, everything. I found a cache of old newspaper articles. This one is about when your grandfather bought the diner." She passed him the brittle article. There was a picture of a young Hank Bennington and his wife, Betty.

"I never knew my grandmother," Sebastian said as he stared at the two young people in the accompanying photograph. "She died before I was born. Once, when Hank was fighting with my mom, he said he was glad she didn't live to see what my mom had become."

"Sebastian, I'm sorry."

He wasn't sure why he'd told Lily that. "No. It's all right. My mother was a drug addict. She blamed everyone for it. She blamed her mom for not being there. Hank for not being enough. Me for being too much. The one person she never blamed was herself. I suspect Hank was right, and she would have broken my grandmother's heart, because it's clear she broke Hank's."

"He was lucky he had you." Lily looked at him as if she really believed that. Despite the way he'd treated her, she believed he was someone of worth.

Sebastian wasn't so sure he agreed with that. He didn't know how to respond, so he read.

> Hank and Betty Bennington bought the old Valley Ridge Diner from John Nauss, who is relocating to Florida. "We hope to carry on Mr. Nauss's fine tradition of providing not only good food at

a fair price at the diner, but making it a meeting place for the community," Mr. Bennington said.

"He did what he set out to do," Lily commented. "The diner is the heart of the community. We have our regulars, but pretty much everyone comes in on occasion. I've met most of Valley Ridge here. As a stranger to the town, helping out here was a great way to begin to fit in."

Sebastian had eaten most of his dinners here when he was younger. He'd sit at a booth with Hank and they'd talk and visit. Then Hank would go back to work, and Sebastian would do his homework. If he ran into a problem, there was always someone around to help. Hank was great with English. Hank's friend Mr. Rooney was a science nerd. "It was a terrific place to grow up."

"I imagine it was." Lily's eyes crinkled, but there was a hint of wistfulness in her smile. "You were very lucky."

Sebastian suspected that Lily wasn't nearly as lucky, and he found it hurt to think about her as a little girl in a bad situation. "Did you know Hank had a degree in English literature?"

She stood up slowly, as if her muscles had cramped from sitting so long. "No, I didn't know that. To be honest, he was much more free with his Sebastian stories than the Hank stories. How did he go from that to this?"

"I asked him that once, and he said literature was, at its heart, the study of people and how they relate to their society as a whole and to each other on an individual basis. Then he grinned and said that's what the diner was. He was able to study people and how they related on a daily basis…and make a steady income to support his family." He shrugged. "And once he told me he liked working with his Betty every day."

"Aw, that's sweet." Now she had her smile lines with a slightly gooey, girly, romantic zest to them. "It must have been awesome to be so in love with someone that you thought working with them daily was a bonus. I don't know if I could stand being with one person all day, every day."

Sebastian couldn't imagine it, either, but he didn't like that Lily couldn't. She was the kind of woman who should have that kind of love. He felt angry that she hadn't had a good childhood and, even worse, that someone hadn't recognized how wonderful she was and snapped her up. And the fact that he should care bothered him. He handed her the article. "I think, if you don't mind, I'm going to get a few of these framed, and then we can put the rest of them in some archival sleeves so they don't deteriorate further."

She set the article down on the desk. "I've been saving all the documents with historical worth. That's what I was thinking. But let's leave it for tomorrow." She yawned and stretched.

Sebastian knew it wasn't meant to be a sexy pose, but it definitely was. Oh, it was time to get out of here.

He should have turned and left, but he found himself saying, "Hank reminded me earlier tonight that a gentleman never allows a woman to walk home on her own."

She stepped over the piles of folders and looked up at him. "Was that an invitation, Mr. Bennington?"

"I believe it was, Ms. Paul."

"That would be nice. Give me a sec to move these piles out of the way or else Hank will knock them over when he comes in tomorrow."

Normally, Seb would offer to help, but his hand was throbbing tonight. He massaged it as he watched Lily nudge the piles against the wall.

"Ready," she said.

He switched off the lights as they left through the back door. He turned around and double-checked that the door was locked.

"Did you check the front?" Lily asked.

When he'd first met her, he might have thought her question was some sort of indication that she didn't trust him, but now he knew she was asking because she didn't trust that Hank did it. "Yes." He paused and added, "He's getting worse."

They started walking side by side toward Hank's house. "The appointment's a week from tomorrow," she said.

At the corner, they left the main street and entered a quiet, residential section of town. Sebastian had always liked being out at night. He liked seeing the houses all lit up and knowing that inside people were going about their everyday lives. Some happy, some not so much. He stared at one particular house that had lights on in every visible room. "And if it's not something they can fix?"

"You're asking what happens if it's Alzheimer's?"

He nodded, still looking at the house, not at Lily.

She stopped and gave his arm a gentle tug until he turned to face her. "If it is Alzheimer's, then Hank's still in an early stage. Noticeably impaired, but not debilitated. The doctor can give him medications that will help."

He'd done some reading on the disease and the medications associated with it, and afterward, he wished he hadn't. "The drugs can help keep him from getting worse, at least for a while, right? They slow down the course of the disease. They don't have drugs to cure it?"

"No. The current medications won't cure the disease, and they won't even help him recover the ground he's lost. What they will do is help slow the disease's progression. The medications can buy him time."

"But if that's the diagnosis, some sort of dementia, how long will he have to still be Hank?"

"I can't answer that. No one can. The medicines might stabilize him for weeks, months or…"

"Years?"

He knew what her answer was when she switched to saying, "Medicine is always changing, evolving. There are new drugs. There are even trials. He might be eligible for something like that. But the truth is, I don't know, Sebastian. Honestly, I don't know." She took his hand in hers.

She'd taken his bad hand, and his first instinct was to pull away, but he didn't. To be honest, it felt nice to know there was still something the hand could manage. It could hold someone. "When I was in the hospital, they wanted me to call Hank, to have him come be there with me at least through the surgeries, but I didn't. I didn't want him to be in California. I needed to think of him here—in Valley Ridge. I needed to know he was still at the diner. I needed to know he was still feeding the town and gossiping with folks. I needed him to be here and to have things normal. Does that make sense?"

He could barely see her nodding.

"Having him here, it helped me. Knowing that he was doing what he'd always done, that Valley Ridge was what it always was, helped. I need to know that even if everything in my life has changed, my grandfather and the town are the same."

She gave his hand a small squeeze. "There's the world the way you want it—maybe even need it to be. And there's the world the way it is. It's hard to reconcile the two. Sometimes it feels almost impossible. But in the world the way it is right now, you've got to figure out a way to cope with that. Hank needs you. No matter what the diagnosis, he needs you."

"And I want to help him, but I don't know how."

"You'll go to the doctor's with us next week and you'll be here for him. That's important, Sebastian."

He realized they'd walked the whole way home. She started toward the house, but he stopped, and because she was still holding his hand, she stopped, as well. "Do you need to get right in?"

She shook her head, and he noticed her dangly earrings tinkled slightly. He hadn't noticed before, probably because the diner was always so noisy. Even when the customers left, the refrigerator and freezers hummed, the ice machine clinked…

She said, "No. I'm going out with Sophie tomorrow and we're not leaving until tenish, so I've got plenty of time."

He wasn't ready to let her go. "Would you sit with me for a few minutes?"

She nodded again, producing more tinkling noises. "Yes."

He took her to the glider and they sat side by side, which tipped the glider at a precarious angle.

"It might work better if you sat on the other side," Lily suggested with a laugh.

He could do that. It might make sense, but he didn't

want to. He found comfort in walking next to and sitting next to Lily. "Maybe, but if I'm on this side, we're tipped back enough that we can see the stars easier."

"You're a stargazer?" she asked.

Well, that just bit him in the butt. Odds were she knew all the constellations. "No. I couldn't pick out a star by name if my life depended on it, but I like looking at them. There's something soothing about them. I remember in school, the science teacher was telling us that the light from the stars takes so long to get here that some of them are long since dead before we ever see them. I like thinking about that."

"About them being dead?"

He shook his head. "About them still being visible even if they're not there. I think when I was in the hospital I wanted to keep Hank here in Valley Ridge because if he was here, I knew he was thinking about me, and somehow, even though I wasn't here, I was. Again, if that makes any sense at all."

"I've found that things that feel right to you don't always have to make sense to anyone else."

"Which is your way of saying it doesn't?"

She laughed. "No, I can understand that the idea of things being the same can be comforting. Sometimes the opposite is true, too."

There was such utter sadness in her voice that it was palpable. "What do you mean?" he asked softly, hoping she'd share.

But the moment passed, and Lily leaned back as if to get a better look at the stars. "I don't know any of the constellations, either, but I'm officially dubbing that cluster there—" she pointed "—the Valley Ridge Constellation." He finger traced what could be considered a big V in the sky. "It represents the valleys and—"

"Let me guess, the ridges?"

She laughed again, and if he hadn't witnessed it for himself, he wouldn't have believed that a minute ago she'd been sad.

"Yes, that's it," she told him.

But that was all she told him.

Lily knew everything about him. Stories from Hank. Things he'd shared.

But he knew very little about her.

And it bothered him.

As they sat on the glider, tipping back so they could look at the stars, he realized that it bothered him a lot.

THE NEXT DAY, Lily listened to Sophie and Mattie chatter happily on the hour drive into Buffalo. She tried to keep up her end of the conversation, but it was tough.

She couldn't help remembering sitting with Sebastian last night. She'd almost told him about her parents.

Almost.

She'd worked so hard for so long to keep her past separate from her present. Oh, she spoke to her mother religiously every weekend, but they were perfunctory calls. She tried to make the distinction between supporting her mother without supporting her choices, but sometimes it was hard. So she kept things superficial. She wished it was different. She wished she had the kind of relationship with her mother that she'd witnessed between Mattie and her mom.

At least it happened for other people.

"We're here," Sophie announced with a squeal, pulling Lily from her thoughts.

They parked in front of a brick building that looked more like a home than a store. The sign out front was the only indication it was a place of business. It read Wedding or Knot, and the *o*'s were Celtic knots.

"Let's go." Sophie practically vibrated with excitement as she got out of the car and hurried into the shop with Mattie and Lily right behind her. Lily entered the shop and had an Oz-like moment. Instead of stepping out of the black-and-white house into the colorful Oz, à la Dorothy, she had stepped into a sea of white. So many shades of taffeta, chiffon and silk. She had never known there were so many shades of white.

Mattie made a small gagging motion, and Lily gave her a poke with her elbow and simply took in the beauty that surrounded her. This was why she was here. To share this with friends. So she forced herself to put thoughts of Sebastian, Hank and even her parents aside and concentrate on Sophie and Mattie.

Growing up she'd hidden in her books. She was on the fringe of school society—not part of any crowd, but tolerated by all. In college, she'd been so busy working and studying that she hadn't really had time for real friendships.

She'd had a few casual acquaintances at work. People she'd call for an evening out or a movie. But Mattie and Sophie were the first real friends she'd ever had. Today was about Sophie—about the three of them. So she shook her head and scolded the still-gagging Mattie. "How on earth did you get like this? You are not a normal woman. Bridal shops are meant to set our hearts aflutter. You didn't even know that bridal showers required pastel colors."

Lily wasn't sure why it had mattered so much to her,

but she had needed Sophie's shower to be perfect. She'd wanted her friend to be excited when she saw the decorations and the cake. And Lily hadn't been disappointed. Sophie loved every pastel-colored winery-themed moment that the party had to offer. And finding pastel wine decorations had been no easy task.

"Showers have to be pastel?" Sophie asked, obviously unaware of the ongoing pastel squabble Mattie and Lily had.

"Aha." Mattie pounced on Sophie's innocent question. "I think that bridal showers require pastel colors only in your head, Lily… What's your middle name?"

"Claire. Why?"

"I've found with the kids using their middle names gives the right emphasis. Watch—that pastel requirement is only in your head, Lily Claire Paul. We don't need to worry about a Bridezilla because we have Bridesmaidzilla."

"I'm not that bad." Lily waited for Sophie to back her up.

But Sophie had obviously wised up and said, "Pastels or not, it was a beautiful shower thrown by two very good friends."

"A perfectly good argument killed by diplomacy," Mattie groused unconvincingly.

"When you get married, I promise, not a pastel in sight," Lily said. "Sophie and I will figure out something very Mattie-esque. Maybe a coffee-themed wedding? Little coffee-mug favors, and—"

"Bridesmaidzilla strikes again," Mattie moaned dramatically.

The shop's consultant was busy talking to an older

lady and held up a finger to indicate she'd be with them in a minute. They took seats by the fitting rooms.

"I'm not that bad," Lily said again.

Sophie remained silent, but her grin said it all.

Mattie obviously caught Sophie's expression, because she gloated. "See, even Sophie's not saying anything. That means she agrees with me."

"I do not agree or disagree. I am the pastel version of Switzerland because I am not getting in the middle of this battle. It was a lovely shower. A lovely day. I don't think you both understand how rare it is to have found friends like you. I'm so very lucky." Sophie looked as if she was on the verge of tears.

Lily was desperately trying to think of something joyful to say, when the bridal consultant approached them.

Sophie's tears dried up and she scolded, "Now, behave, both of you. Here's Harper."

Lily had met Harper Akina when they'd all gone dress shopping. The woman had been wonderful to work with. She hadn't made them feel pressured; she'd never once asked if this was *the dress.* She'd simply asked questions about what they were looking for and then worked to find it.

She was petite. Shorter than Sophie, who at five-two was tiny. But both times Lily had seen her, Harper had been wearing towering heels that helped disguise her lack of height. She was today as well, but she wasn't smiling as she had been on previous visits. She was pulling her sleek, dark hair back into a severe ponytail, twisting the band with far more force than required.

"Problems, Harper?" Sophie's expression became

concerned. “Tell me there’s nothing wrong with our dresses.”

Harper took a long, deep breath, then shook her head. “Sorry. It was only a rude customer.”

“Ugh, Harper.” Mattie’s voice was awash with understanding and sympathy. “I work with the public, and while most of our customers are lovely, some are…well, not so much. I had a guy come into the coffee shop the other day and yell at my mom because she put whipped cream on his hot chocolate. Mom’s been working at the coffee shop, learning the ropes so that she can fill in more readily if I need her. She learned how to make the whipped cream and was treating everyone to a sample.”

“You make your own whipped cream?” Harper asked. “That sounds like my kind of place.”

“Park Perks, in beautiful downtown Valley Ridge.” Mattie grinned. “Of course, our downtown is only a few blocks long, but still, we have great coffee, whipped cream—”

“And homemade muffins,” Sophie added.

“Thanks, Soph,” Mattie said. “We buy our cream locally. Anyway, Mom’s customer was a jerk. I finally stepped in and told him he had three options. He could scrape the whipped cream off, drink it as it was or I’d make him a new one.”

“Which one did he pick?” Harper asked.

“He slunk away, whipped cream on the cocoa.” She smiled at Harper. “Most people are lovely. That’s what I remind myself.”

“Most are,” Harper agreed. She scowled as she looked over her shoulder where the older woman had been, as if the lady had left some bad smell behind. When she turned back to them, she offered a genuine smile. "You three are quickly becoming my favorite customers. That woman won't be coming back anyway. She kept me hopping for two hours and finally told me she wasn't interested."

"We won't keep you that long," Sophie promised.

"That's not what I meant at all. To be honest, I've been so anxious for you all to get here. Wait until you see the dresses. Follow me."

The woman's good mood instantly restored by the thought of the dresses, Harper hurried them into a spacious viewing room where three dress bags were hanging on hooks.

"Start with the bride's," Lily said. She felt as excited as Sophie looked as Harper unzipped the bag and took out a knee-length, white silk wedding dress with thin, wispy straps. Sophie had complained that since she was so tiny if she tried to go with a traditional princess-style dress she'd get swallowed in it. Still, she'd worried that maybe Colton would be disappointed if she went with something less traditional, but Lily had assured her that Colton wouldn't care what Sophie wore as she came up the aisle as long as she came up the aisle.

Sophie and Harper disappeared into a dressing room. Lily found herself tearing up as she waited with Mattie, which was ridiculous. Sophie hadn't even come out yet.

"Are you okay?" Mattie asked her.

"Fine. It's stupid. I know it's stupid, but I can't help it. I don't cry as much as Sophie, but I do cry at weddings and, apparently, at bridal shops." She brushed at her eyes with the back of her hand.

"If you're this emotional over Sophie's wedding, imagine how you'll be when it's your own."

"Maybe I'm so invested in Sophie's because I'll never

have a wedding myself." Once, Lily had thought differently. She'd thought she could forget her past completely and marry. But that short-lived moment passed and she knew the truth—she'd never be able to trust someone enough to give them her whole heart. A marriage without that kind of love wasn't a marriage.

She wouldn't settle.

But thinking about relationships made her remember the strange vibe she'd gotten off Mattie and Finn when she'd witnessed that kiss. If it had been Sophie giving someone a quick peck, she wouldn't have thought anything about it. But Mattie wasn't a casual-kiss kind of woman.

Lily was going to ask Mattie about kissing Finn, when Mattie asked, "What do you mean..." However, she was also interrupted as Sophie came out of the dressing room.

Lily felt the tears well up again, and even Mattie seemed moved.

The dress was perfect in its simplicity. It was the wedding dress Sophie belonged in. "Sophie, you look so beautiful." Lily dug in her purse for a tissue.

Sophie walked over to the large three-way mirror and admitted, "I do." Then she turned around. "I didn't mean that to sound like—"

Lily stopped her. "Don't apologize for stating a fact. That is the perfect dress. You are going to be the perfect bride. And your wedding is going to be—"

"Let me guess, perfect?" Sophie teased.

"Yes," Lily and Mattie said in unison.

Harper whisked Mattie away next, and finally, it was Lily's turn. Soon all three of them were wearing the dresses in front of the large mirror.

Lily studied her reflection. The dark blue fabric made her eyes look bluer. She hadn't been sure she'd like the one strap, but she had to admit that it was a good choice. Sort of Grecian. Mattie wore a different style of dress with two straps, in another shade of blue that bordered on navy.

"I won't need anything blue for my wedding. I'll have you both bookending me."

"Blue?" Mattie asked.

Lily knew that Mattie wasn't very girly, but still, she hadn't grown up under a rock. "Really? You don't know 'Something old, something new, something borrowed, something blue'?"

Mattie shook her head.

"You are bridally challenged," Lily concluded. "The bride's supposed to have all four represented for luck."

"I grew up with brothers," Mattie said, as if that explained everything. "And Bridget and I were far more interested in keeping up with my brothers and hers than messing with stuff like weddings."

They all laughed. A split second later she realized something important. They were talking about Bridget and able to laugh about it. Lily knew they'd all miss her at the wedding, but the pain wasn't as fresh. It wasn't so sharp that they couldn't find the good memories and share.

"Well, I have you two for the blue," Sophie repeated, "my grandmother's locket for the old, the dress for new. I'll have to find something to borrow."

"It's perfect," Lily insisted. "The wedding and you and Colton...perfect."

Mattie scoffed, "Nothing's perfect. Don't let her build up your expectations. Something could go wrong."

"Mattie," Lily scolded.

"No, seriously, something could go wrong," Mattie maintained. "What you have to remember is the wedding…well, it's only a day. As long as you and Colton say I do, the wedding will be perfect enough simply because you'll belong to each other."

"Mattie, I apologize," Lily said. "That sounded almost romantic. Could it be that Cupid's shot another arrow in Valley Ridge?"

This time she had Mattie on the spot, but Mattie didn't have a chance to answer because Harper announced they had to be back in their civilian clothes.

"Time for lunch," Sophie proclaimed.

Lunch would be an ideal time to ask Mattie about what was up with her and Finn Wallace.

Because something was definitely up.

Lily might not be planning any romance for herself, but that didn't mean she couldn't meddle in her friends' romances.

And meddle she would.

CHAPTER SEVEN

SOON LILY AND HER FRIENDS were being seated at a table at Betty's, a fun, funky restaurant in Buffalo. The place made her think of Sebastian. His grandmother had been named Betty. She remembered him looking at the old article about his grandparents and saying he wanted to save it and some of the other historical things she'd found.

She didn't like the way her thoughts seemed to find their way to Sebastian so often.

She was here with her friends. It was such a beautiful early May day. That was where her mind should be.

They opted to sit at one of the outside tables. The restaurant's brick exterior was painted red, and the trim was green. The umbrella of their table was a darker green, and the trimmed bushes beyond the railing gave their table a feeling of privacy.

The waitress had served their drinks when Lily took her opening salvo. "So, Mattie, how are things with you and Finn?"

"He's been around more for the kids' sake," she said. "Zoe, Mickey and Abbey really need to have him involved. I'm so glad he's making them a priority."

"And how about you?" Lily asked.

Mattie looked confused. "Pardon?"

Lily spoke slowly, enunciating every word. "How. Are. You. And. Finn. Getting. Along?"

Sophie looked as confused as Mattie, who answered, "Fine. We're getting along fine, despite a rocky start."

With utter delight, Lily dropped her bomb. "I saw you kiss him."

Rather than immediately deny the possibility, Mattie took a long sip of her drink before replying, "When did you see me kiss Finn?"

"At the picnic the other day. You and Finn were talking, but the kids had put that saddle on Bear, and as you rushed off to help, you kissed his cheek."

Mattie blushed, though Lily didn't think her friend knew it.

"That was nothing," she said. "I kiss the kids on such a regular basis that it's almost second nature to me now."

"If I'd seen you kiss Zoe, Mickey or Abbey, I wouldn't have thought anything of it. But Dr. Finn Wallace isn't a kid…not by a long shot. Until recently, I didn't even think you liked him."

Sophie glanced at Lily, then at Mattie, then back at Lily. "How on earth did I miss the fact that Mattie went and fell in love with Finn?"

Lily had wondered that same thing. Sophie even had romance on the brain, so how had she missed Mattie falling in love? But Lily hit on a reason. "You're in a wedding fog. You're not expected to notice things like that." Lily turned to Mattie. "So spill."

Mattie sputtered, "There's not—"

Lily waggled her finger at Mattie. "Uh, uh, uh. Friends don't fib to friends."

"Today is about Sophie. It's not about me," Mattie tried.

Sophie shook her head. "Today is about friends sharing a day. Listen, I'm not the kind of bride that thinks the entire universe has come to a halt because of her wedding. I'm still me. I still work. I still go out with friends. I still care what's happening to you two. I cared when Abbey was sick. I care that Lily's worried about Hank even though she hasn't said much about it. I care. So tell us."

Mattie sighed. "I'm not used to this." She waved her hand at Lily and Sophie. "I always had Bridget, but she was almost more of a sister than a friend. She knew all my stories. She never had to pry. And when I moved around so much, sure, I always had people I was friendly with, but they never pried, and I never pried."

"You explained the difference in those sentences. You were friendly with them. Friendly isn't friends. You're friends with us. Friends pry. They get to the bottom of things, even when others wouldn't. Listen, I get it. I was never one of the cool kids at school," Lily said. "I kept to myself. I studied."

Being friends didn't work for her as she grew up. If you were friends with people, they invited you to their homes, and they expected you to reciprocate. Only, Lily wouldn't—couldn't—have anyone at her house. In college, she'd had a roommate who had come to school more for the parties than for studying and was always encouraging her to do the same. Lily studied and worked...worked and studied. After a while, her roommate didn't ask her to go out with her anymore.

At the hospital, she'd been pleasant and friendly with the other nurses, but when she punched out, she went home to her quiet, peaceful house. She wasn't sure she could ever explain to anyone else how much looking forward to going home meant to her. She hadn't cultivated friends in Buffalo because she reveled in spending time with herself.

Maybe she'd done all she needed to do with that, because when she agreed to work for Finn and come to Valley Ridge to care for his sister, she'd become friends with her patient, Bridget Langley. And through Bridget, she'd met Sophie and Mattie…and they'd all become friends. When Bridget died, having someone to lean on, to count on, was novel.

"I understand," Lily told her. "I've never had friends like the two of you before."

"Me, either," Sophie said.

Mattie chortled. "Soph, I find that hard to believe. You are one of the most open, loving people I've ever met."

Sophie frowned. "Where I come from, open and loving are not considered positive attributes."

"I don't think I ever want to go there," Mattie said.

"You don't. You're so lucky, Mattie." Lily joined in. "I saw you with your family at the engagement party. You love them and they love you. And I guess most families do love each other. But you like them, too."

"I do," Mattie agreed.

"I don't know what that's like—liking your family," Lily said softly. "And I suspect neither does Sophie."

"No, I don't. Love? Yes," Sophie said. "But like? No."

"Are they coming to the wedding?" Lily asked. She was new to this kind of intimate friendship and obviously had a lot to learn. While she and the other women had bonded in a unique and intense way while they helped Bridget, Lily acknowledged they hadn't shared much about their pasts. About their families.

Sophie shook her head. "No, I won't have anyone from my family at the wedding." She took Lily's and Mattie's hands in hers. "But I'll have the two of you, and that means more than you'll ever know."

All three of them were teary-eyed when the food

arrived. They talked about the wedding, the dresses, the flowers and decorations. As the food and wedding prep talk wound down, Lily said, “Mattie, don’t think we’ve forgotten about you and Finn. We’re still waiting on an explanation.”

Mattie hefted a mock put-upon sigh. “You’re not going to let it go?”

“No,” Lily and Sophie said at the same time.

“Fine,” Mattie huffed with resignation. “We’re…together. Not only for the kids, but…”

“You love him,” Lily said. “You love Finn Wallace.”

“Yes,” Mattie admitted.

Suddenly, Lily knew what that could mean to their friendship. After so many years of friendly, she treasured what she’d built with Mattie and Sophie. So she asked, not really wanting to hear the answer, “Are you taking the kids to Buffalo, then?”

“No,” Mattie said.

Tension that had wound tightly in her chest relaxed as Mattie continued, “Finn will still work with his partners but open a satellite office here. He’ll go into Buffalo a few days a week, but for the most part, he’ll be in Valley Ridge.”

“With you and the kids,” Sophie said with a grin. “Like it should be.”

“Yes. I didn’t want to say anything until after the wedding. This is your time, Sophie. We don’t want to usurp that.”

“Mattie, love is something that should always be celebrated,” Sophie said softly. “Knowing you and Finn are in love only makes my wedding more special.”

“More perfect,” Lily whispered.

She’d looked to Sophie and Colton as proof that the true and everlasting kind of love did exist, and as she looked at Mattie, she saw even more evidence of that kind of love.

Lily knew she'd never have that kind herself. She wasn't foolish enough to blame her past. She put the blame firmly where it belonged…on herself. She simply wasn't the kind of person who was meant to open herself up and share all her secrets with someone.

That being said, she wouldn't mind a quick interlude with someone. Maybe it was time to throw caution to the wind and have a fling with a guy who wasn't looking to settle down.

With someone who was only in town for a short while.

And as she thought the word *someone,* it was Sebastian's face that came to mind. He was only here until the wedding and he'd made it clear he wasn't looking for a happily-ever-after, either.

That was something to think about.

SEBASTIAN TOLD HIMSELF he wasn't really waiting for Lily to come home. She'd been gone all day with Sophie and Mattie. He'd known it would be for the whole day, but somehow, not having her in her apartment at the back of the house felt wrong. Most days, she stopped in between clients. But today, not a glimpse.

He felt…

Oh, hell, he sort of missed her.

She'd gone on a very early call in order to have the rest of the day for the fitting, so he hadn't even seen her at breakfast. She'd left some muffins on the counter with a note.

Hank and Sebastian,
Mattie made them, so you know they're healthy—but they're also good. See you tonight.

She'd left one muffin for his grandfather and one for him, as well.

She'd included him in the note.

They hadn't needed him at the diner today, but he couldn't stand the quiet house another minute, so he'd come in during the dinner rush to hang out with Hank… and watch for her.

When Lily finally walked into the diner around four-thirty, smiling at everyone and hugging Hank, something inside him unwound.

He felt…relieved.

"Hi, Sebastian," she called out as she breezed through the place. He grabbed the box he'd bought and followed her into the office. "How was your day?"

"Wonderful." She threw her bag into a file cabinet drawer and thumbed through the mail, still talking to him. "The dresses need a few alterations, but Sophie looked beautiful. No shock there."

"I'm sure you looked beautiful, too."

She looked up from the mail, surprise registering on her face, then she shook her head. Her dangly earrings sounded as she moved. Sebastian knew that she didn't see herself as beautiful. But he did. Instantly, he felt as nervous as a schoolboy.

"I got you something." He thrust the cardboard box at her.

She looked even more surprised. She dropped the stack of mail on the desk and took the box. "For what?"

"You'll understand when you see it." He'd spotted it at Quarters and known she'd be delighted. He hadn't even thought twice about picking it up. He'd felt like a kid putting cookies out on the plate, waiting for Santa.

Lily eyed the small box suspiciously.

"I promise it's not going to bite you."

She opened it and pulled out a giant binder.

"All the paper and the plastic sheets are acid-free. Marilee called them archival. It should help protect the articles and stuff you found."

"Sebastian, this is so sweet."

Her laugh lines were back in their proper places, which he knew meant she was genuinely pleased. Knowing he'd made her happy made him happy, and that realization left him flustered. "I'm not sweet."

She laughed. "I'm sorry. You're a marine. That means you're all huzzah and semper fi, right?"

He tried to look stern, but in the face of her amusement he couldn't quite manage it.

She grew more serious, but her laugh lines stayed in place as she said, "Really, thank you. It's a very thoughtful gift."

He'd wanted her to be pleased by the gift, but witnessing her happiness made him anxious, though he wasn't sure why. He wanted her happy, but he didn't want her to look at him as if he were a hero. He knew that was a lie. A hero would be fighting next to his buddies, not home. He knew he had an excuse. He flexed his stupid left hand. But knowing and feeling, Lily had said, were two different things.

"It's more for the diner than for you," he said, trying to hide from the intimacy of giving her a gift.

"Sebastian, you can't take it back. You got me a very sweet gift. Sure, it's for the diner, but more specifically, you were thinking of me. That's a very sweet thing to do." She kissed his cheek, still laughing.

She'd reminded him that he was a marine. He was prepared for anything. Ready to face anything. But this? He didn't know what to do with Lily. So he scolded her. "You said the word *sweet* again."

She set the binder down and, with dramatic flair, crossed her heart like he used to do with Finn and Colton. "Here's a promise," she said solemnly. "From now on, I might think the word *sweet* on occasion, but I'll try not to say it out loud. Uh, when I think you're being pigheaded or basically annoying, is it okay to tell you that?"

"Could I stop you?"

So much for serious because she chuckled and said, "Probably not."

Now that he'd given her the gift, he wasn't sure what to do—what to say to her. So he settled for the first thing he could think of. "I should get back out front."

She glanced at the schedule she had posted on the wall. "You're not on the clock tonight?" she half said, half asked.

He shook his head. "No."

"So you could go back out front, or you could take a stack of papers and help me sort." She pointed to the piles that littered the floor.

Sebastian wanted to stay. He wanted to sit on the floor and laugh with Lily as he looked through the diner's history—his grandfather's history.

But she was staring at him in a way that made him feel uncomfortable

"No, I should let you get to work. Glad you had a good day and that you liked the album." He hurried out before she could say anything else.

He'd been so excited at the prospect of pleasing her, yet once he did, he'd felt awkward and disingenuous.

The word *disingenuous* sounded like something Lily would say. Why the hell was Lily Paul dominating his every thought?

He didn't like it.

He didn't like it at all.

LILY WASN'T SURE what had happened yesterday with Sebastian. He hadn't come down for breakfast. And when she stopped at home in between visits, he hadn't come by and said hi, even though his car was in the drive.

His mood swings in general were understandable. But she found his hot-and-cold attitude toward her grating; still, she tamped down the feeling and tried to concentrate on being caring.

Hank had never talked about what happened to Sebastian as a soldier. And he rarely talked about what Sebastian had done after high school when he'd left to go to college.

She thought about going into the diner that evening but opted not to. She wasn't sure which Sebastian she'd find…the amicable one or the not-so-much one.

There was a certain Jekyll-and-Hyde quality to Sebastian. She smiled at the thought but decided it might not be wise to mention it.

She changed her clothes, and since she'd already decided the diner was out, she wasn't quite sure what to do. She could visit Mattie and maybe pitch in with the kids. Or she could head over to Sophie's.

She could sit in her apartment and read, or even clean.

What she ended up doing was sitting on the glider. She couldn't believe how quickly the year had gone.

There was a sweet scent on the breeze as she sat on the creaky swing. She leaned back and let the rhythmic rocking soothe her. Maybe when she finished cleaning the office at the diner she'd sand this down and repaint it.

She fingered a huge paint peel. Her cell phone interrupted her ruminations.

She didn't check her caller ID. She simply said, "Hello?"

"Lily Claire, it's your mother."

"Hi, Mom. How are you?" She rocked the glider.

Her mother didn't answer her question. She didn't inquire how Lily was or what she was doing. Without any preface, she said, "I need money."

"Mom, I love you, but you know I can't." She rocked the glider with more force than necessary.

"You won't," her mother argued.

They'd had this conversation before. Sometimes frequently. Sometimes less frequently. But it always came back to this. "Fine, Mom. I *won't* give you the money."

"Your father—"

Yes, Lily understood that her mother had acquiesced for so many years—she'd bowed and groveled—that it was second nature. If her father said jump, her mother asked how high. She felt sorry for her mother. But even if she gave her mother everything she asked for, her father would never be happy.

She interrupted her. "Mom, I'll help you leave. I'll come get you and we'll move you somewhere he can't find you. There are organizations. Programs—"

"And what would I do for money, Lily Claire?" she asked wearily, with no rancor. "I've never supported myself. I've never worked—"

"You've never worked because he wouldn't allow it. If you left, you could do what you want. Be what you want."

"What I want is some money to tide us over. He says you have your bonus from that rich doctor. You should share. Please, Lily."

Everything in Lily wanted to say yes. She'd said yes so many times before. She'd sent money she didn't have, scrimped and made ends meet in order to send the money. If it would make her mother's life easier, improve it in some way, she'd find the means now to send it, but she knew it wouldn't really improve her mother's lot. She knew exactly where any money she sent would go—exactly where it had gone in the past. So Lily steeled her resolve. "Mom, I don't have any of that bonus left. I bought into a business. But even if I did, I wouldn't send it. I told you that last time was it. I'll help you leave—"

"I won't leave," her mother said softly. "I take my vows seriously."

"Mom, I don't think anyone expects you to stay in a situation like that."

Her mother sighed. "I called for help."

"I'm sorry, but I can't help you. But call if you change your mind. Otherwise, I'll talk to you on Sunday like we always do."

"What good is talk?" her mother said. Again there was no anger, only a bone-deep weariness.

"Mom, you can be in charge. You can change things. You just have to take that first step. If you do, I'll help in any way I can. But I can't send you more money. I'm sorry, Mom. I'll call this weekend."

The phone went dead.

"I love you," Lily said to the dial tone.

It would be easier if her mother got angry at her. If she could learn to get angry at Lily, maybe she'd finally get angry with Lily's father, and maybe if she did, she'd finally leave him.

Lily shoved her phone into her back pocket, pulled her legs onto the glider's seat and wrapped her arms around them as she allowed herself to be calmed by the glider's motion.

She chanted the Serenity Prayer over and over. It was her private mantra. She couldn't make her mother take action now any more than she could when she was a child.

Her mother had locked herself into a situation. Lily could point to a door. She could even open it. But her mother had to be the one to make the decision to go through it.

So she'd continue to call on Sundays. She'd send gifts for birthdays and holidays. But she wouldn't send money. She hoped that someday her mother would decide she'd had enough and walk through the door for good.

Tears slid down Lily's cheek. Normally, she wouldn't allow herself to cry. She knew from years of experience that it didn't do any good. But sometimes…sometimes she couldn't help it. She knew she was doing what she could, but it didn't make it easy.

She brushed away the tears and willed herself to stop.

Maybe someday her mother would be ready to leave. Until then, Lily would hold open the door and wait.

She continued rocking, knowing she'd done the right thing, the only thing she could do, but aching from it nonetheless.

A giant crash from inside the house pulled her from her misery.

She brushed the remnants of her tears aside and raced toward the house, thinking Hank had left the diner early for some reason, that he'd fallen or hurt himself.

"Hank?" she called as she rushed through the open doorway.

"He's at work" was the response. But not from Hank. Sebastian.

"Sebastian, are you okay?" she asked, finding him seated at the kitchen table.

"Oh, I'm fine. Absolutely freakin' perfect. I'm feeling better, and I thought, *I'll start running again.* It always made me feel fantastic. I told myself that the first few days would be more of a brisk walk, but that's fine, because you gotta start slow. My leg injury hardly bothers me. But do you know what, Little Lily Sunshine? In order to go out running, or even brisk walking, one should have on sneakers, not the freakin' loafers I've taken to wearing. But though my leg is improved, my hand isn't. I can't tie my shoes. Something every kindergartner does."

His frustration rolled off him like waves. She wanted to reach out and touch him. Maybe pat his shoulder. Something to reassure him and soothe him. But he didn't appear to be in a mood that would welcome that kind of comfort. Instead, she asked, "The shoe tying explains the frustration, but the crash?"

He pointed to the shoe on the counter, and the shards of the stoneware container Hank used as a holder for utensils.

"Temper tantrums don't look good on two-year-olds and they look worse on adults." She retrieved the shoe and tossed it at him. He caught it with his right hand. She picked up the broken container and put the spoons and spatulas and things into the sink.

Any other time, she might have tried to offer Sebastian a pep talk. She might have told him it would be okay. Things would get better. But coming on the heels of her talk with her mother—with listening to her mother's inability to help herself—Lily had no sympathy or pep talks left over.

"Hold on one minute." She walked back to her apartment, opened up her laptop, did a quick search, and when she found the right page, she went back into Hank's kitchen. She handed the laptop to Sebastian. "There. You can borrow it."

He looked at the computer as if it were an alien device. "What is it?"

"YouTube. There are all kinds of videos on how to do things with one hand. How to tie your shoes, typing and opening bottles are a few. Stop breaking things and start figuring things out."

She started to storm out of the kitchen, but then stopped and faced him. "You scared me tonight. I thought you were Hank and that he'd fallen or hurt himself. He called me Leanne yesterday and asked me to stay, to never leave. It only lasted a moment. I said, 'Hank, it's Lily,' and he came right back, but..." She paused. "But I thought that he'd come home and hurt himself."

"He called you Leanne?" Sebastian asked.

She nodded. Sebastian recognized the name, and she could see that it hurt him. Her annoyance with him faded.

"Leanne is—was—my mother. She broke his heart time after time. Asking my mom to stay was something Hank did often."

Lily sat down in one of the chairs. "Did you ask her to stay?"

Sebastian's expression grew hard. "No. I was a kid and I'd spent more and more time here with Hank. She'd drop me off, and then she'd show up out of the blue to get me. The last time she brought me here, Hank told her she could either leave me with him on a permanent basis and sign the papers he'd had drawn up or take me for good. She signed the papers and that was the last time I ever saw her. We got word a few years later that she'd OD'd."

Lily felt horrible. Horrible about not being able to help her mom, horrible about not being able to help Hank and horrible for the man next to her. But she also felt a sense of kinship with him. She knew what it was like to not be able to save a parent. "I'm sorry."

"Don't be" came his clipped response. "Leanne was an awful mother who didn't love me. I was better off here with Hank."

"Or," Lily said softly, drawing the word out, "or maybe she did love you. I mean, she left you, but she left you with Hank. She saw to it you were safe, cared for and loved. Maybe that doesn't seem like much to you, but that might have been the best thing she could have done for you."

Saying the words to Sebastian eased the hurt in Lily. She was reminding herself that her mother loved her.

She formed the words with purpose in her head. *My mother loves me.*

Lily knew it. Her mother wasn't strong enough to leave her father—she hadn't been strong enough when Lily was growing up, either. But she'd put herself between Lily and her father countless times. She'd taken blows that were meant for Lily. She'd told Lily to go out to the swing when he came in drunk.

It was a warped sort of love.

It certainly wasn't healthy.

But it was love.

Lily had taken some psychology classes in college, and she'd given the subject of her mother a lot of thought over the years, especially since she'd decided not to fund her father's drinking habits by sending more money home.

She couldn't save her mother. But whether or not her mother ever left her father, her mother did love her.

It wasn't the kind of love Lily had wanted from a parent, but it was something.

"Maybe—" she started, ready to tell him, to share with him.

"REALLY?" SEBASTIAN ASKED, incredulous at her suggestion. "Really, you're going to find some bright and shiny silver lining in a drug addict who deserted her own son? Do you always look for the best in everyone?" he spat. She took a quick step backward. He tamped down his anger and asked in a calmer voice, "In your silver-lining world, does anything bad ever touch you?"

Lily snapped, "You don't know me."

Her annoyance reminded him of a kitten trying to hiss at another. It was a valiant try, but it wasn't the least bit intimidating. "Oh, I know you, Pollyanna. You live in a world where nothing bad ever happens. Where there's always a happy ending. Where birds sing and little rabbits play in your garden. Well, in the real world, sometimes things simply suck. Sometimes kids get dumped by mothers who don't care. Sometimes people die. Sometimes those damn rabbits hopping in your garden are actually eating your crop and leaving you hungry."

There was no retreating now. She was angry. "Like I said, you don't know me, Sebastian. You don't know where I've come from or what I've overcome. How dare you say those darn things to me."

"I—"

"So what? You've got a wounded arm. You've had a couple surgeries. So what? Do you remember that boy we played basketball against the other day? Joey's mom left town and his father got injured at the plant. He's had to take care of his dad, his younger sisters and the house, as well as keep up his grades. That boy has shouldered a man's responsibilities. That boy knows what trouble is. You have trouble tying your shoes? Well, boo hoo. Throw another tantrum. Other people have problems, too."

She stormed toward the door, leaving him with an untied shoe and a laptop opened to YouTube. She turned, and for a moment, he thought he saw the sheen of tears in her eyes.

The idea of Lily being upset enough to cry undid him.

No, he convinced himself. He must have imagined the tears. Even at the height of her anger, the best curse word she could manage was *darn*. It was cute. Kitten-hissing sort of cute.

But a more sobering thought followed that. For the first time since he'd met her, he'd seen her lose her temper. As he sat there, he confessed she was right on both counts.

That kid, Joey. He'd shouldered a man's responsibilities.

And Lily was right about something else, too. Not a surprise, he was discovering.

This time she was right that he didn't know much more than a few cursory facts about her.

So what did she do for fun?

He'd ask himself what made her laugh, but pretty much everything did. A few minutes ago, he would have said she probably lived an idyllic life, but now he wasn't so sure. The idea that her life was once unhappy truly bothered him. He found himself hoping he was wrong, but the pain he'd seen in her eyes told him he wasn't.

He wanted nothing more than to see to it nothing hurt Lily Paul again.

Ever.

He wasn't sure how he'd manage to do that.

Hell, he wasn't even sure how to tie his own shoe.

He clicked on the YouTube page Lily had found and saw a man with a prosthetic arm demonstrate how to tie a shoe one-handed, step by step. He laughed as he thought the words. *Tying a shoe—step by step.* He wished Lily was here. She'd have laughed, too.

Since she wasn't, he watched the video alone, and fifteen minutes later, with two tied laces, he got up with a new goal. Find out more about Lily Paul.

CHAPTER EIGHT

LILY DECIDED THAT THIS had been one of the oddest Saturdays in her life. She'd gone on two house calls. The first was a new patient. Katie had a two-day-old baby, Ben, who had jaundice.

Lily had picked up a BiliBlanket at the medical supply store and had taken it out to their house. She hated poking Ben's heel to check him, but she'd loved cuddling the newborn while Katie took a shower. After that, she'd gone to see Mrs. Burns for her breathing treatment.

The house calls weren't the weird part. It was afterward, when she went to the diner, that things got odd.

She spent the rest of the afternoon reviewing more of the diner's old records. Hank had kept absolutely everything. Old phone bills and other utility bills. Invoices. She decided to throw out anything that was more than a decade old. She had a shredder and a file. Most of the older papers went into the shredder, but anything of historical significance went into the file.

And that also wasn't the odd part.

The odd part was Sebastian Bennington. He'd been different since the incident with his shoes, which she now thought of as the YouTube Incident. But today, he lingered in the diner, supposedly helping Hank, yet finding his way into the office on a regular basis.

Even that wasn't so bad.

No, what got to her was that he kept looking at her. Long, piercing looks. She'd read the term *piercing look* before, but she'd never really experienced a piercing look, at least not to the best of her knowledge. But Sebastian had certainly taught her what one was. She'd never read the term again and not think of him.

He couldn't have seen her crying, could he? Sometimes, she forgot to be optimistic. She forgot to find the silver lining. Those were the times she cried.

She was now back under control, and that was what was important because she was the only one she could control. She'd never been able to control her father—his drinking or his temper. And she couldn't control her mom. Her mother's actions were her own. All Lily could do was be there and look at the bright side.

And there was a bright side. Her mother hadn't ever closed the door on her. She was always at the house on Sundays, waiting for Lily's call. The calls were short, but every time, Lily asked if her mother wanted to leave. Every time, her mother said no, but someday, maybe she'd be ready.

And as for Sebastian? Well, she couldn't control him, either. But really she wished she could because his lingering and piercing looks were getting on her nerves.

"Do you mind my going through the records?" she finally asked as he hovered by the doorway, watching her. She thought he might have reverted to his hostile attitude.

"No. Why would I mind?" He seemed genuinely confused by the question as he took a seat.

"I don't know. Maybe I'm searching for millions that

your grandfather squirreled away and I've got some nefarious plans to abscond with it."

"Uh, Webster—"

That stopped her short. She had no clue what he was talking about. "Webster?"

"As in Webster's dictionary. You used the words *nefarious* and *abscond* in the same sentence. That qualifies as a definite Webster moment."

She felt the need to defend not herself, but her choice of words. "*Abscond* and *nefarious* are both perfectly good words."

"They are. But they're not everyday words. When I was in the marines, I don't think we were ever advised about the enemy's nefarious plans."

She sighed. "I like words. Some feel so right tripping off your tongue. Back in school, a classmate asked how a test had gone and I said it was long and arduous, which made him laugh."

"So you've always been a Webster?" He had an aha sort of look, as if he'd discovered something he'd been trying to find out.

Lily couldn't figure out what was going on with him. "Just what are you doing, Sebastian?"

His aha look was replaced by an innocent one—too innocent. "What do you mean?"

"You've been giving me—" she considered saying *piercing,* but thought he might label it a Webster sort of thing, so she settled for "—weird looks all day, and now you're wearing an aha sort of expression as if you were Columbus stepping foot in America. You're here chatting with me. One might even say teasing me in a chummy sort of way. Only a few days ago, birds were helping me dress in my Pollyanna morning."

"Birds were singing—they weren't helping you dress." His voice was soft, calming even. "Why would birds help you dress?"

Lily recognized that he was deliberately trying to change the subject. "Sorry, that was Disney's Cinderella. I wouldn't want to put insults in your mouth when you do such a fine job of it on your own."

He raked his right hand through his hair. "Look, there's nothing wrong with being positive, but you're..."

"I'm Pollyanna? Someone who always sees the bright side of every situation? Yes, I am. I try, at least. That doesn't mean I don't have crappy days. Well, not whole days, usually, but moments." Talking to her mom recently had been a moment, and Lily's being upset—that was simply a blip. "Being an optimist doesn't mean I don't work at overcoming personal flaws, or my past. Some days I'm better than other days. Today, obviously, less than better. So if you don't think I'm out to take advantage of your grandfather and somehow rob him blind as I clear out decades of old paperwork, I'd appreciate it if you excused me."

He stood as if he was going to leave, then stopped. "Lily, I'm sorry."

"Sorry for what, Sebastian? Sorry you came in here when I'm obviously not in a very good mood? Sorry for acting as if you know me when you don't have the slightest notion of who I am and where I've come from? Sorry for taking someone's optimistic attitude and thinking it makes them somehow less intelligent? Trying to find a bright side doesn't make me stupid. It doesn't mean I don't recognize that some things are just crap." She thought of Hank and the upcoming doctor's visit. Yeah, some things were absolutely just crap.

Sebastian nodded. "Sorry for all of it. Despite my behavior, you've been a very good friend to me."

She snorted her disbelief.

"No, I mean it. Only a good friend would challenge me to a one-hand-tied-behind-her-back basketball game, or force me to stop feeling sorry for myself and sort out new ways to tie my own shoes, or open a jar. I'm used to seeing a problem and addressing it. But I'm too close to this particular problem." He waved his left hand at her, exposing the scars from what must have been a horrific injury.

Everything in Lily wanted to offer some sympathy. She wasn't sure of the extent of his wounds, but if the scars on his hand were any indication, they'd been severe. But she sensed that Sebastian didn't need sympathy. "You've already made improvements. You need to realize that you can't force it. This is one of those obstacles that takes time to get over," she offered. As the words left her mouth, she regretted them. She waited for Sebastian to shoot them down.

"Listen, since I've come home I've had a hard time keeping a lid on my emotions. I thought that once I was in Valley Ridge everything would reset…that I'd go back to being the old Seb. The old Seb who joked around, who never took anything seriously. The guy who believed life was exciting and fun…that life was filled with opportunities. Despite the fact his mother left him, that old Seb had Hank, and that allowed him to think that the world was all…" He hesitated, searching for the right words.

"The world was all sunshiny rainbows?" she supplied.

He looked a little chagrined, but nodded.

"But that's not what happened?" she asked, though she already knew the answer.

He sat back down. "No. I'm not that kid anymore. I can't go back to being him—to being Seb. And after him, I was Lieutenant Bennington in the United States Marines. He's gone now, as well. I don't know who the hell I am. What I've found so far doesn't thrill me."

"What have you found?" she asked.

"A man with a short temper and a crippled hand who's adrift. I'm here until Colton's wedding, but then?" He shrugged. "I'm not sure."

"You could stay."

He shook his head. "I don't think so. This was Seb's home. The marines? Well, that was Lieutenant Bennington's home."

She totally understood what he was saying. "And you need to find Sebastian's home?"

She saw the relief in his expression. "Yes."

"I get that," she said. "I left home and went to school, then went to work in Buffalo. It was far enough away from…" She almost said *home,* but living with her parents had never been that. "It was far enough away from where I grew up and it was exciting living in a city, not a small town. But I missed walking down the street and waving at friends and acquaintances." Okay, frankly, she didn't have many friends. She'd held people at a distance, but she'd had plenty of acquaintances, and she'd waved at them.

"I missed a feeling of community. Where I grew up, even though I was on the fringe of things, I was still part of the town, part of someplace. A real community is what I found here in Valley Ridge. To be honest, I'm more a part of Valley Ridge than I ever was where I grew up. I've got friends and a place I belong."

"What did you overcome?" he asked.

She didn't understand his question. "Pardon?"

"What was in your past that you've worked to get over? I saw evidence of something before you mentioned it. Ever since you shoved a laptop with a YouTube video at me, I've been wondering about you, about where you're from…about *what* you've come from."

She shrugged. "I can't…no, I won't share that." Her family was none of his business. She didn't want to talk about them. It felt like if she did she'd be bringing those old problems to Valley Ridge. She didn't want that. She didn't want to be poor Lily Paul, whose father drank too much and used her mother as a punching bag. She didn't want to be that lonely little girl hiding in the backyard on the swing waiting until it was safe for her to go back inside.

No.

Sebastian obviously didn't like her answer. "You know practically everything there is to know about me. Before I even came here, you'd seen pictures and heard stories from Hank. And now that you've met me, you know I'm a short-tempered, frequently frustrated man who doesn't know where he belongs."

Tell someone about growing up? She'd thought about it—by the time she was in high school, she knew if she called social services and reported the situation that she could probably get out.

But the question had been, where would she land?

In the end, the devil she knew was better than the devil she didn't. So she'd waited and bided her time.

She'd studied. Got good grades. Tried to stay under her father's radar. And the second she could do so, she left.

She might call her mother weekly, hoping someday she'd find the strength to leave, too, but she'd never gone back home. "I guess you know all you need to know about me. I work at being an optimist, at finding glee in…well, everything. And I'm someone who longed for a place to belong…. I don't have any grand scheme. I've simply found my true home. It's here in Valley Ridge. And it's Hank, too…if you'll share him."

"You may find it hard to believe, but I can see that you and Hank have something special."

She got up and walked around the desk to where he sat. "So we have his appointment in a few days."

"And the diagnosis isn't going to be good, is it?" Sebastian's voice said he knew that much without seeing any doctor.

"Who knows? Maybe his issue is something that's easily rectified. We've talked about it. There are medical conditions, drug interactions that can cause these kinds of problems. But if it's not, if it's some sort of dementia, I want you to know I'll be here with him… if you'll let me. I know I've pushed my way into your family…even into the business. It's only that I connected with Hank. He was lonely. He missed you and his Betty. I gave him someone. And he gave me a family… the kind I've always wanted. The kind who loves you unconditionally and, more than that, cares about you."

"You never had that before?" he guessed.

"I have it here and that's enough. I have friends—good friends—in Mattie and Sophie. And a family in Hank. At least, I will if you'll share your grandfather with me and you'll let me help."

He stood up and nodded. "I will. It will be a comfort to know when I'm not here you will be."

"Well, then, I guess we're back to our truce." She extended her hand.

He took it in his and they shook. "I guess we are. Why don't you tell me about this boy, Joey..." He left the question hanging.

"Joey's amazing. His mom left the family." Lily couldn't understand how anyone could leave Joey and his younger sisters. But Sebastian had to feel a connection. "His dad hurt his back and is recovering slowly. He can't lift anything yet and for a while could barely get out of bed. Joey's been getting his sisters to school, taking care of the cooking and cleaning...and he's an honor-roll student. I've taken over dinners a few times, trying to help out. And Hank and I have the kids over now and again for a meal here. We send something home for their dad."

"Of course you do," he muttered.

Lily related to Sebastian's frustration while trying to tie his shoes. She felt it now trying to deal with him. "I thought we'd called a truce."

"We did. We do." He sighed. "But here's the thing.... You're annoying."

What was she supposed to say to something like that? "Ouch."

"No, I mean it. You take care of Finn's sister, help out my grandfather, and now you take meals to sick families. Plus, you find gimp-handed ex-soldiers YouTube videos and even play a mean game of one-handed basketball. With all of that, you make it impossible for me to wallow. You are too good to be true."

"When you put it like that, I think I want to barf right

now. That's what you see? A Goodie Two-shoes? It's not an accurate picture of me."

"But you do all that," he pointed out.

"Maybe." She nodded. "Yes, I guess I do. But there's a lot you missed."

"So tell me," he challenged.

Lily laughed. "Yeah, that's right. I should tell you about all my flaws and weaknesses." Her nightmares. She could tell him that while she'd had friends, she'd never let any of them get too close—until Mattie and Lily. And even with them, she hadn't shared her past. She could tell him that she'd once thought she could fall in love, but in the end, she couldn't go through with it. She'd left the man who'd asked her to marry him. No. She wasn't sharing any of that. "You're a soldier. I'm not going to arm you with ammunition you can use against me. You already do a good enough job at taking swipes. And if that's how you see me, then I'll let your picture of me stick."

"Maybe I'll make it my business to find out more."

"You can try." It occurred to her that challenging him might not have been the best way to go.

He appeared thoughtful for a moment, then said, "How about I try tonight…at dinner? Somewhere other than here."

Lily was sure she'd misheard him. "Pardon?"

"Did anyone ever mention that you're cute when you're knocked off guard? You go all prim and proper. You say things like *pardon.* And it might not be quite a Webster-worthy word, but it's awfully close the way you say it. So let me be clear, I'm asking you out to dinner."

When she didn't respond immediately, he clarified, "Dinner. Tonight."

That didn't make her feel any less confused. "Like on a date?"

"You could call it that. I mean, not in a 'looking for a long-term relationship' sort of way, but rather a 'two single people hanging out and having a good time' way. Maybe we get to know each other better. Not that you need to know any more about me."

Friendly. That was the description of every relationship that she'd had since college. Sometimes it was friends with benefits. If things ever got too serious, she always cut the connection, so it was the *get to know each other* that gave her concern. But Sebastian had made it clear he was leaving after the wedding.

Shocking as it might seem, Sebastian Bennington might be her perfect match in Valley Ridge.

A man who was going to leave.

A man she'd liked immensely when she'd heard Hank's stories. A man she occasionally still liked… when he wasn't infuriating her to the point of screaming.

"You're sure you're not planning on falling in love with me?" she half teased, half asked. "I mean, after you've listed all my glowing attributes, how could you not?"

"I swear I'll manage," he replied with a grin. "That is, I can if you can promise not to fall in love with me."

"Uh, Sebastian, I'll grant you that you're easy on the eyes, but most women want something more than that. And by more than that, I mean someone who doesn't throw things—"

"I knocked it over," he protested.

"Yeah, if you say so," she teased. "Still, women want a man who can keep their temper in check. I know that would be important to me if I were looking for someone long-term."

"You're not?" His tone said he found that hard to believe.

"No. I'm not. I can say that emphatically and categorically. I'm not looking for anyone long-term. But it does seem that I have a date tonight with a guy who's leaving after Sophie and Colton's wedding. For now, shoo. I want to get a bit more done around here before I go home to change for dinner."

SEBASTIAN HADN'T INTENDED to ask Lily for a date. But his curiosity won out. At least, that was what he told himself. It was merely curiosity that moved him to issue the invitation.

He might have stayed and tried to uncover more about her, but as if on cue, his cell phone rang. Mrs. Dedionisio asked if he had a couple hours to assist her neighbor.

He closed his phone and said, "Looks like I have a job. Let's say I pick you up at six on the front porch?"

"Six works fine," she said.

And with that, he left before he embarrassed himself further.

He walked the few blocks to Mrs. Dedionisio's.

She was out at the edge of her driveway, picking up debris and dropping it into a small wheelbarrow with another elderly woman. Mrs. Dedionisio smiled when she looked up and saw him. She wiped her hands on her purple housedress. "Sebastian, have you met my neighbor of thirty years, Margot Esterly?"

The other woman looked familiar. That was the thing about Valley Ridge—even if you didn't know someone, you generally recognized them. Well, you did if you worked in the diner.

Rather than answer that she only looked vaguely familiar, he said, “Hi, Mrs. Esterly. What’s up, ladies?”

“Some hooligans knocked down her mailbox last night.” Mrs. Dedionisio’s voice was laced with indignation on her friend’s behalf. “I thought you might put it back up for her?”

He saw that the debris they’d been picking up was the splintered post and dented metal mailbox that had been hit so hard the flag and door had been knocked off.

He thought about asking why they had called him. However, he then realized that asking for help got easier once you’d done it the first time. He’d carried Mrs. D’s bags, and maybe that made it easier for her to ask for his help now. “Sure. I’m on it. I’ll have to run over to the supply store and pick up materials, but yeah, I can get this back up for you.”

“I’d be happy to pay you, and of course, the costs,” Mrs. Esterly offered.

“Don’t worry about paying me. I’ll bring you the receipt for the supplies, though.”

Mrs. Dedionisio pushed the wheelbarrow toward the house. “See, I told you that he might have been a hooligan back in the day but he grew into a fine man….”

Sebastian was glad when she moved out of earshot because he’d felt like a fraud listening to her glowing compliment. He’d felt just as uncomfortable when he’d met Lily, who’d heard one too many stories from Hank.

He decided that even though the Farm and House Supply was a few blocks away he’d probably have to get his car in order to bring the materials here. Plus, he’d need a posthole digger and some other tools.

A police car pulled up next to him. Well, actually, *the* police car. Valley Ridge only had the one. Dylan Long got out of the cruiser. He looked more like a surfer than a cop. Tall, lean, with sandy-blond hair. "I heard you were back," Dylan said.

Sebastian nodded. "Yeah. Thought I'd have seen you at the diner."

"I've been there. It seems our paths haven't crossed until now. Want to tell me what happened?" He gestured at the stump where the mailbox had been.

"Mrs. Dedionisio called me to see if I could help her neighbor fix her mailbox. Someone knocked it over last night."

"Someone walloped the hell out of it," Dylan said, toeing some splinters of wood.

"Probably some kids."

"I'll go in and talk to her, then file a report. But you know how these things go. Thankfully, we don't have much mischief like this in Valley Ridge, but even small towns aren't immune."

"I don't think Mrs. Esterly is expecting miracles, but I do think she's hoping for a new mailbox."

Dylan started for the house and turned around. "Heard you got Mrs. Dedionisio to let you carry her groceries. I can't tell you how many times I've tried to get that woman to let me help. I've offered her a ride, or even to walk with her and carry them."

"I played the injury card—" he extended his messed-up hand "—and told her I'd feel emasculated if she didn't let me help."

Dylan choked on his laughter. "Brilliant use of an injury."

Sebastian couldn't help but think that Lily would be

impressed with his looking at the silver lining. Hell, he might not have even noticed there was a silver lining if he hadn't met her.

It occurred to him that he no longer hid his hand in his jacket pocket. Here he was flashing it left and right without a thought.

Thanks to Lily.

"Not everyone would use their free time to help out like that…like this." Dylan waved at the mailbox.

"There's a lot I can't do, but carrying a couple bags and putting in a mailbox are things I can, so I did, I am." That realization—that there were still things he could do—came courtesy of Lily Paul, too.

"Well, thanks," Dylan said. "As long as you know someone appreciates it. If everyone helped where they could, the world would be a better place." He waved as he headed up the driveway.

Sebastian drove his car over to the supply store. He found that Jerry, the owner, was still exactly where Sebastian remembered him—behind the counter, helping a customer. He looked the same, too. Old. Frankly, Jerry had always looked old.

He relished the things that stayed the same.

He borrowed a posthole digger from Jerry, dug the hole, placed the post, then poured dry concrete around it. He doused it with water, then backfilled dirt on top of it. He was getting ready to mount the mailbox onto the post when he spotted Joey and one of the other kids from the basketball game. "Hey, Joey. And Cameron, wasn't it?"

"Yes, sir," Cameron said politely. Too politely.

"What's going on?" Sebastian asked.

"Cam's got something to say." Joey elbowed his friend.

"I did it." The kid gestured to the mailbox. "I was out with some friends last night, and they dared me, so I got a branch and whacked it."

"You whacked the post down with a branch?" That would have been one hell of a branch.

Cam shook his head. "No, that part I kicked."

"Why?"

The boy shrugged. "It was stupid, I know. But they dared me, and I didn't want to seem like a wuss, so I did it. I came to apologize to the lady and ask if I could fix it and pay for the damages, but I don't have any cash right now. I can make it and pay her back."

"Why don't you two help me finish up with the mailbox? I was trying to figure out how I could hold the screws with my bad hand."

"Yeah, did you see his hand the other day? It's messed up," Joey told Cameron. They both admired his scars.

"Gross, but cool," Cameron agreed.

Sebastian had felt the scars were gross, but he'd never really thought of them as cool…until now.

Cameron and Joey actually mounted the mailbox under his supervision and they cleaned up the mess just as Mrs. Esterly came out of her house. "I see you have some helpers," she said, extending a plate of cookies at them all. "I thought you deserved a treat."

Cameron eyed the cookies guiltily. When Joey elbowed him for a second time, he said, "I don't deserve them, ma'am. I messed up your mailbox and came to say sorry. I wanted to fix it, but Mr. Bennington had it almost done when we got here."

"He helped, though," Joey threw in.

"And you are?" Mrs. Esterly asked.

"His friend. Joey Williams." He held out a hand and shook Mrs. Esterly's in a very adult manner.

"He wasn't there," Cameron assured her. "There were some other guys, but I'm not here to rat on them. They didn't do it. I did."

"They dared him," Joey explained.

"But I took the dare," Cameron said honestly. "It was stupid, ma'am. I told Mr. Bennington I was gonna offer to fix it, but since it's done, I'll pay for it. I don't have the cash right now, but if you'll give me a chance to earn it, I'll pay you back."

Mrs. Esterly studied Cameron, then slowly said, "Well, it just so happens I have a very big garden in the back. I'm always behind on the weeding. Maybe we could work out a deal?"

Cameron and Mrs. Esterly worked out their deal, which basically amounted to Cameron visiting for an hour or so on Saturday mornings for a wage that he would apply to his debt. "And afterward," Mrs. Esterly said, "if you want, we can talk about you keeping the job for the summer and keeping that money. I'll need to tell the police, though."

Cameron looked scared spitless and Mrs. Esterly patted his shoulder. "Don't worry. I'll tell him that I'm not pressing charges, so it's okay," she said. "What made you confess?"

Sebastian had wondered that.

Cameron eyed Joey, then addressed Mrs. Esterly. "I told Joey, and he said I had to man up and tell you. He said that everyone makes mistakes, but a real man tries to make up for it."

Joey seemed embarrassed. "My dad says stuff like that all the time. I only passed it on."

"Your dad's right," Mrs. Esterly said to Joey. "And, Cameron, it takes a real man to own up to his mistakes. I'm proud of you."

"Your dad's a very wise man," Sebastian agreed. He said goodbye to the boys and Mrs. Esterly, then suddenly realized he hadn't come up with anything for tonight's date. He'd take most women to a nice restaurant. Valley Ridge didn't have anyplace that would suit, but they were close enough to Erie or Buffalo that he could find someplace. But that idea didn't seem quite the thing for Lily Paul. An idea finally came to him and he texted her, Wear something casual.

Well, good or bad, he'd set his first date with Lily in motion.

CHAPTER NINE

BY THE TIME Sebastian returned Jerry's posthole digger and went over to explain the situation to Dylan, he was running late getting home. He made one quick stop at the grocery store before arriving at Hank's place. He had a quick shower and raced out the front door at five minutes to six. There was a very real chance that his palms were sweating. He wouldn't be surprised. He was feeling like a teenage boy on his first date. And that was ridiculous. He was a grown man. He'd fought for his country. He'd dated women before.

And yet…

He stood waiting with sweating palms, a roaring heart and hopes that he'd made the right choice.

Lily came from around the back of the house in jeans, some flat shoes and a big, billowy top that pretty much hid any assets she had—and he knew she had assets—but she looked all the sexier because of its modesty. And like that first day he'd met her, she had on big jewelry.

But it was her hair that drew the bulk of his attention. It was down again and hung in dark waves behind her shoulders. A few strands crept forward, and everything in him wanted to push them back into place, if only for a chance to touch her.

"I'm so glad you texted me the appropriate attire.

I'd planned on wearing my slinky designer dress." She grinned and he knew she was teasing.

He teased back, "Nothing's written in stone. I could wait while you go change, because try as I might, I can't picture you in something slinky. You're more flowy and wild."

"Is that a good thing?" she asked.

"A very good thing."

"Then thank you." Those wrinkles at the edges of her eyes fell into their happy places. "So you didn't say where we were going."

"It's a surprise." He didn't know Lily well enough yet, but he sensed she wasn't a conventional-date kind of woman. In fact, he was counting on it. She didn't say much as they rode through Valley Ridge, then down toward the lake. Actually, she didn't say anything.

With some women, that might have been awkward, but the silence felt comfortable with Lily.

There was something easy about being with her.

As the car reached the top of the ridge, Sebastian could see out over Lake Erie. It was warm for May. The evening sky was a well-worn-pair-of-jeans sort of blue that was reflected in the lake's color. Sebastian realized how much he'd missed the lake.

Yeah, he knew missing a lake, even if it was one of the Great Lake, might seem odd, but he'd spent his childhood roaming its shores with Finn and Colton. He'd watched sunsets, he'd gone parking with girls from school, gone swimming…

Lake Erie was a big part of his childhood memories.

And hopefully, if tonight's date went well, it would become a part of some of his adult memories, as well.

Lily finally spoke and startled him from his reverie. "This is the way to the Nieses' cottage."

"It is. But that's not where we're going." Well, not exactly. He turned onto the dirt drive that wove back toward the lake.

"You look suspiciously proud of yourself, Sebastian Bennington, and I find that makes me nervous."

He glanced over at her, yet nothing about her looked nervous. Her eyes sparkled and her smile was broad enough he could tell she was enjoying the surprise. "Now, why would my being proud make you nervous?"

"Because it's kind of a cat-that-swallowed-the-canary sort of pride. And while the cat had every reason to be proud, the canary…"

"So I'm the cat and you're the canary?" he asked innocently.

She chuckled. "Let me say *tweet, tweet* in response."

He refused to humor her by meowing and was saved the embarrassment as he parked at the Nieses' cottage.

"I thought you said we weren't coming here," she said skeptically.

"Hang on." He got out of the car and pulled out a picnic basket from the trunk. A real wicker basket. He saw her staring at it and offered, "It's Hank's. He used to say taking a woman to a restaurant doesn't show any particular investment. But if you pack her a picnic, she knows you gave it some thought and put some effort into it."

"You packed the basket?" Lily sounded unconvinced.

"Who else?"

"Someone at the diner?" she asked.

He scoffed, "No. I packed it myself. I went to the grocery store on my way home and shopped."

"Hank's right about the picnic versus restaurant. I'm impressed."

"Wait until you taste it before deciding." He carried the basket with a blanket on top in his right hand. Part of him wanted to reach out and hold her hand. But he knew he couldn't manage the basket with his left hand and he didn't want that hand holding hers. He knew it was irrational. Lily was a nurse. She hadn't even blinked at the scars. Still, he didn't want to hold hands with it.

He thought of the boys' assessment this afternoon—gross but cool. He still didn't reach for her hand, but he did feel better as they walked in companionable silence. Okay, it wasn't exactly silence. They weren't talking, that was true, but noises abounded. The sound of the lake's waves beating against the rocky cliffs, which comprised most of the shoreline on this stretch of water. Birds calling. There was enough of a breeze that he could hear the leaves and grasses being blown about.

He stopped at a particular bluff.

"This is where we met," Lily said with no hint of fondness.

"Yes, this is where we had our first, infamous meeting. I thought maybe we should erase that less-than-stellar introduction and replace it with a better memory."

She smiled. "That's a nice idea."

He spread the blanket, opened a bottle of wine from Colton's winery. They sat and ate the pasta salad and cold fried chicken. He kept glancing at Lily. She seemed content, sipping her wine and watching the lake.

He stared out at the water, as well. He'd looked at Lake Erie from many points. From Erie's bay and from Presque Isle, the peninsula there. From Cleveland's lakefront. From Buffalo. From Freeport Beach in North East. From Put-in-Bay in Ohio. Each vantage point had its own particular appeal. But the view from this bluff was his hands-down favorite.

He focused on the woman sitting next to him and realized that now it would hold an even bigger attraction…it would remind him of Lily Paul.

"This was my spot, growing up," he offered. "When I was away, I'd dream about this view. It was always a day like this. A warm spring evening. Windy enough that the sound of the waves breaking against the rocks below carried. But not too blustery. In my dreams, I'd sit here and watch the sunset, like I've done a hundred times."

"That's comforting," she said as she looked out over the lake.

"It was." He didn't mention that suddenly, sitting here with her, he wasn't nearly as captivated by the view of the lake as he was by the view of the woman next to him. "Now it's your turn."

"Pardon?" she asked with that prim-and-proper tone that she'd used before, much to his delight.

"That's how it goes with friends," he instructed, smiling. "Friends take turns sharing. And the way I see it, you've got a lot of catching up to do."

"You've only told me one thing."

"But Hank told you hundreds of stories."

"Doesn't count. Those were his stories—his memories—he shared. So they don't count for you." Her eyes crinkled as she instructed him.

"Fine," he agreed. "But you owe me one, at least."

"Fine."

He watched as she thought, searching for something she would share. He suspected she was searching for something that wasn't too personal. Despite her smile and her ever-present optimism, Lily Paul was a closed book.

"Here goes. I grew up reading books."

He almost laughed that even as he was thinking she was a closed book that was what she opted to share. She read books? Not a deep insight. "Come on, Lily."

"Hey, if you're going to complain about what I share, I'll stop."

"Continue." She wasn't just a closed book…she was like one of those diaries Finn's sister, Bridget, used to keep. The kind with the strap that locked, so prying brothers and their friends couldn't read it.

Of course, they'd learned to pick the lock, but really, Bridget hadn't said much other than that boys were exasperating and little tidbits about her life. There had been no huge secrets or drama.

Lily kept her attention on the lake. "I learned pretty much everything I hold dear from books. I learned to be inquisitive from Trixie Belden." She turned, maybe to gauge his reaction to what she was revealing.

He must have looked lost because she clarified, "Trixie Belden was a teenage sleuth. She solved mysteries, dealt with brothers, memorized license plates, learned to ride horses at her friend Honey's house."

"Do you ride?" he asked.

"No, but let's see, where was I? Reading. Helen Keller taught me that no matter what the obstacle, with perseverance it can be conquered. Lazarus Long taught me that family isn't necessarily made up of the people you're related to. You can make your family."

"Is that it?" He didn't have a clue who Lazarus Long

was, but he didn't ask. She was on a roll, and he wanted nothing more than to have her continue.

"And Bilbo and Frodo Baggins…they taught me that even if you're small and not up to the journey, you have to do your best and put one foot in front of the other. I think I learned the most from the Hobbits. There's this poem in the books. It's about how the road goes on and on. In the first version, Tolkien talks about pursuing it with 'eager feet.' In a later version, he talks about 'weary feet.' I understand that. When I left home, I was eager to get away—to be anywhere else but there. And right before I came to Valley Ridge, my feet were indeed weary. I didn't like the anonymity of the city. I wanted to be somewhere people knew me and I knew them. I wanted to build a community."

"A family," he said with clear insight.

"Yes. I know you accused me of glomming on to Hank with ulterior motives. Maybe I did. I see in your grandfather everything I wanted growing up. He was kind when I moved in. He'd invite me in for a cup of coffee some mornings. As Bridget got sicker, I stayed over at her house most nights. One day, he asked if I'd call when I wasn't coming home because he worried about me.

"You don't know what that's like—having someone worry about you in that sense. He was lonely, and so was I. He was a friend at first, but now he's become family to me. The kind of family who would never abandon you. I know it sounds dumb, but—"

He took her hand. "It's not dumb at all. I had a family of sorts in the marines. Not the family I was born to, but they were still family. I know if any one of my buddies called me even now and said, 'I need you,' I'd do everything I could to be there. I have the same relationship with Colton and Finn."

"So now you know something about me. Though I'm not convinced that it matters."

"It matters," he said.

She looked uncomfortable, as if regretting she'd shared anything with him.

If it bothered her that much to tell him about books she read, he wondered what other stories she had that she hadn't spoken of. And more than ever, he wondered where she came from. Her yearning for a family, for someone like Hank, was so strong. She'd obviously never had anything like that. And that broke his heart.

"Do you know Maeve Buchanan?" he asked.

She smiled and the lake breeze caught her wild hair, blowing it across her face. She brushed it aside, which was probably good because he'd almost done it for her and he wasn't sure she'd welcome his touch, even if they were friendlier now.

"Sure, I know Maeve," she said. "She comes into the diner sometimes."

"She was like you," he told her. "Always had her nose stuck in a book. However, she spent so much time in the principal's office that it always seemed like an anomaly."

"People are complex. My job has taught me that. If you look deep enough, you can find something to admire in almost everyone. When I worked at the hospital, it was sort of a game I played, especially if I had difficult patients."

"How?"

"Well, there was one woman who threw her cane at me, then tried to punch me. As I called for help, I found myself thinking, *Wow, she's got great teeth.* They were all pearly and white. Of course, a moment after that thought, she tried to bite me with those pretty teeth."

She was staring at the lake again as she told her story, and that allowed him to study her. As she talked about the patient with pretty teeth trying to bite her, she laughed, not out loud, but with her eyes. Those laugh lines grew more intense and seemed to say everything.

She didn't seem to notice he looked at her as much if not more than he looked at the lake. He'd always found Lake Erie fascinating, but he had to admit he found Lily Paul even more so.

He pointed at the water. "It's almost sunset. Finn used to work with this doctor and he'd visit Valley Ridge. He came once with his kid Aaron, and we spent a day at Colton's farm. He started bugging his dad to hurry to the lake, though, because tonight might be the night. When Colton, or maybe Finn, asked what night, the doctor said his wife used to tell them that if you're quiet enough, you can hear the sun hiss as it hits the water."

Lily laughed. "I love it. Maybe we'll get lucky tonight."

She reached out for his hand as the sun sank nearer and nearer to the horizon. Her voice dropped to a whisper, as if she didn't want to take a chance of missing the hiss. "Did they ever hear it?"

"Aaron said no. Then his father said that's half the fun...they keep on trying."

He and Lily sat on the cliff, watching the sun continue to sink closer to the point where the water and the sky seemed to meet. Sebastian let go of her hand and hesitantly put his arm around Lily's shoulders.

But she didn't pull away. In fact, she leaned in closer.

It always amazed him how quickly the sun sank the last few inches. One moment, it sat just above the water's edge; the next, it was almost touching.

"There," Lily whispered, then held her breath as if she might really hear a hiss and cocked her head as if to get a little closer.

The sun sank and she breathed in. "Well, I didn't hear it. Did you?"

There was a sense of hope in her voice.

He laughed. "No. I guess we'll have to try again sometime."

She nodded and looked up at him. "I'd like that."

The wind whipped a piece of her hair up again, but this time, since she sat so close, it brushed across his face. She reached up and brushed it off for him. Her finger ran lightly across his lips, then she froze.

He did, too.

Their eyes met as they sat there, staring at each other. He eventually breathed in because he realized he'd forgotten to. And when he leaned down to kiss her, there was no question in his mind that she was receptive, just as there was no question in his mind that he had never wanted anything as much as he wanted this moment.

It was a gentle kiss. An introduction as much as any of the stories they'd shared with each other.

Sebastian could have kept kissing her for a long time—maybe indefinitely—but she pulled back. She didn't look happy. He couldn't tell if her expression was thoughtful or annoyed. "Lily, I'm sor—"

"Shh," Lily informed him. "We kissed. And you were either going to say, *Wow, Lily, I'm sure that kiss rocked my world* or *Wow, I sure didn't feel that kiss.*

Either of those are acceptable. But if you were to apologize for that kiss, that would not be acceptable. Kissing me either worked or it didn't, but it's not something you're sorry for."

"I didn't want you to get the wrong idea," he explained. "I don't know who I am or where I'm going, and I would never want to lead you on—"

She laughed. "Wait, answer this…it rocked, or it didn't?"

He couldn't help it—he laughed, too. "It rocked."

"Then no problem. I meant what I said before. I'm not looking to ever settle down. I'm loving helping Sophie with her wedding, but I have no desire in that regard. However, I wouldn't mind a…" She looked for a word. "A tryst."

"Webster," he teased.

"It's a good word. And it implies a secret meeting. And that's what I'd want. I don't want to date in the open. I don't want people in town knowing."

Well, talk about keeping him in his place. "Wait, are you embarrassed—"

"Don't be an ass. But I know how it is with small towns. One minute we're dating, and the next they have us walking down an aisle. And the only aisle I plan to walk down is the one Sophie's going to be married at the end of. So what I'd like is…"

"A tryst?" he finished for her.

She nodded. "A no-strings, not-meant-to-last-long tryst."

He nodded. "I'm leaving after the wedding."

"And I'm staying."

Sebastian should have been thrilled. After all, having a woman who wanted nothing more than a tryst, who said she never desired a long-term relationship, was almost every single guy's dream. And he understood where she was coming from. He'd dated women throughout his career, but he hadn't been looking for anything like what Colton and Sophie had. Simple and uncomplicated—that was how he liked his relationships.

And yet, something about Lily's willingness to enter into a *tryst* with him made him uneasy. Not because he didn't want her, but because…

Well, hell, he had no idea why. He felt that Lily deserved the kind of relationship Sophie had with Colton, but if that wasn't what she wanted…

"It's getting dark," she said, interrupting his whirling thoughts.

They gathered up the remnants of their picnic and headed back to the car. "That was the best first date I've ever had," he told her.

LILY COULDN'T HAVE been more pleased about the way their date had gone. "Me, too," she assured Sebastian.

They rode in silence to the house, but Lily felt abuzz with anticipation. She was confident that Sebastian would be amenable to what she was going to suggest. "You want to come in?"

They both knew what she was asking. Sebastian said, "More than anything."

She felt giddy, young, as if something new and special was about to happen. "Hurry?" she asked.

"Hurry," he agreed.

They dashed from the car, around the house, to the small door at the back of Hank's house. She unlocked the door.

"I've just realized I've never been to your place before."

"I'll confess I don't invite people over." That, too, was a leftover of her childhood. She knew it, but still, it didn't alter the fact that she didn't invite people into her personal space. Not even Sophie and Mattie. She went to their homes or Colton's farm. She visited at the coffee shop. Saw them at the diner, but not here.

And the few men she'd dated had not been invited to her house. Ever.

The thought of having someone over should be making her a bit crazed, but all she could think of was getting Sebastian into her bedroom…into her bed.

She opened the door of the small efficiency apartment and stepped in, reaching for the lamp…and squished.

"What…" She flipped on the light switch and looked down. "There's water everywhere."

She sprinted to the kitchenette at the other side of the room. "Nothing here."

"It's coming from here." He pointed to where the water was seeping from under the bathroom door. "Do you mind?"

"Please."

He opened the door to the bathroom and it didn't take a plumber to see what the problem was. Water dripped from the ceiling.

Lily knew that directly over her bathroom was Hank's bathroom. There was another separate bathroom in the hall that served the other two bedrooms.

They both rushed toward the door to the main house.

"Hank?" Sebastian called as he sprinted up the porch stairs.

Lily followed and was relieved when she saw Hank standing at the top of the stairs. "Sebastian, what's wrong?"

Sebastian zoomed past him, heading for Hank's bathroom. "It's the tub," he said. Lily watched as he turned off the taps.

"Did the faucet break?" Hank asked.

"No," Sebastian called.

"No, Hank, you didn't turn the water off," Lily said gently.

The older man bristled. "I'm sure it wasn't me."

"It's in the master bathroom, Hank," Sebastian said as he came over to them. "Your bathroom."

"But I—" Hank walked to the doorway and looked at the water that pooled at the wall opposite the tub. It was obvious that was where it was leaking down into Lily's bathroom.

"It's okay, Hank," Lily said. "It's only some water. We'll get it all fixed up soon enough." She turned to Sebastian. "Why don't you work up here and I'll start cleaning downstairs? If you can get the water off the floor here, at least it will stop raining in my place."

"Got it. I'll help you as soon as I've got this under control."

Lily nodded and went back to her apartment.

She stood and considered the small living-dining-kitchen area. Water still ran across the bathroom into the living room, but in the short time they'd been gone, it had also started dripping from the living-room ceiling. She tried to decide where to begin and opted for the bathroom. As she crossed the living area, a portion of the ceiling plaster fell, and with a loud splat, it landed on her couch.

She opened her bedroom door and saw more pieces of the ceiling had fallen in there and landed on her now-soaked bed.

Feeling overwhelmed, she figured the first thing to do was move what she could outside. She started with the sodden ceiling tiles. She piled them in the driveway. Next, she picked up her coffee table and end tables.

She kept moving things into the backyard. All the small furniture and cushions. She started dumping her wet bedding and the clothes from her closet on the corner of the porch. She'd borrow Hank's machine tomorrow and get them all washed and dried before they started to mildew.

Load after load of wet and mangled objects were transferred outside.

Sebastian stood in the doorway surveying the wreck. "I'm so sorry, Lily. Hank seemed fine this afternoon."

"Anyone can forget to turn a faucet off," she said, knowing he didn't want her to bring up dementia again. He was settling into the idea it was a possibility, but it wasn't smooth by any means. He needed time to adjust. "He was probably tired."

Sebastian gave her a look that she understood meant *Don't sugarcoat things for my benefit* and she sighed. "You're right. He was confused. But he did seem okay earlier. There's the phenomena called sundowning, or sundown syndrome. Basically, patients with dementia—"

"You can say the word. Alzheimer's. You think it's Alzheimer's."

"Dementia is a symptom, Alzheimer's is the disease. As for sundowning, I saw it with patients in the hospital. They got worse at night. There are all kinds of theories, and there's no rhyme or reason as to when or why it happens. There's simply confusion, or anxiety, shifts in moods. It's no one's fault, and there's no need to apologize."

Sebastian nodded but didn't say anything else or ask any questions. "I'm afraid your apartment got the worst of it."

"Almost everything's soaked. The clothes in my dresser did okay. And the shelves sheltered most, if not all, of my books. But everything hanging up, as well as all of the bedding, is wet. All the hard-surface furniture should be okay, but the couch and my mattress were soaked through. I don't know if they'll ever be serviceable again."

"I'll call the insurance company first thing tomorrow," Sebastian said. "They'll take care of everything."

"They'll take care of the house stuff, after the deductible, but I'm a tenant, so I'm on my own for my personal belongings." She almost laughed at the words... she'd been on her own her whole life, it seemed. "I thought about rental insurance, but frankly, most of what's here came with the apartment. Even with whatever's mine that needs replacing, I'll still come out ahead. Buying rental insurance would have made sense if I had more stuff."

"I couldn't help but notice that the apartment was rather..."

"Spartan?" she said with a laugh.

"Webster," he teased. "But yes."

"I found out a long time ago that things are only things. Would I like nice things? Sure. Sometimes I can almost picture what my house will look like someday. Antiques everywhere. But not fussy ones. Comfortable pieces meant for living. I want an overstuffed chair with an arts-and-crafts style lamp for reading. And bookshelves with old, leather-bound volumes, not my predominately paperback collection."

"You don't have anything like that now." Sebastian scrutinized her again, as if he were trying to figure her out.

Good luck to him, because most days she couldn't figure herself out.

"No, I don't have anything like that now. I paid my way through school with student loans and have worked to pay them off. I'd been saving for a down payment on a house when Finn asked me to take care of Bridget. I moved in here and met Hank. I decided to invest in the diner. I'm hoping my business takes off soon. When I have a better, reliable stream of income, I'll start a new house fund."

"You gave up your dream of owning a house to help Hank?" Sebastian's brow furrowed at the thought.

She laughed off his concern. "Don't make it sound all noble and self-sacrificing. It was a business decision. A very sound one, I think. Helping Hank out was secondary."

"Liar," he said in a tone that was partially teasing and partially something else she couldn't quite identify. "You would have done it without any hopes of financial return."

"Wow, way to look down on my business savvy." She grabbed the last kitchen chair and carried it outside.

Sebastian followed, dragging a soggy area rug. "No. Way to look at your very large heart."

She found a free spot for the chair and made a gagging motion. "Oh, man, you're going all sappy on me."

"No, I'm getting to know you," he insisted. When she looked displeased, he added, "Maybe not all the nuts and bolts. I'm hoping someday you'll share those with me. But in the meantime, I've got a very good overall picture of you, Lily."

"I know. Sunshiny rainbows. Unicorns and talking birds." She leaned against a stack of cushions that squished.

"I don't think I ever mentioned unicorns, but yeah, those, too. But here's something I hadn't suspected before. You don't get a rainbow without the rain. You've let me see the sunshiny rainbow—maybe someday I'll get to see the storms."

She walked over to him and wrapped her arms around his neck. "Here's the thing, Sebastian—you won't be here that long. After the wedding, you're leaving. And that's good for me. I don't want to show you my storms.... I simply want you." She looked at the waterlogged furniture. "But probably not here, not tonight. I'll see if JoAnn has a room at the B and B. You need to stay with Hank."

"You're not getting a hotel. We've got extra rooms in the house. You can bunk with us until I can get this place fixed up. The water even ran along the joists. That's why the ceilings are in such a bad state. The walls are wet, which means the drywall in them will be ruined, too. The rug's trashed, but maybe if I get a company with an industrial..." He searched for the word.

"Water-sucker-upper?" she suggested.

He laughed. "Close enough. I'll see about getting the insurance company out here first thing in the morning, but it will probably be a couple weeks until you can get back into the apartment. And if you don't have any renter's insurance, you can't afford a room for that long, and like I said, we've got extras."

"You're sure?" she asked, mainly because she wasn't sure. She wanted Sebastian, but part of that desire came from the knowledge that he'd be leaving and that they both had their own space. If she were living in a room next to his, there wouldn't be much space between them at all.

"I'm sure." He sounded certain.

And because he was right, she couldn't afford a room at JoAnn's for weeks, and she wouldn't want to intrude on Sophie or Mattie, she found herself saying "Okay."

SEBASTIAN HADN'T LIKED the idea of Lily living somewhere else and felt relieved that she agreed to stay with them.

They got the bulk of the water cleared up. Lily was a trouper. She carried the drawers of her dry clothes into the house, along with any other salvageable items, including a small library of books. If she hadn't told him she was a bookworm, he'd have known it after toting those stacks.

Afterward she put a load of her soaking clothes into the washing machine. She worked with him, side by side, and didn't complain that his grandfather had ruined her home.

No, not Lily. "You know, I've hated that couch. Don't tell Hank, but that couch did not sell this apartment. So now I'll get a new one. My own couch. Something that reflects my taste."

Sebastian rarely acted on impulse, but without thinking, he pulled her over to him and kissed her. This was no gentle hello. It was a kiss that spoke of desire. And though he did desire her, it went deeper than that. He wanted to hold her, keep her close.

"Wow," she murmured when they ended the kiss.

"Bedtime. We all need to get some sleep tonight. We're going to have our work cut out for us with the apartment."

"Not to mention Hank's appointment on Wednesday. He really needs to get to this one."

"He'll be there," Sebastian promised.

Sebastian had grown accustomed to having Lily at the house and at the diner. He'd find her with Hank, laughing, or sitting at the kitchen table, sharing coffee and the paper in the morning. But now following her up the stairs felt strange. She'd gone beyond the common parts of the house and was now in the private area. It was odd. Not bad, not as if she were intruding, but different.

"You can have the bathroom first," he offered. "Sorry you'll have to share it with me."

"No problem. And thanks."

She went to gather some things from the pile she'd put in his childhood room, and he walked down the hall to Hank's room, cracked the door and peeked in. Hank was sound asleep.

Sebastian stood there for a few minutes. His grandfather appeared younger in the dim light from the hall. Not that Hank appeared much different than he had during Sebastian's childhood.

He was sure Hank wouldn't like hearing that, but there it was. His grandfather had been an old man when his mom had abandoned him here. He'd never complained about having to take care of a kid, though.

Overflowing the bathtub didn't mean anything. Anyone could have an accident.

Anyone could have a momentary lapse and forget something.

But when Sebastian paired it with the other things he'd noticed, it didn't look good.

He could see the light shining under the bathroom door. He went into his room and could hear Lily moving around.

It was torture listening to the shower being turned on and knowing she was in it, only a wall away.

It was something he hadn't really considered—having Lily in the house and not being able to touch her because his grandfather was here.

She started to sing in the shower.

He couldn't quite make out the words, but it was a happy tune. Well, not exactly a tune. It was supposed to be, but frankly, Lily had already proved that singing wasn't her talent.

Here she was flooded out of her apartment, her things soaked, some completely ruined. And instead of complaining, she was singing.

Sebastian flexed his hand, and not for the first time, he wished he was more like Lily Paul.

LILY WENT FROM DREAMING to wide-awake in literally the blink of an eye.

She sat straight up in bed and stared at the strange room.

It took a few more blinks to orient herself.

She was at Hank's, in one of the spare rooms upstairs. More specifically, in Sebastian's childhood room.

He'd taken the other room, with the queen-size bed, when he'd come back to Valley Ridge. Frankly, she couldn't imagine him fitting on a double.

She remembered the state of her small apartment and realized that she was going to have a busy, busy day.

She should get going now. She had a few home visits, but she could finish the laundry before she had to leave.

She walked over to the drawers and noticed for the first time the shelf on the wall. It was filled with trophies. A big state championship for basketball. Another for soccer. Behind them, propped against the wall, were honor-roll awards. There was a picture of a basketball team. Sebastian was there, standing in the center. The two boys next to him could only be Colton and Finn. Even then, Finn wore glasses. It was a bit disconcerting to see Colton without the cowboy hat.

She looked around the rest of the room. There wasn't much childhood paraphernalia. Just the trophies, certificates and a few pictures.

There was one other photo on the dresser. It was of a very young Sebastian, a younger Hank and a girl on the cusp of adulthood that could only be Sebastian's mom. Leanne. Lily traced the girl's face. She had to have been practically a baby herself when she'd had Sebastian.

Leanne smiled down at him, and in her expression, Lily saw love.

Maybe it wasn't the kind of love that stuck around. Maybe it wasn't even enough love to stay away from drugs. But it was love. And it was because of love that she'd left Sebastian here with Hank, where he'd be cared for and loved.

Lily knew he'd wanted more. She knew because so had she. Her mother hadn't left—not Lily or her father. She wasn't the kind of mother Lily had dreamed of. But her mother loved her, too. She'd done her best to protect Lily.

Someday, Lily hoped her mother learned to love herself and recognize she deserved more out of life than she had.

Time for her morning ablutions. As she thought the word, she grinned and called herself Webster. If it were Sebastian teasing her, she'd inform him it was a superb word that always made her think of a Regency romance. But he wasn't and she sort of regretted not having him there to debate the word's merit.

She was barefoot but dressed when Sebastian came downstairs.

"Seriously, this is how you look the morning after a disaster like last night?"

"How is that?" she asked.

"Good enough to kiss good-morning…if that's okay?"

"Promise you're not going to fall in love with me?" she teased, repeating their words from last night.

"I promise if you promise."

She crossed her heart with her hand. "I do."

She stepped into his arms and gave him a proper good-morning. "Now, I don't mind starting my days like that…at least until Colton and Sophie's wedding."

"How did you sleep?" he asked.

"Like a stone. You?"

"Not so good. You see, I knew you were nearby. So close, but…"

Hank came clunking down the stairs, and Lily took a step out of Sebastian's arms. "But," she repeated, nodding at the door as Hank walked through.

"Good morning," he sang out as he helped himself to a cup of coffee. "What's on everyone's agenda for today?"

"I'm calling the insurance company and will store the rest of the furniture in the garage," Sebastian said to Lily.

"I can help after my house calls."

"Why are you moving Lily's furniture?" Hank asked.

"Because my place got flooded last night," Lily said gently.

For a moment, Hank looked blank.

She continued, "The tub in your bathroom overflowed?"

"My bathroom's fine," he said. "I just used it."

"Yes, it is. Sebastian cleaned it last night. All the water ran down into my apartment. So I'm staying here for a few days while we get it put to rights, if that's okay with you?"

He didn't say anything more about the flooding. "Sweetie, you've always got a home with me. I told you that over and over. This is your home."

"I know, Hank. It's good to hear, though." She hugged him.

Hank went to get coffee and Sebastian whispered, "He didn't remember."

"Wednesday. We'll get some answers on Wednesday." But even as she said the words, Lily was certain she knew what the answers would be, and she didn't believe it was something a prescription could cure.

CHAPTER TEN

THE NEXT THREE DAYS were hectic fixing up the apartment. Sebastian and Lily spent Sunday taking out the rest of whatever was damaged. Furniture and flooring. Sebastian got Jerry at the Farm and House Supply to open on Sunday, and he bought two new dehumidifiers. He'd lost track of how many times he emptied them. On Monday, an insurance agent inspected the place and a Dumpster was delivered. He and Lily cleared the debris out of the drive, then Sebastian started pulling down plaster. When he got the plaster away from Lily's exterior wall, he saw that even some of the insulation had gotten wet.

He worried that they didn't have a big enough Dumpster.

By Tuesday night, Sebastian was exhausted and his arm ached, but he knew that he'd been very busy, and he'd been concerned about the doctor's appointment right up until Lily hustled them to it first thing Wednesday morning.

Sebastian sat in the doctor's private office on a couch next to Lily. Hank sat on a chair across from them.

"Let's go," Hank said, fidgeting. He'd been agitated since breakfast when he'd started to leave for the diner, and Lily had reminded him of the appointment. "This doctor's rude. We've been waiting for twenty minutes."

"Hank, he stopped in to apologize for keeping us

waiting and will be here soon," Lily said. "It's rare that doctors think to apologize for keeping patients waiting. I think that says a lot about him. He's busy, but considerate."

"He's rude." Hank harrumphed and sat back in the chair.

His grandfather was generally one of the most easygoing people Sebastian knew, but obviously not this morning. Sebastian didn't blame him. He didn't want to be here, either, but Lily was right—avoiding the problem wouldn't make it go away. "Hank, it'll be fine."

His grandfather rose and he muttered, "I know it'll be fine. There's nothing wrong with me. I'm old. I know it. If I forget something now and then, it's to be expected."

"Humor me, please, Hank?" Lily patted the seat on the couch between them, and Hank grudgingly came over and sat down.

"Fine, we'll see your doctor, but he's going to tell you I'm old."

They sat in uncomfortable silence a few more minutes, then Dr. Flint came into the room. "I'm so sorry to keep you all waiting. I had an emergency this morning and it's thrown my whole day off."

"No problem, Doctor," Lily said.

"It was a problem," Hank griped. "I need to get back to work."

Dr. Flint didn't seem to take offense at Hank's less than cordial attitude. He smiled and said, "Then let's get going."

Lily had taken Hank for a CAT scan before their previous missed appointment, and the nurse had already taken Hank's vitals. The doctor scanned the chart and pulled a chair up opposite Hank. "Mr. Bennington, can you hold your hands out in front of you?"

Hank complied.

"Great. Now, I'm going to push against them and try to push them down. You don't let me." Hank held his own as the doctor pushed down.

Dr. Flint made some notations on Hank's chart. He asked, "Can you tell me the date?"

The tests went on like that. *Can you tell me what month it is? Who's the president?* Then the doctor switched to giving Hank lists of words to remember. Then he had Hank draw a clock.

Hank complained that he wasn't in school anymore, but obliged.

Sebastian watched as Lily's optimistic smile faltered. He knew why. He didn't need a medical degree to see that Hank wasn't doing well.

"Oh, and here," Lily said, handing the doctor a sheet of paper. "I made a list of all the drugs Hank takes, their dosage, and I included the multivitamin he has daily."

Sebastian knew that Lily was grasping at straws. That she wanted the doctor to look at the list and say, *Aha, this is it.* But he didn't. He simply took the sheet, glanced at it and said, "Thank you." When he looked up again, the doctor did a double take and studied Lily for a moment. "You look familiar."

"I worked at the hospital until last year. I've seen you around the halls. Finn Wallace recommended you."

"Lily, right?" Dr. Flint asked.

Lily nodded. "Right."

It didn't surprise Sebastian at all that the doctor would remember her. He didn't know how anyone could meet Lily Paul and ever forget her.

"You took care of Finn's sister." She nodded, and the doctor continued, "I know he appreciated it. We were all sorry she passed away."

"I was, too. It's only been three months and there's already so many things that she's missed and I ache with it." Sebastian could hear the sorrow in her voice. He could tell that Lily had loved Bridget. He might not know as much about her as he wished he did, but he knew that when Lily loved she did so wholeheartedly.

"I heard that Finn's moving," Dr. Flint said, as if talking about Finn was easier than delivering the diagnosis that Sebastian knew was coming.

"Yes," Lily said. "He'll still be in the hospital for surgeries a couple days a week."

"Good. If I needed surgery, he'd be the man I'd see."

Sebastian was gratified when the man turned back to his grandfather. "Mr. Bennington, I've reviewed your CAT scan, and there's no evidence of a stroke or TIA. Your physical tests were all well within normal parameters."

"I still bus tables. Those bus pans can be heavy," Hank said with pride.

"Well, it shows. But I do see signs of cognitive decline. We caught this early. There are medications that may slow the progression. We can..."

The doctor kept talking about medications and side effects. About promising new research and having hope.

But all Sebastian could register was that bit by bit, he was going to lose his grandfather.

He felt sick to his stomach at the thought of watching Hank disappear.

Lily sat there talking to the doctor about drugs and courses of action. Sebastian knew he should join in. He should engage in the conversation. He should ask questions or make comments, but neither he nor Hank said a word.

Then the discussion ended and the doctor stood up.

He extended his hand to Hank, then Lily and finally to Sebastian, who extended his hand in return by rote and shook.

Lily gathered up the prescription and some other papers the doctor had left for them and maneuvered him and Hank to the outer office to set up the next appointment.

They'd talked about going out to lunch, but Lily seemed to sense that neither he nor Hank wanted to.

"Hank, do you have any questions?" she asked as they all settled in the car.

"No."

Those were the last words spoken in the car on the trip home. At one point, Lily turned on the radio and they listened to country music on The Wolf. She hummed along to a few songs.

Crooning country music only made Sebastian feel worse, so he leaned over and switched the station to Star 104. Some guy was rapping. Normally Sebastian wasn't a fan, but there was an angry undercurrent to the song that matched what he was feeling, so he left it.

He glanced back at Hank and wanted to say something to his grandfather. Something comforting. But he couldn't imagine what those words would be.

He wasn't even sure Miss Webster herself had any words that would suit the purpose.

She pulled into Hank's driveway and switched off the engine. "I know you both are upset. I am, too. But we can get through this. We'll get the prescriptions filled and try those drugs, and we'll..."

"I've got to go to the diner," Hank said as he opened the car door and walked toward Park Street.

"Sebastian, we should go after him and—"

"No. Give him time. I know you're trying to help,

Lily. I know your first instinct is to look for a rainbow, and maybe tomorrow I can look for one, too, but today, I need to let this all sink in. I knew. Of course I knew. You pointed out Hank's problems, and after that, I couldn't write them off or overlook them. I guess I was better prepared than most for the diagnosis. And we'll talk it over soon. But not today."

"I understand." Lily rounded the car after they'd both climbed out. She took his hand in hers. "I'm your friend and I'm here for you."

He couldn't face her comfort and her rose-colored glasses yet. His plans to leave after the wedding—at finding out where he belonged—faded at Hank's diagnosis. Hell, they didn't fade—they popped and disappeared.

He pulled his hand away. As he did, she stepped back again, and that made him even angrier. "I'm not mad at you," he said as much to her as to remind himself. "I don't want you doing that weird little step-back thing you do every time I'm pissed."

"I don't know what you mean," she said.

Her statement pissed him off even more. "Really? When I've lost my temper—and I know I've lost it around you more than once—you put distance between you and me. As if you're afraid I'll hit you. And then I watch you give yourself a little mental shake and you step forward."

"I don't—" she started to deny.

"You do. And listen to me when I say that even though I might be tightly wound since I've got home, this isn't me. I'm trying to get it all under control and it's taking time, but I'm working on it. You have to believe me, Lily, even at my worst—when I'm pissed at the world in general and so frustrated I can't see straight—I would never, ever hurt you."

Her voice was as quiet as a whisper as she said, "I know that. Really, I do, Sebastian."

"Knowing and feeling are two different things," he replied gently, trying to keep his frustration and anger at the circumstances out of his voice. "Someday will you tell me what the hell happened to you?"

She shrugged her shoulders.

"You hold yourself back. You don't trust me to know your history. You give me stupid stories about the books that raised you, but fail to mention the parents that did. Do you think anything you tell me is worse than what I've imagined?"

It didn't take a rocket scientist or a degree in psychology to see that Lily had been hit before. It was there every time she moved out of his reach. He'd known it, but like Hank's diagnosis, he hadn't really voiced it in his own head until now. The thought of anyone hurting sunshiny-rainbow Lily made him ill.

"My past is not pretty," she said, "but so many had it worse. And my past doesn't define me. At least, not anymore. I think we need to concentrate on the present…not on what may happen to Hank. We need to live in the here and now. We need to treasure the fact that Hank's still as he is. That this medication might buy him time. We need to look at our friends and how happy they are as they start a life together. We can't change the past, and we can't know the future. We've only got now."

"Lily…"

She took his hand. "I'm not pulling away. Hank's gone to the diner, and even though my apartment's trashed, the house itself is fine. More specifically, your room is fine. The insurance adjuster was coming back today, but not until three. That leaves a few hours…"

Given everything his personal Pollyanna could have said in this moment, he hadn't considered this.

When he didn't respond, she said, "I'm stepping forward, Sebastian." She walked into his arms and kissed him. "Come into the house and take me to bed."

Sebastian claimed her hand and led her to the house. Before he opened the door, he asked, "You're sure? I can't make this more—"

"I don't want more. I simply want you. For now. No talk of forever and always. I think you and I both understand that there's no such thing anyway."

Of all the women he'd ever known, Lily Paul was the most forever sort of one. Those words coming out of her mouth sounded incongruous.

He thought about asking her, about checking again, but she was kissing him and then he was kissing her, and after that…

Well, the questions would wait.

LILY LOOKED AT SEBASTIAN. She'd never known him to look so peaceful. Everything in her wanted to reach out and touch him again, but she didn't want to wake him, so she lay on her pillow and watched him sleep.

He'd been so crushed after the doctor's diagnosis.

Lily had known what the doctor would say. She'd known for a long time. But that didn't mean hearing him say the words didn't hurt. She didn't want them to be true. She wanted him to say, *Look, I can fix this.* Even though she'd known that wasn't likely, she'd had hope.

Now she didn't have that hope—she had a diagnosis.

The one thing she could hang on to was the fact that there was no timetable. The new medications could level out the spread of the disease and keep Hank where he was right now for a long time.

That was her wish.

And then…

One step at a time, she scolded herself.

"You're awake," Sebastian stated without opening his eyes. "You were thinking so loud I could hear you."

"You're awake, too," she said and laughed, although nothing either of them had said was really funny. She laughed because despite the pain they both felt, they'd found solace in each other's arms. A respite.

He opened his eyes, leaned his head on his hand, his elbow pressed into the pillow, and grinned at her. "I shouldn't have fallen asleep. It was rude, really."

Lily laughed again because she was completely content in this instant. More than that, she was happy, regardless of everything. She was happy to be here with Sebastian. "No, your falling asleep was a compliment. Just your way of saying, *Lily, you were so good that I need to recoup.*"

He reached out and ran his finger lightly along the line of her neck and said, "You did that."

"Ditto."

He looked disappointed. "Oh, come on, Webster. The best you have to offer me is *ditto?*"

"Way to put my word power to the test," she teased. "Okay, how about *magnificent, astonishing, amazing, impressive*—"

"*Impressive?* Oh, I like that one," he said with mock seriousness.

"I could try phrases, not only words. Uh, you rocked my world. You…"

He leaned over and kissed her forehead. A gesture

of affection that felt overwhelmingly intimate to her. "Let me just say ditto."

And she watched as the fun, teasing Sebastian gave way to the man who was worried about his grandfather. He massaged his left arm. Lily reached over and gently touched along the scar. Then on to right below his rib cage where there was another long scar from a surgery. And though it was half under the covers, she'd seen the long scar from his knee to almost his hip on his left leg.

"What happened?" she asked as she kissed the scar on his stomach. "Never mind, forget I asked."

"Right. You don't want to ask, because if I told you, it might mean there was an intimacy here between us. Something more than sex. Maybe it's even deep enough that you might have to reciprocate and share something deep with me?"

She threw back the covers, intent on escaping his new mood. Only, this time she wasn't backing up because she was afraid; she was running because he was right. If he answered her question, they'd move to a more personal level than sex had taken them.

He caught her hand and tugged her back onto the bed. "You asked—now you sit here and listen to the answer."

"I know that it's hard for veterans to talk about the war—"

"You think that's what this is? That I was injured fighting for my country and I can't talk about it? I think it would be easier if I had been. If I'd been wounded fighting for my country, then maybe all this would make more sense. I knew that could happen when I enlisted."

She stopped trying to pull away. "No one in town knows what happened. I assumed… But you weren't hurt there?" And here Lily had thought there was a chance that Hank had known and forgotten. She'd assumed, like everyone else in town, that he'd been injured overseas. In her imagination, it'd happened in a desert and Sebastian was lying on the sand, wounded and bleeding.

"No, I came back from Afghanistan uninjured. At least, not physically. The things we saw..." He shook his head as if to clear those memories. "But we were home, back at Miramar in California. I had a place off base. I was driving in one day and...that's all I remember until I woke up after the surgery."

He got quiet. Lily wasn't sure what to say, but before the silence went on too long and got too awkward, he blurted, "A stupid accident! That's what they told me. The driver drifted into my lane, and I swerved to avoid him, and the car went over the side of the road. A road with no guardrails, so I dropped, only twelve or so feet, but my car flipped and I was pinned..."

"Sebastian..." That was all she could manage. The man was pouring out his heart to her, and all she could say was his name.

"My left side was a mess. I didn't just break my leg, but shattered it, and my arm...well, you've seen that. Internal injuries. They patched me together. Told me that my injuries, being what they were, meant my career was over."

She ached for how much pain he must have been in. "But you're here. You're home."

"Oh, yes, I'm here. I'm home because of some fluke accident. I'm here and my friends have all gone back overseas without me. They'll be fighting and risking their lives and I'll be here. I'll be home and safe. That's the problem. Don't you see?"

He was practically begging her to understand. "You didn't want to quit."

"I knew when I joined the military there was a chance I'd be hurt or even killed, but this isn't what I expected. Some random car accident? Just some young kid on a dark road? Where's the honor in that?"

"Sebastian, you've said I know more about you than anyone. Well, if that's true, then maybe you can trust me when I tell you that you are one of the most honorable men I've ever met." She looked at this man next to her in bed and realized how true that was.

"My unit is seeing combat and I'm here because of an accident. I'm here with friends and family, and they're risking their lives." His voice escalated until he practically shouted the last few words. "I'm here in bed with you."

"Maybe this makes me a very small person, but I'll admit I'm glad you're here. I'm glad you're safe. I'm glad you won't be fighting anymore."

She tried to lean over and kiss him, but this time he was the one who pulled away. She was hurt he wouldn't let her console him. But he'd trusted her enough to share something with her. Something he'd obviously not told many, if any, people. And she felt selfish for wishing he hadn't. It felt as if she now owed him. And she knew she couldn't repay his confidence with one of her own.

She'd tried to share her past, tried to open up once before, but the words wouldn't come.

She'd read self-help books with absurd titles like *You Are the Captain of Your Lifeboat.*

She wasn't the captain of anything. She knew that much.

But she wanted to share with him, and that was more than she'd ever wanted before. Most of the time she bundled up her past into a dark corner of her mind and ignored it, except when she called her mother once a week.

"Thank you for telling me," she whispered. "You should know that you are an amazing man. You really are. And you're going to have to trust me on that until you can feel it for yourself."

"I don't know if I'll ever feel anything more than..." He hesitated, searching for the word. "Furious at the hand I was dealt. Literally."

He'd tried for a joke, and Lily couldn't offer even the smallest smile for the attempt. "It's more than that."

He nodded. "And guilt. At first, it was anger, but more than that, it's the guilt. I feel guilty that my friends are fighting and I'm here in bed with the most beautiful woman I've ever met. Guilty that I'm home. And now guilty that I can't help Hank. He gave me everything. A home. Stability. Love. And I can't stop this disease from taking him away from me."

"But you can love him."

"That's a given," he agreed, then grew silent. He watched her and she wondered if that was expectation in his eyes. Did he think that because he'd shared she'd reveal all her pain and fears?

Lily knew that she wanted to do just that. And for a moment, she tried to force the words—some words. Any words. She wanted to give Sebastian some bit from her past. Something meaningful. Something personal.

He'd noticed her flinching, her stepping back. He said he had an idea of what happened to her in the past.

"My—" *father was a drunk,* she wanted to say. *I grew up thinking that bruises were part of a stylish woman's fashion accessories.* She tried to force the words out. *I grew up sitting on a swing and listening to my father beat my mother.* But she'd bottled the story, the words, up for so many years, and like the one other time she'd tried to share them, they got stuck and she couldn't speak, no matter how much she was tempted to.

She trusted Sebastian Bennington more than anyone she'd ever met, and still she couldn't tell him the truth. Instead, she frowned and said, "I like ice cream."

Maybe that was the right thing to say because Sebastian laughed. "What kind?"

SEBASTIAN HAD ACCEPTED Lily's kindness when he told her about his car accident. He'd told her about his anger, that he'd felt guilty, and she seemed to understand. She'd called him honorable. And for a second, he thought she was going to tell him who'd hit her. Who had taught her to fear anger. He'd hidden his disappointment and forced a laugh when Lily told him she liked ice cream. But he was upset.

When she left for a house call, he left, too.

Sebastian crisscrossed Valley Ridge. He avoided Park Street. There were too many people he knew that might stop and want to talk. And talking was the last thing Sebastian wanted to do.

He'd been angry for so long that the feeling was like an old friend. And after talking to Lily today, he admitted that it was more than that—it was guilt. That he was here at home and he was safe, while his buddies were not.

He clenched his hand hard—the pain was almost welcome. He could deal with it so much easier than the awful feeling churning inside him.

Lily wouldn't let him in. She'd have sex with him, but she wanted to keep it casual. She'd be his friend and Hank's friend.

Thinking about Hank made not only his anger but also his guilt flare.

The neurologist had asked his grandfather a million questions. *What's the date? Repeat these five things back to me. Who's the president?*

Hank had laughed about his inability to name the president. He'd said that after Kennedy he tried to forget all of them. But Sebastian had seen how much his grandfather had been covering. And even if he hadn't, Lily's expression would have told him how bad the tests were going.

In his back pocket, Sebastian had one of the pamphlets the doctor had given them. *The Seven Stages of Alzheimer's.* Hank fell somewhere between the third and fourth stage. He was still functioning but had some impairment. Impairment that Sebastian might have simply written off as old age if not for Lily.

Lily had stressed that the medication the doctor gave Hank couldn't help him buy back the ground he'd already lost or stop the disease's progression, but it could help stabilize him. It could buy him time.

Sebastian played the appointment over and over in his head. He needed to process the fact that this was as good as Hank would get and that things would get worse. How quickly they'd get worse, he couldn't tell. There was no way of knowing, really. But the grandfather he knew and loved would surely fade away.

Sebastian knew that his plan to leave and discover the next chapter in his life was gone. His next chapter was here in Valley Ridge.

He didn't have a notion as to what he'd do here. He knew that Seb, the wild child of his youth, was behind him. Lieutenant Bennington of the marines was gone, too. Now he was Sebastian. A man who owed his grandfather more than he could ever repay. He'd be here for Hank and figure out the rest somehow.

And maybe while he was figuring things out he'd be able to figure out Lily Paul, too.

She had completely surprised him after the doctor's appointment. Instead of jumping into the what-are-we-going-to-do-now mode, she'd given him the space he'd asked for and had come to his bed.

Despite being so confused, he couldn't help but smile at the memory.

He knew he hadn't been himself since the accident. He'd spiraled out of control. He'd thought being in Valley Ridge for Colton's wedding would help him find his feet and decide what he was going to do next, but instead, his life had continued to be topsy-turvy. When he was with Lily, he felt—

"Hey, Sebastian," someone called.

He looked up and tried to decide where he was. He'd been walking so long without paying attention that he wasn't sure.

He turned and spotted Joey. The two girls following after him had to be the sisters that Lily had mentioned.

He forced a smile. "Hi, Joey. And these beautiful ladies are?"

"Oh, that's Allie and Mica, my sisters. They're not beautiful, or ladies. Mica ate a quarter yesterday. Who does that?"

The two tiny blondes eyed him, not sure what to make of him. He knelt down. "I'm a friend of your brother's. We had a great game of basketball not too long ago. How old are you ladies?"

They both giggled as he called them ladies for a second time, and Joey grimaced.

"I'm Allie and I'm seven, almost eight." The younger

one held up five fingers. “And that’s Mica. She don’t talk much, but she’s five and in kindergarten. I’m in third grade, even though I’m seven.” Her voice dropped to a stage whisper. “I’m very smart.”

“Oh, it’s nice to meet you both.” He stood up. “How’re things with you?” The boy was frowning so fiercely that Sebastian suspected they weren’t all that good. “Problems?”

“You girls can go in. Dad’s car’s here, so he’s back from therapy.”

The little girls bolted for the house.

“What’s wrong?”

“Some lady in town was looking for a babysitter, and I applied, but she told me she wanted a girl. That’s discrimination, but no one ever says anything about that. I mean, I’ve been watching the girls since forever. I used to walk Allie home from school and stop at the neighbor’s for Mica, then babysit them both until Dad got out of work. I can change diapers, and I’ve read the *Wild Baby Book* so many times I can recite huge chunks of it by heart. I’ve even had CPR classes, but the lady didn’t want to hear about any of that.”

Sebastian felt another surge of frustration. He couldn’t help Hank. He couldn’t get Lily to share more than her love of ice cream and reading, but maybe he could do something for this kid. “Do you need a job for a reason?”

“Well…” Joey scuffed his shoe on the ground.

“Joey, I know we’re not exactly friends, but if I can help, I will.” What he wouldn’t give to be able to help someone.

“It’s only that Dad’s been off work for a while. He gets disability money, but it’s not as much as his normal paycheck and things are tight. Allie wants to go to Girl Scout Camp this summer and I thought…”

"And you didn't get the babysitting job."

"No."

"Would you consider some other jobs?"

"Like what?" Joey asked. "I don't want pity."

"I don't blame you," Sebastian said. "But it just so happens that Lily rents an apartment from my grandfather and there's been some water damage. I could use an assistant while I fix it up."

"That's like charity."

"That's not what that is." Sebastian held up his left hand. "It's getting better, but I still have a lot of problems with small motor skills. That means holding a screw so I can put up drywall might be an issue. And dozens of other things that I'll need help with. No sympathy here. Maybe some admiration, though. I like seeing someone who doesn't moan about their circumstances but picks up and does what they can." Even as he said the words, Sebastian realized that he'd done a lot of moaning.

Maybe it was time to start concentrating on what he could do rather than what he couldn't. "I thought that between the two of us, we could get most of the work done."

"I have to look after my sisters."

"We'll work around that. I don't have a proper job anywhere," he said, but thought that was going to have to change. Hank's diagnosis changed everything. However, right now he would concentrate on Lily's apartment. "My schedule's open. Could we start Saturday?"

"Yeah. I'll do a great job for you," Joey answered excitedly.

"Maybe you should introduce me to your father. We'll run it by him."

"Sure, come on."

They went into the modest bungalow. The girls were sitting at the table, eating apples, and a man was talking to Mrs. Lorei.

"Mrs. Lorei," Sebastian greeted Maeve Buchanan's mother. She used to work at the diner and still brought in fresh eggs from the farm she owned with her second husband. "Nice to see you. How's Maeve doing?"

"Seb Bennington, what mischief are you up to now?" she scolded as she gave him a hug and kiss on the cheek. "My daughter's doing fine. Thanks for asking." Never one to beat around the bush, she took his scarred hand in hers and examined it with all the care of a surgeon. "I heard you got hurt. Are you okay now?"

"Getting better every day," he said and realized it was so. "I'm having to relearn things like tying shoes—"

"I can tie my shoes," Mica, the younger sister, said. "I can show you how if you want."

"Thanks, Mica." He smiled down at the young blonde. "I might take you up on that."

"So what brings you here?" Mrs. Lorei asked.

"I came to meet Joey's father." He addressed the poor man who hadn't been able to get a word in edgewise. "I'm Sebastian Bennington. I met Joey the other day on the basketball court."

"Miss Lily was playing against him, with her hand tied behind her back," Joey added. "I told you, Dad."

"You did. It's nice to meet you. I'm Ron."

"Sebastian offered me a job," Joey said. "His hand is messed up and he's got to fix Miss Lily's apartment. He said I'd be a help."

"I need to hang new drywall and maybe replace the floor. I can handle the big stuff. It's the smaller things that do me in."

"I didn't get that babysitting job. Seems moms only

want *girls,*" Joey said, making the word *girls* sound like a curse. "What do you think?"

"I'll vouch for Seb," Mrs. Lorei offered. "He was a hellion growing up, but he's now a fine, respectable man. He's a marine."

"Was a marine. Right now I'm in…flux." When he used that last word, he thought of Lily, aka Webster, and smiled.

"I don't see why not," Ron said.

"Sebastian said he can work around when you need me for the girls," Joey pressed.

"Hey, we can help," Allie said, and her little sister nodded in agreement.

"This is a paying job," Joey scoffed. "Dad never took kids to his paying job."

"Dad," Allie wailed.

Ron chuckled. "Your brother's right."

Sebastian saw a stubbornness in Allie's eyes that reminded him of Lily, and it won him over. "I'll tell you what, I may find a job that might work for two little girls, if you know any who'd be interested?"

"We would," the girls said in unison.

"Only, we're not little," Allie informed him.

Mrs. Lorei rose. "Now that I'm done with providing this rascal his references, I'm off to city hall to complain to another reformed imp."

"What's wrong?" Sebastian asked.

"There's been a tree down on Longhorn Street for the better part of three days. I have to weave around it when I do the egg deliveries, and that's not exactly safe. Someone was supposed to come get it, but no one has. We pay taxes and I expect—"

Sebastian interrupted her. "How big a tree?"

"It's only a branch, but far too big for me to handle

on my own, and big enough that even if he took a chain saw to it, my husband would probably kill himself trying to lift the pieces."

"Why don't I come over and check it out? If I can manage it, I'll take care of it and save Mr. Lorei from doing himself in and the mayor from a tongue-lashing."

"I'll help," Joey offered.

"Us, too," the girls yelled.

"I'd offer, but..." Ron gestured to the prominent brace on his back.

"Well, if you can spare the kids, we'll all walk over with Mrs. Lorei and see what we can do."

"Them, too?" Joey asked.

"I'm thinking if the branch is that big, we'll need some stick-picker-uppers." He'd probably have to borrow Colton's trailer and a chain saw. "Let's go take a look and formulate a plan."

CHAPTER ELEVEN

"THIS IS WAY COOLER than babysitting," Joey said as they carried sheets of drywall into Lily's apartment.

Sebastian studied the boy, who was balancing the other end of the drywall, and said, "I'd never thought about it, but yes, it probably is cooler than babysitting. Drywall doesn't cry."

"Or throw up, or wake up crying 'cause they miss their mom." Joey spoke with authority.

"Sorry, kid." Sebastian felt a kinship with Joey. They'd both lost their moms, but Joey had it worse because he was trying to pick up the slack for his younger sisters.

"'It is what it is,' my dad says." They set the piece of drywall on the pile.

Sebastian flinched. His hand was definitely getting a workout. He massaged it gently.

"Sorry about your hand."

Sebastian smiled, then started back outside for another sheet of drywall. "Lily's been hounding me to find the silver lining."

Joey laughed. "That sounds like her. Have you found one?"

"Maybe." Sebastian nodded. "Definitely. For instance, if I hadn't been frustrated because of my hand,

Lily wouldn't have challenged me to a game of one-handed one-on-one."

Joey chuckled at the memory. "We still talk about her with her hand tied behind her back."

"She wanted to prove I could still do things. I had to find new ways of doing them. I had to think outside the box. And then you and your friends came along."

Joey grinned as he lifted his end. "So what you're saying is, if you hadn't hurt your hand we'd never have met?"

"Possibly. And that would have been my loss because you are a super kid." They balanced the sheet of drywall and walked through the door to the apartment. "No, I take that back," Sebastian said as they put the piece down.

"You take it back that I'm super?" Joey didn't seem insulted.

"I take back the *kid* part." Sebastian patted his shoulder. "You're no child. Your friends are out running around and, if they're anything like I was at the age, causing mayhem. While you're here, keeping an eye on your sisters—"

"Actually, Lily's keeping an eye on them." Lily and the girls were in Hank's kitchen.

"And you're working here, earning money to send Allie to camp. You've been helping your dad at home, too. Those aren't the things a normal kid does. Those are things a man does."

Joey chewed on that for a while as they maneuvered the last piece of drywall onto the pile.

"Joey," Sebastian started to say, then stopped. "Joe."

The boy caught the distinction. "Why'd you call me Joe?"

"I had this friend Pontz in the marines. I went home with him one leave, and his family didn't call him that. They called him Ponto and he kept correcting them. He said he'd outgrown his childhood nickname. He was Pontz now. When I came home this time, people called me Seb, and I discovered I wasn't him anymore. Seb was a young boy. I'd left him behind and was Lieutenant Sebastian Bennington. That's what I wanted to be called—not the whole thing, mind you, just Sebastian." And who the hell that was going to turn out to be, he didn't know.

"Names define you, I guess," he continued. "You were Joey when you were a kid. But you're not that kid anymore. You shouldn't walk around with a kid's name—it no longer suits you. So, unless you object, I'll call you Joe."

Joe mulled that over. "Thanks, Sebastian."

"Anytime, Joe."

"And thanks for saying that other stuff. I mean, it sucks my mom's not here and that Dad got hurt, but maybe Lily's silver lining is I grew up because of it."

Sebastian remarked, "You grew up *well* because of it."

"And I know the kind of person I want to be."

"Which is?" he asked.

"Someone like Lily—she always smiles, no matter what's going on. When Dad had his accident, he was kind of tough to be around. She never noticed. She'd come to the house for the doctor, and Dad, he'd yell at her, and she just kept smiling and doing what she needed to do and acted like she didn't know he was being mean. One day I came in and she was telling him a story and he was laughing. It was the first time I'd heard him laugh since Mom left."

"Being as much like Lily as you can be would be a wise decision." Sebastian realized that as he dealt with Hank's health issues and with trying to figure out what to do next, he wanted to be more like Lily Paul, too.

"And I want to be like my dad," Joe said. "He'd never leave, not like Mom did. Normally, he's the nicest guy ever. No matter what pain he's in, he'll always take care of us and love us."

Sebastian nodded and was surprised when Joe said, "And I want to be like you."

"Me? Hey, be like Lily and your dad. I think those are much better choices."

"Nah. You came home to Valley Ridge to be in a friend's wedding. You're a good guy. And you fought for your country. You even got hurt."

Sebastian started to argue he didn't get hurt fighting for his country. All the bitterness and guilt rose in his chest, but Joe continued talking. "You're figuring out how to work around your problem. I've watched you trying different ways to do stuff 'cause of your hand. And you've been nice to me—some kid you didn't even know. You even helped out Cam. He's working for Mrs. Esterly now, for real, since he paid off his debt. You didn't have to do that. Yeah, I think I'm adding you to my list."

"I'm honored but, Joe, the only reason I'm here trying to think outside the box is because of Lily." Honored as well as embarrassed. Joe saw him as something that he knew he really wasn't. He'd been as short-tempered and ornery as Joe's father.

Lily might feel sympathy, but she didn't coddle anyone. She did what needed to be done…and did it with a smile.

He felt silly, but he also felt inspired to be more… more like Lily and more like Joe.

LILY STOOD OUTSIDE her apartment's open door and listened to *Joe* and Sebastian, the tray with cookies and iced tea almost forgotten. Their assessments of her made her feel like a fraud.

Sure, she tried to look at the bright side, but sometimes she couldn't find one and she just faked it. When she'd first gone to Joe's house, his father had been one of her most difficult patients. He'd been depressed about his wife leaving and in constant pain from his back. He'd forgone strong pain medications because he didn't feel he could take care of the kids if he was knocked out—and he was right. But he'd been so miserable and had lashed out at her almost every visit. She'd forced a smile and got on with her job, but…it had been hard.

That day Joe had heard his dad laugh out loud wasn't really because of anything she'd said. He'd reached a turning point in his recovery and felt better. She'd told him some goofy story—she couldn't even remember which one—and he'd cracked up.

Joe and Sebastian both seemed to think that her smiling and staying positive made her someone they should emulate, but she knew better.

The fact that she'd thought the word *emulate* made her smile.

Fraud or not, Sebastian and Joe seemed to set a lot of store in her good mood. So rather than admitting to the eavesdropping or her occasional lapse of sunny disposition, she checked on the girls. Allie and Mica were playing on the glider. "Be careful on that, girls. It's seen better days."

She pasted a smile on her face as she went into the apartment. "Wow, you guys are making progress."

"We brought in the last of the drywall. Your place is almost done," Joe said. "I know how to score and break the drywall now. Sebastian said he'd teach me how to tape the seams and mud them and the screws."

"Sounds like you've learned a lot."

Joe looked at Sebastian with admiration. He nodded. "Yeah, I've learned a lot."

"Well, you guys enjoy the snack. If you don't mind, the girls and I are heading over to MarVee's. I have a couple things I need to buy."

"You don't have to babysit them," Joe said. "That's my job."

"I've always enjoyed your sisters, Joe." She saw him puff up a bit as she used his name. "You'd be doing me a favor."

"Okay, then. We're only working a little longer."

"Great. I'll bring them back as soon as we're finished."

Sebastian shot her a look—another one of his piercing looks. She felt her cheeks warm as she realized that not only did he know she'd eavesdropped, but he also knew she'd heard the nice things they'd both said about her.

He gave the very slightest nod, which she knew meant he was telling her that he stood behind all the things they'd both said about her. So she smiled at Joe, then at Sebastian, as if she were agreeing with Joe's assessment of Sebastian.

The entire exchange took a mere second, and Lily

would have liked to blow it off as a figment of her imagination, but as she reached the doorway and turned back, Sebastian was not only giving her a piercing look, he was smiling, and she knew that they'd pretty much had a conversation without saying a word.

The idea of that sort of understanding made her uncomfortable. She brushed it aside and called the girls. "Do you guys want go to MarVee's with me?"

"I love Miss Mar and Miss Vee," Allie said. Her little sister nodded in agreement. "Sometimes they give us candy. Dad and Joey say, 'Tell the ladies thank-you, girls.' And we do. Well, I do. Mica's shy. She's not shy at home. Daddy says her mouth waddles like a duck's behind."

Both girls giggled at the word *behind.* Lily couldn't help but giggle, as well. As they went along Park Street, Valley Ridge's main avenue, she listened to the girls prattle and knew that her current sunny disposition had nothing fake about it. It was impossible not to be enchanted listening to life from their perspective.

She waved at Mattie through Park Perks' window as they passed and then crossed the street to MarVee's Quarters.

"Miss Mar and Miss Vee," the girls cried as they spotted the two older ladies behind the counter.

Within moments, the girls were behind the counter with the women. "You go do your shopping, Lily," Marilee said. "We need some assistance from these special helpers. Oh, and Sophie's back there somewhere."

"Thanks, ladies. Girls, you behave."

"Yes, Miss Lily," Allie answered, and Mica nodded.

The "back there somewhere" was a very apt description of the store. There were no orderly rows here. And although the ladies had divided the shop into sections—kitchen, bath and the like—there was still the sense of organized chaos in the randomly stocked shelves.

She scanned the aisles and followed a haphazard path to the back of the store. She found Lily in a section that was supposedly Miscellaneous.

"Sophie," Lily called, and her friend popped up from behind a table that contained stacks of material, ribbon and silk flowers. She had a big dust smudge on one cheek and the general appearance of a person who'd been out on safari and found her quarry.

"Yay," she squealed, holding a large roll of lace aloft.

"Indiana Jones, I assume that's the Holy Grail?" Lily teased.

Sophie clutched the lace to her chest, her expression ecstatic. "It is. I wanted this for the chairs at the wedding. I found this awesome idea on Pinterest. They did it in really bright colors, but I'm doing the chairs at my wedding in shades of white."

"Shades of white?"

"Oh, there are so many kinds of white. White-white. Ivory-white. Cream-white. I want to use all of them. We're borrowing folding chairs from everyone we know, and of course, none of them will match, but I thought the white ribbons and lace streaming off the back would bring it all together."

Lily wasn't sure what Pinterest was, but she nodded enthusiastically about the concept. "Shades of white, bringing it all together. It'll be beautiful, Soph."

"No idea what Pinterest is, right?" Sophie asked, as if reading her mind.

Lily shook her head. "None. But I do like the idea of the streamers on the chairs. It will look so romantic."

Sophie added the hard-won bolt of ribbon to a giant box at her feet. "You know, you could enter the twenty-first century. I mean, you don't even have a Facebook account."

"I know. I'm an anachronism." She'd never tell Sophie, but the truth was, she'd never started any online social media because she didn't want old friends to find her. She didn't want her past spilling into her present. She'd buried her childhood, and as far as she was concerned, it could stay buried. "I see all my friends on a regular basis. I don't need Facebook."

Sophie frowned and gave up the idea of making a social-media convert out of Lily. "So what are you doing here today?"

"I wanted to see if there were any sheets or blankets. It seems that since Sebastian's renovating so much of the apartment that it might be time to do some updating of my own." When she'd first come to Valley Ridge, she'd spent more time at Bridget Langley's than at her apartment. And after that, she spent more time at Hank's and at the diner. But as she watched the place get rehabbed, she wanted to make it hers. To put some kind of stamp on it.

"I'm buying new furniture, too," she said. The couch was totaled. It had drowned to death. But the rest was okay. There were a few new water marks on the end table and coffee table. She'd lived with worse.

But suddenly she didn't want to do serviceable. She wanted nice. "Yep, a new living-room set at the very least."

"Do we get an invitation when you're done redecorating?"

Lily felt a surge of anxiety at the thought of having

guests. She forced herself to ignore the sour feeling in the pit of her stomach. "I'll tell you what, I'll make dinner one night. We'll probably have to eat outside at a picnic table. I don't think I could fit everyone in the apartment. But you'll get an official tour."

"That sounds wonderful. Now, let me leave my stuff at the counter, and I'll help you shop."

Twenty minutes later, new sheets, curtains and a bedspread had been purchased, and Lily started home with the girls, who not only had enjoyed cups of milky tea with Marilee and Vivienne but had brought home three Gobstoppers. "We got Joey one, 'cause he's working."

"That's very considerate of you both," Lily said.

Mica tugged on Allie's sleeve, then whispered something to her. After which Allie said, "Oh, no, we didn't get you or that guy one."

Lily knew "that guy" was Sebastian. "I think once you're over twenty you're too old for Gobstoppers. It's a rule."

"Oh." Both girls nodded as if that made perfect sense to them. As if more than twenty was so ancient that neither she nor Sebastian would be able to handle an entire Gobstopper.

They saw Joe waiting in the front yard as they came down the block.

"Joey, we got you a present," Allie yelled, and Mica raced ahead of her older sister.

Sebastian came up behind Joe, spotted her and hurried to help with her bags. "Thanks."

"Did you buy out the store?" He hefted the bags for effect.

"No. Sheets and bedspreads are bulky." Lily felt a surge of excitement. Her apartment was going to be more than a location to eat and sleep. It was going to be her home. The idea appealed to her.

"Redecorating?" he asked.

"Since it's being remodeled, I thought I'd continue the theme."

"Lily, I saw your apartment before. You'd have had to *model* in the first place in order to *remodel.* Heck, Colton's barn looked opulent by comparison."

"I was only here short-term at first," she defended, even though she knew Sebastian was right. "That's why I rented a semi-furnished place."

"When Hank advertised *semi-furnished,* he meant there was a bed and a couch."

"That's all I needed. I'm thinking of a trip to Erie or Buffalo to buy some new furniture."

He set the bags down on the kitchen table and let out a long, low whistle. "Wow, this is serious. Would you like company on your furniture-shopping trip?"

"Are you offering?" she asked.

"Indeed I am."

Lily looked at the tall, handsome man, who was smiling, and had two opposite reactions. One was she'd like nothing better than to take him up on his offer, and the other was it was a good thing he'd be leaving soon, since the strength of her first reaction scared her.

The first reaction won. "Yes."

"If you play your cards right, I might even treat you to dinner. Like a real date." He did a Groucho Marx sort of eyebrow wiggle.

Lily clasped her hands together on her chest. "Be still my heart."

Sebastian looked past her and found Joe loitering on the porch. "I'm taking the rug rats home, Sebastian.

Miss Lily. I saw Hank and he's heading over to the diner and we thought we'd walk with him." He pointed to where Hank stood on the sidewalk, talking to the girls.

"Thanks for helping, Joe."

He took off after his sisters and Hank.

"You told Joe about Hank?" Lily asked.

"Yes. I think folks should be aware of it. Looking out for him is a good thing."

"I've told the staff at the diner," she admitted.

"I talked to Dylan, too. As a cop, he's a good one to keep an eye on Hank. The word will spread on its own now."

"I read an article in a nursing journal about tools, tricks and tech for Alzheimer's patients. Hank's dementia is moderate right now, but it wouldn't hurt to set things up for later."

Sebastian listened as Lily talked about what they could do to make the house and the diner safer for Hank. "...maybe some sensor for overflowing sinks and tubs? And an intercom between here and the big house?"

Sebastian caught her in his arms. "There's a lot to do, but as of this minute, the house is empty. Hank's at the diner, my assistant and his sisters are on their way home. That means it's me and you...alone in this quiet house. What do you think we should do with that alone time?"

Lily laughed. "Look at paint swatches?"

"I'm thinking we could come up with a better idea." He took her hand and nudged her toward the door.

"Better than paint swatches? I don't know, Sebastian. Better than paint swatches is a lot to ask for. It would have to be something big and special to rival paint swatches." He shut the apartment door and they walked around the corner.

"Oh, I think I can manage that. If my arm were stronger, I'd pick you up and carry you into the house and into my room. But I'm afraid I'd drop you. So I'm going to improvise. This wonderful woman I've met has been pounding the fact that there's more than one way to do something into my thick head, so..." He leaned over, scooped Lily over his right shoulder and hooked his arms behind her knees. "It's not nearly the most romantic method to carry a woman, but hey, I make do."

"And you didn't break anything or get frustrated," she called.

"I think I'm making progress."

"I think so, too," she said.

Sebastian carried her toward the main house and then directly up the stairs. "And you're right, I've found that there are some things I can still manage with no problems, even with a bum hand." He'd reached the hall, strode into his room and deposited her on the bed.

AFTERWARD, SEBASTIAN held her close in his left arm. Yes, he'd found something his arm could still do. Something that he could still do. He leaned back, and his eyes felt heavy. Just as he was about to let them close and enjoy the peaceful feeling of holding Lily, she bound out of bed, collected her clothes, and leaned down and kissed his forehead. "Thank you. That was lovely."

"You don't have to leave. Hank won't be home for hours and I'm not scheduled to be at the diner. We have—"

She smiled. "I do have to leave. We're friends with benefits until you're gone. And now that our benefit is over, I'm going to shower and then go to the diner for a while."

She was gone before he could protest further. And as she shut his bedroom door, the true implication of her words sank in. She thought he was still leaving after the wedding.

She hadn't realized he was staying. After Hank's diagnosis, Sebastian hadn't come out and said he was staying because he hadn't thought it was necessary to. His grandfather would only get worse from here on in.

He'd read all he could about Alzheimer's and he knew that there was no measurable rate of decline. Hank could stay where he was for a long time or for a week. He could decline in slow increments or tumble down the rabbit hole.

How could Lily think he would leave his grandfather?

He'd been paying attention and gleaning small things about her. Lily Paul didn't do long-term relationships. She was convinced she'd never marry. She was the most open, giving woman he'd ever met.

She'd had a very bad childhood.

He could tell her. He should say, *Lily, I'm not going anywhere.* Hell, he should be pissed that she thought he'd walk away.

He'd bide his time and let her figure out that he was staying. He'd ease her into the idea. And maybe, while he was easing, he'd also ease her into the idea that whatever they had was more than friendship with benefits.

He wasn't ready to label what they had, but he knew it went deeper than that.

He'd poured his heart out to her. He'd told her things

he hadn't even told the shrink the hospital had made him talk to.

Why? Because he trusted her.

Maybe someday she'd trust him enough to really talk to him.

An image of Lily smiling and telling him not to fall in love with her flashed through his mind.

And suddenly he knew that he was in danger of doing just that.

Was it already too late?

That image of Lily repeated itself again and again in his mind.

Sebastian considered a trip to the diner, but he rejected it. Rather, he went and sat on the glider and waited. He understood why Lily gravitated to it. The swinging motion was very comforting.

He watched as the sun sank behind the neighboring houses and the sky grew darker. Nighttime insects started to make their evening noises, and something black flew overhead. A bat. He found himself thinking they were lucky they had bats because they helped control insect populations. The idea made him grin because it was very Lily-esque. Looking at the bright side.

He started tallying how much money he had available. He'd talk to Hank about buying a share of the business. As things got more difficult, he'd be able to step in and keep things afloat. He wasn't sure how Lily would feel about him not only staying but working side by side with her at the diner.

He spotted her walking on the sidewalk with Hank. Their arms were interlinked and she laughed at something he said.

"Good night?" he called out.

They both turned toward the glider. "Great night," Hank replied. "But it was almost too much for an old man. I'm off to bed." He kissed Lily's cheek and smacked Sebastian on the shoulder as he strolled past him.

"Are you going in, or can you sit for a few minutes?" Sebastian asked.

Lily claimed the seat opposite him.

"So how was your day?" he asked. "I know about our—what's the word? Tryst? But otherwise?"

"I visited a new mom. The baby had jaundice, but now he's a bit colicky. I don't think she's caught more than a couple hours of sleep most nights. So when she dozed off, I couldn't leave."

"So you stayed and sat rocking the baby?" Sebastian couldn't imagine Lily sitting still too long.

He couldn't really see her eyes clearly, but he knew they crinkled in just the right places as she admitted, "Okay, maybe I did a few dishes and dusted. He was happy as long as he was held. I'll confess I got a touch of what you go through trying to figure out how to do various tasks one-handed."

"Bet you didn't throw a hissy fit. You studied the problem until you found a solution." When she didn't say anything, he added, "Pollyanna."

"Stop making me seem like a saint," Lily said with a hint of anger. "I work at—"

"You work at being upbeat," he finished for her. "Yeah, I know you paint on your sunshiny-rainbow exterior to hide your deep, dark interior."

She laughed, which Sebastian didn't inform her was not the least bit in keeping with a hidden dark side. Even in the murky twilight, he could see her looking at his injured arm. He stopped massaging it.

She moved across the glider and sat next to him. “Let me see if we can get those muscles to relax.”

“I thought that touching outside the bedroom was frowned upon in this weird little relationship—oops, wrong word, right?”

She took his arm and started to gently treat the knotted muscles. “Wow, someone’s a bit snarky. Do you feel better?”

“No.” He hated her friends-with-benefits rules. And he hated that she thought so little of him that she seriously believed he would leave Valley Ridge and Hank.

“I need to say, to tell you…” He paused and pulled away from her. He wasn’t sure which topic to broach first, but he didn’t think he’d be able to do either justice while she was touching him.

“So go ahead and vent at me, but while you do it, give me your arm again.” She reached for him.

He shifted from her grasp. “Stop touching me. I need to talk to you.”

She sighed long and loud and said, “Fine. Talk.”

Something was different. It took him a minute to determine what. “You didn’t react this time.”

“What?”

“When I’ve gotten frustrated and yelled, you always step back. And after that instinctual step back, I’ve watched as you force yourself to step forward again. To stand your ground. Am I close?”

She shrugged. “Maybe I know that you’re all bluster. Maybe I understand that you came home expecting everything to be the same as when you left—that you’d be the person you were when you left. It’s been hard finding out that things continued to move and change while you were gone. I've noticed that you haven't vented at anyone else. Not Hank, not your friends. Only me. So maybe I've decided to take it as a compliment that you trust me enough to voice your frustrations at me."

"There you go, all sunshiny rainbows on me."

This time she didn't laugh but seemed to consider his words. "Maybe. But, Sebastian, I know that coming home after being in the service is hard—you're not the same. Coming home injured is harder. Coming home and finding that things have changed for your family—and changed for the worse—is even harder yet."

"And knowing there's nothing I can do to make it better...the hardest. Hank always took care of me, but I can't stop this disease. I can't make things better for him. My whole life I've had Hank in my corner. He needs me now, and there's not a damn thing I can do to help him." Perfect segue into telling her he wasn't leaving. Part of him was afraid that when she heard that she'd pull back on their relationship.

Before he could say anything, Lily spoke. "When I was little, my mom took me on a walk almost every afternoon after work. We had a favorite route that went by this big white house with a garden next to it. There was this statue of Mary they kept in the center of it. I was still real little and I begged to be allowed to walk around that block myself. It was two or three times bigger than most. I begged and whined and wheedled, and eventually she said yes and gave me a lecture about not crossing or even setting foot on the street. So I took off. I was so little and most of my memories are blurry, but this one is so clear. I was on top of the world. But

I came to a driveway that had these very high curbs, like a street…"

"And because you were a Goody Two-shoes, you didn't cross." He realized that Lily was sharing something from her past with him. And he wished he could apologize for what he'd said earlier, but he didn't want to ruin her mood.

"No, I didn't. I'm sure you would have."

He nodded. "Probably."

"Well, I didn't. I turned around and went back to look for Mom, who'd waited for me at the garden, but when I didn't come, she started back around the block—in the direction I should have been coming from—and when I backtracked and got to the statue, she wasn't there."

"Did you freak out?" he asked, though he was fairly sure he knew the answer. Lily wouldn't freak out over being lost because in her sunshiny world, she knew she'd be found.

"No, I didn't freak out. I simply sat down and waited. I was sure she'd come find me, and she did. She picked me up and snuggled me in her arms and held me. I think I remember that moment because I felt so safe, so protected. So loved."

"And the point is?" he asked. He figured Lily didn't get along with her mother because of whatever was there in her past, but that was not the picture she'd painted.

"The point is, Hank's lost," Lily told him. "He's a little more lost every day. He's standing by the statue and trusting that we're going to find him. We can't take this disease away. We can't make it better. We can be there, though. We can hold on to him and make him feel safe."

She said *we.* The impact of that stuck with him. Maybe it had occurred to her that he was staying.

"We can meet him by the statue, Seb," she said softly. "You can hold him and make him feel safe. And once you're gone, you'll call. And I'll be here."

She still thought he was leaving. The warm glow that he'd felt when he realized she was talking as if they were a team didn't fade—it disappeared in a flash. Replaced by anger. "Lily, I'm not—"

A phone rang and interrupted him. Lily pulled it out of her pocket and said, "I have to take this."

He got up and left her to the glider and walked back toward the house. The kitchen light was on. It illuminated the back stoop.

That was the door he'd used when he came to Hank's with his mom. His mom had stayed in the back apartment because she didn't like to feel that Hank was watching her every move, and he'd stayed with Hank. He'd walk between the two places.

When he left the apartment to come into Hank's well-lit kitchen, he'd felt safe. Just like Lily felt when her mom came to find her when she'd been lost.

When his mother did have him with her, they moved from place to place. Living on a friend's couch, or occasionally she'd have enough money for a dive of their own. But without fail, they always ended up back at Hank's. And when they did, Sebastian had felt safe—he'd felt as if he was genuinely coming home.

How could Lily think he'd leave Hank? He owed his grandfather that same kind of safety net.

He headed back to the glider. It was time he had this out with Lily once and for all.

She was still talking on the phone. "No, Mom, I can't send you any money."

There was a pause and she said, "I did have some

put aside, but I've spent it. I don't have anything to send. But, Mom, even if I did, I wouldn't. We've talked about this."

Okay, he needed to go. He wanted to know more about Lily, but not like this. "Mom, I was talking to a friend about when we used to go for walks when I was little and that first time you let me walk around a block by myself. He asked if I was scared when I couldn't cross the street to meet you, and I said no. I went to the statue and waited, sure you'd find me. When you did, when you hugged me, I felt loved and I felt safe. Mom, I can't find you, but I'm here. I'm waiting. When you're ready, I'll still be waiting. Until then, I'll call every week."

Lily set her cell phone down next to her on the swing.

There was no point trying to give her privacy now. "Lily, are you okay?" he asked as he sat on the glider.

She sniffled.

"You heard?" she asked, her voice full of sorrow.

"A bit. I didn't mean to."

She shrugged. "It doesn't matter. When I told you that all you could do was be here for Hank, I said that because that's all I can do. I won't send my mother any money. It doesn't do any good. But I can't cut her off. I love her. So I call, I offer options. And I wait."

He knew that story she'd told him meant more than he'd originally thought. "You're still waiting at the statue, aren't you? But this time, you want to be the one to hold your mother and make her feel safe."

She nodded and he knew without a doubt that her mother was in a bad relationship.

"Is it your father?"

When she stepped back, she was putting herself out of harm's way. It was a response she'd learned as a child.

She nodded again to confirm his thoughts, but she didn't offer anything else. "Tell me why it is you tend to come out here to make your calls. The swing here and at Colton's. What is it about swings?"

That garnered a small smile. "You noticed that?"

He smiled back. He didn't want to tell her how much he'd noticed and how much more he would like to learn.

He wasn't sure she was going to answer, but finally she said, "When my father came home you could tell if he'd been drinking simply by how he came into the house. If he stumbled or was loud, if he couldn't get his key in the door, we knew. And Mom would say, 'Why don't you go outside and swing for a while, Lily Claire? You love the swings.'"

She rocked the glider a little harder. "Mom never said he drank. She'd say, 'Your dad had a hard day.' I could hear them. I'd be out on the swing, and I could hear him yelling. I saw that he hit her."

"Oh, Lily." Sebastian didn't know what to do. Should he comfort her? He reached across the glider, but she resisted, as if she was caught up in the past and had forgotten the present. She'd forgotten that Sebastian would rather cut off his arm than hurt her.

"She loved me," she said. He wondered if she was attempting to convince him or herself. It wasn't the kind of love she'd wanted, but her mother did love her. "Once, he hit me. I was little. I don't know how old and the memory is hazy, but I remember my mom telling him she'd leave if he ever touched me again. I knew she meant it. So did he, I guess, because he always left me alone after that. But she didn't love herself enough to get out, to understand she deserved better. She tells me now that he doesn't drink as much and that he doesn't hit her. But I hear him sometimes when I call, and I don't believe her."

"I could go with you," he offered.

She shook her head. "I wish she'd leave—but I can't make her, and neither can you. She has to be the one to decide. I wish she'd left when I was little. I wish we had a different relationship. I see Mattie with her mother, and I feel so jealous. That is definitely not a sunshiny-rainbow sort of thing."

It was an attempt to lighten the mood, but it didn't work. She reached across the glider and affectionately patted his hand.

"I remind myself I can't control my mother. I can't force her actions. But I can be here for her. I can call every week and make sure the lines of communication are open. And I can love her. I don't have the best relationship with her, but I do have a relationship. That's enough."

He had a sudden blast of insight. "Your parents are why you don't do long-term relationships?"

"It sounds rather pathetic when you say it like that. I don't know if that's precisely the right answer. I have a lot of the psycho-jargon memorized. It boils down to the fact that I can't control anyone else's actions. My father's drinking wasn't my fault. My mother's willingness to continue living with a man who abuses her isn't my fault."

She paused. "I thought I could trust someone enough to marry them once. I was engaged, you know."

He didn't know and felt an unexpected surge of jealousy. He didn't try to sugarcoat it. He was jealous of this unnamed, unknown man Lily had obviously been in love with. However, he didn't say any of that. "What happened?"

"He took me to meet his family. They lived in Connecticut and were so nice. The house was beautiful and sat on a pond. They had a dog named Ted. A small, scruffy thing. He was ugly, actually. When I saw them all together, laughing and having a great time, I wanted to belong to them so badly. Then, the second day we were there, we were outside and Justin's father pushed his mother off the small pier into the pond as they were goofing around. It was August and more than warm enough for a swim. But when I saw his hand come up to push her, I screamed no and started running. They were still joking and playing as I charged him and pushed him into the pond, too.

"I stood on the end of that pier and cried. All three of them stared at me. Justin came over to calm me, but I ran away.

"Maybe if I'd told him. Maybe if I did something else. But I ran away from his embrace, and within weeks I broke off the engagement."

"God, Lily."

"I heard he got married a few years later. I'm glad. He was a very nice man."

"Just because you were upset and ran away, you convinced yourself you'd never marry?"

"I realized I'd never trust anyone enough to marry," she corrected.

A million things flitted through Sebastian's mind. So many things that he could hardly pin any of them down. "You trust me."

"Pardon?" she asked in that cute way of hers.

"You know that I'd rather cut off my arm—my good arm," he added with a grin, which made her smile in return, "rather than ever harm you."

She stopped and faced him, looking deeply into his eyes, as if to his soul. "You're right. I do know that."

"And you told me about your past," he added. She hadn't told this Justin she'd thought she could marry.

That was enough for now. Sebastian wasn't going to push her. But he'd realized so many things. Lily thought she wore her sunshiny exterior as a cover for her dark past. That wasn't the case. She hurt for her mother, but in fact, she'd overcome her past. Not forgotten it, but moved on and made a good life for herself. She was the most amazing, caring woman he'd ever met.

He also knew that Hank represented to her exactly what he'd always represented to Sebastian. Safety. Family. A home.

When he'd first come to town, he'd thought she'd wormed her way into Hank's life in order to get something. Instead, she'd found somewhere she belonged. Not only with Hank, but here in Valley Ridge. That was why she'd stayed. She'd found sisters in Sophie and Mattie. A father figure in Hank. She'd found a community, and everything she'd done had been to carve out a space for herself here.

He'd never do anything to take that from her.

Hell, he'd fight to see to it she kept it all.

So no, he wasn't telling her right away he was staying.

Because he wanted her to realize that there was more here than she thought. More than family, friends and a community.

He was here.

And he…

He had feelings for her.

Feelings that grew stronger every day.

"Come to bed," he said. "Just for tonight, let me hold you. Be with me, this once."

She nodded.

And that was when the million swirling things coalesced in his mind. He was going to woo Lily Paul. Slowly. He was going to convince her that he'd never hurt her, that she could trust him. Lily had said that knowing and feeling were two different things.

She'd trusted him with her story…with her past. That said something.

He slipped an arm around her shoulders and they went inside the house, up the stairs and, after they both checked on Hank, into his room and bed.

One night at a time. That was how he would win over Lily Paul.

One night at a time.

CHAPTER TWELVE

LILY SMILED AS SEBASTIAN came into the kitchen. She marveled that it had only been a little over a week since she'd told him about her parents. For so many years she hadn't been able to talk about it. She hadn't been able to tell her fiancé. She'd never even thought about telling her friends.

But she'd told Sebastian.

She wasn't sure what she'd expected to feel, which was good because she didn't know what she felt.

But she did know that being with Sebastian was easy. He didn't push her for more revelations. He didn't ask her probing questions. And he no longer was shooting her piercing looks.

It was bright and early on a Monday morning and he greeted her with a simple smile.

"Good morning, sunshine," she quipped.

"Good morning, rainbow," he responded. "'Morning, Hank."

Hank grunted from behind the sports section.

It was a stupid ritual. Schmarmy even. But over the past week, it had become their standard greeting.

She'd heard the shower kick on and had poured his coffee so that it was waiting for him next to the national news section of the paper. As Sebastian sat down, she knew that he'd become a comfortable part of her and Hank's morning routine.

They sat in silence, reading the paper, sipping coffee. Lily grinned behind her sheets of newsprint.

Sebastian pulled down a corner and peeked at her. "What are you smiling about?"

Lily folded back the corner of her paper. "How did you know I was smiling?"

"I could hear it as I read." He picked up his mug in his left hand, and while it wasn't quite steady, he managed to bring it to his lips without spilling. He took a sip and put the mug down with a small clunk.

Lily wanted to say something about how much stronger his hand was getting, but she opted to carry on their morning banter. "You could not hear me smile."

"Hank, tell her that she's got the loudest smile ever."

Hank's paper went down and he nodded. "You do, Lil. Sometimes, when you come into the diner and are in the office, I can hear you smile all the way at the front counter."

"Cut it out, you two." She resumed reading her paper, totally aware that she was indeed smiling loud enough that they could hear her.

A few minutes later, Hank folded the sports section, rose and announced. "Red's picking me up today." The cook had been great about pitching in where Hank was concerned.

If Hank noticed that he was getting more rides and more offers from people to walk to and from work with him, he hadn't commented.

"You coming in this afternoon?" Hank asked Sebastian.

"I have to finish painting at Lily's, then I've got an appointment. Afterward, I'll be in."

Hank waved and left.

She and Sebastian sat quietly until they heard Red say something, then the front door close.

"He seemed good today," Sebastian said. "It's been better the last few days. Maybe the medicine is having an effect."

Lily wanted to warn him that Hank wasn't better. Mornings were always the best part of the day. By evening, Hank grew more tired and he slipped more often. They'd probably have to think about having Hank go into work only for the morning shifts.

She'd learned a long time ago not to live in the past, and now she was going to have to learn to not live in the future. Worrying about what might or would happen wouldn't help anything.

"So what are your plans?" Sebastian asked.

"It's Monday, so I'll be at the doctor's office. Oh, and I have to run out to see Miss Helen."

"But afterward?" he pressed.

"I'll be at the diner." She speculated whether she was maybe spending too much time with Sebastian. She was already living under the same roof as him. Even working at the same place, too.

Honestly, though, when Sebastian left Valley Ridge, she'd miss him. And the wedding was only weeks away; he'd be gone soon. So she decided not to borrow trouble and worry about after the wedding when it actually happened. For now, she would enjoy and appreciate their time together. "What meeting do you have?"

He shrugged. "Mattie's brother Ray wants to see me,

then I promised Jay Markham I'd give him a hand with his ditch. It needs to be shoveled out."

"You're sure your arm's up to it?" She'd noticed him massaging it.

"Probably not. It will probably ache like crazy tonight. I'll probably require a bunch of medical attention."

"Oh, will you?" She leaned over and kissed his cheek. "I happen to know this nurse who, while she's not a physical therapist, might be convinced to give you a massage."

SEBASTIAN COULDN'T HELP but replay what had happened at breakfast. He thought he was gaining ground with her and couldn't wait to see her later. He noticed that when he wasn't with her, he thought about her nonstop.

He went to Valley Ridge's small mayor's office. There was no staff to greet him, though there was an outer secretary's office. Mayor Ray Keith hollered from the room right beyond it, "Seb, is that you? Come on in."

Ray Keith was tall, with dark hair and a rugged complexion. He looked nothing like his sister, Mattie. While Ray was younger than Sebastian, he did remember him as a snotty-nosed kid who frequently tagged after Mattie and Bridget.

"Mayor Ray," he said, shaking his hand. "Finn told you about the bachelor party?"

"Colton wants women there, too?" Ray's expression said he doubted the wisdom of that decision.

"They call them Stag and Drags in Erie. Finn's rented a huge party bus. It'll leave from the library, then take us into Buffalo for wings and a night on the town."

Ray sat down in his chair and waved Sebastian to

the chair on the other side of the desk. He murmured, "You had me at *wings*."

Sebastian took the seat. "But that's not what you wanted to see me about?"

"No. Your name's come up a lot lately."

"How so?"

"You've fixed Lily's flooded apartment?" Ray half stated, half asked.

"It's my grandfather's place, so sure I did."

"Rumor has it that not only are you giving the Williams boy a job but you've single-handedly Paul Bunyaned a tree, as well as repaired various property. Not to mention helped Colton out at his place and kept Dylan from having to take serious action with respect to that Sturgis kid."

"Sturgis?"

"Cameron. Cameron Sturgis, smasher of mailboxes."

"Oh, Cam." Sebastian felt uncomfortable, as if he'd bragged and been called out for it. He knew that was ridiculous. He hadn't said a word to anyone, and honestly, why would he? "I've helped out a bit where I can."

"More than that. You found a creative way to make Cameron own up to what he did, but you also made a difference for an older resident."

"Cam felt guilty about it. I spoke to Dylan, and as long as Mrs. Esterly wasn't pressing charges, he was fine with that as a solution."

Ray leaned back in his overstuffed leather desk chair. "No, I wasn't complaining. I'm here to ask something else from you."

"You've got a ditch that needs digging out?" Sebastian asked. "Or a place that needs drywalled?"

"There's going to be a vacancy on the town council. Stan Tuznik—"

"The former mayor?" He'd seen Mayor Tuznik near the school, sporting a bright orange vest and a stop sign.

"Yes." Ray told him, "I tried to talk him into running for council, but he's enjoying his retirement. He crosses the schoolkids a couple times a day and says that's enough. I think he was worried about stepping on my toes, but I want to see Valley Ridge thrive. I want to keep everything that makes it special intact while making sure we don't get left behind. The election's this fall. We need a person who takes initiative, someone with their roots firmly planted in Valley Ridge. I know you weren't planning to stay on after Colton's wedding, but I heard about Hank—I'm very sorry for that—and figured you weren't going anywhere now."

Sebastian studied Mattie's little brother. Here was a man who barely knew him. Someone he'd known as a kid but hadn't had so much as a cup of coffee with since coming home. Sebastian had seen him at Colton's picnic and a few other times around town, but that was it. And yet Ray knew without asking that Sebastian couldn't leave his grandfather given the news. How could Lily not know that?

He was trying to be patient with her. Trying to ease her into the notion of him living here permanently, of them having more than a—what was the word Miss Webster had used?—tryst. Yes, he wanted to show her they were more than a tryst. But right now, he was glad she wasn't around because he was pissed that Ray knew he'd stay, while Lily hadn't.

"I'm staying," he confirmed. "Though I have no idea what I'll do."

"I thought you'd take over the day-to-day at the diner." Ray made it a statement, but there was a question hidden in it.

Sebastian hadn't given much thought to an occasional shift at the diner. Work there full-time?

He liked working at the diner. He liked seeing old friends come in for a meal and a bit of companionship.

He liked working with Hank…and Lily.

He liked feeling as if he was a part of the town. More than that, part of the town's hub.

He loved the marines. And he'd imagined he would find some sort of career after he retired from the corps. He had a business degree and that seemed a logical path. And yet, he couldn't picture what kind of job would provide him with the same sort of satisfaction that he felt working at Hank's.

No, Valley Ridge Diner didn't require a suit and tie.

He would be a simple, ordinary guy going about his ordinary life, working at something he was good at and loved.

That was why Lily had moved to Valley Ridge. She'd made more money, steady money, nursing at the hospital in Buffalo. But here, she'd found home. She'd found a community she loved.

"Yes, if Hank's amenable." As he said the word, he thought of Lily, aka Webster, and some of his annoyance drained away. "I'll probably work at the diner full-time."

"And if you do, you'll know everything about Valley Ridge, about the problems and the issues that will have to be dealt with. Which means you'd be a perfect addition to the council. You'd have your finger on the pulse of the town. Add that to your military ability to see a problem and address it. Well, you'd be a good fit."

Government? Politics? “I'd never thought about anything like that.”

Ray leaned forward over the desk. “Well, I think you should. You're a man who's proven that you know what serving others means. You were a marine, serving your country.”

“That's over now.” He still couldn't quite believe that a stupid accident was keeping him from doing a job he loved—one he felt was important. But for the first time, he realized that leaving the corps when he did meant he was able to be here for Hank. “There's no going back.”

Ray nodded. “No one should go back, but you can move forward. You could serve Valley Ridge now. We need you.”

Ray was handing him a chance to do something else important—a way to serve his community. “I'll think about it.”

Ray stood and extended his hand. “That's all I'm asking.”

Sebastian rose and shook hands with him. “Could you do me a favor and not mention this to anyone? And by *anyone,* I mean especially your sister. I haven't told folks I'm staying yet.”

“I don't think it will come as a surprise. We're all sorry about Hank's condition, and you should know that everyone will be keeping an eye on him for you.”

“To be honest, I know for a fact that not everyone's realized I'm staying, and I'm not sure how a few people are going to take the news.”

“A sentence like that could only mean one thing—a woman.”

“I didn't—” Sebastian started to protest.

“No, don't. I'm not asking, and you don't need to

tell me. I find it best to stay out of all things that concern women. I've become the target of any number of matchmaking mothers since I became mayor. I've tried to tell them that mayor of a town as small as Valley Ridge isn't all that impressive. But that doesn't seem to dissuade them. Mainly I'm a farmer who does some community service."

"And I'd be a business owner doing some community service?" he asked.

Ray smiled. "Exactly."

"I'll get back to you soon." Sebastian had a feeling he knew what he'd decide, but he wasn't ready to commit without really thinking it through.

He left Ray's office and waved at Benjamin Michaels, who was sitting in front of the Volunteer Fire Department. He crossed the street diagonally and stopped in at Park Perks.

Mattie was behind the counter and grinned when she saw him enter. "Sebastian, how are things?"

"Great," he answered. He was finally ready to move forward and had been handed a wonderful opportunity.

"What can I get you?" she asked.

"A double espresso."

"Cream?" she asked. His expression must have given her an answer because she shook her head. "I forgot who was I was asking. Mr. Tough-as-Nails Marine."

"Not that tough anymore." And not a marine. The thought didn't sting nearly as much as it once had.

"I think that someone who can face their challenges head-on is as tough as they come," she said as she busied herself behind the counter.

"Thanks." That was a lie. He'd railed against his accident, against fate, until Lily had shown him to look on the bright side.

"You're welcome. Oh, and Finn booked a bus last night. He's going to call you to see if we can get together and put the finishing touches on the Stag and Drag."

"That sounds great."

"He'll call," Mattie promised.

Sebastian waved goodbye. As he walked toward the diner, he sipped his espresso.

Mattie had said he was tough, but he knew that Lily was the true tough one.

He would like nothing better than to talk to someone about Ray's offer.

And by *someone* he knew he meant Lily. Maybe that was a way to bridge the idea of staying in Valley Ridge? Obviously, they'd have to discuss it sooner rather than later.

And when she did find out he was settling down here, she'd kick him out of her life. But hey, just because she kicked didn't mean he'd go.

When he got to the diner, Lily and Hank were in the office.

"I found more records in the basement, and Hank said to have at it. We agreed he didn't need canceled checks from 1972. But in among the checks, I found a box of old photos. This one's amazing." She passed Sebastian a picture of Hank in a suit, next to a woman in a bridal dress…his grandmother. And another photo, this one of Sebastian in his dress blues. "You two could be twins."

"I was telling Lily about the day Betty and I got married…."

Sebastian had heard the story before. His eyes were

on Lily. She leaned close to his grandfather as she listened to the tale of the whirlwind wedding his grandmother had pulled off in a week's time. "Just seven days from when I proposed to when I said *I do.* My buddies laughed and said she didn't want to take a chance on me getting cold feet, but I knew the truth. Neither Betty nor I was willing to wait because we loved each other so much. So much so that being apart caused physical pain. I lost the best part of myself the day she died."

Lily's gaze met Sebastian's, and he could see her unshed tears. Tears for Hank's loss, but also tears for herself, possibly? Because she truly believed that she'd never be able to trust someone enough to marry him—enough to love him.

Yet, she was trusting him with her feelings. She was letting him see a side of her he doubted any man had ever seen. Which meant that no matter what she said, she…

Sebastian stared at her hard as she oohed along with his grandfather over another picture, and he knew he wanted more because…because he loved her.

CHAPTER THIRTEEN

LILY TOOK THE LAST of her dresser drawers out of Sebastian's childhood room. When she first met him, that was how she'd thought of him, as the young boy from Hank's stories. A good-natured scamp. That wasn't the man she'd met that first day on the cliff.

Sebastian had grown from the boy in Hank's stories into a man. A man who felt guilty and frustrated. A loyal man who loved his grandfather and friends. She thought she'd met Seb that day, but as time went on, she knew that she'd met Sebastian on that cliff overlooking the lake. And she'd shared this house with him.

Not only a house; she'd also shared his bed.

Now that she was moving back into her own apartment, she should think about calling things off. The wedding was only a few weeks away.

She'd planned on waiting until Sophie and Colton said *I do,* but her instincts told her it might be better to break things off sooner. There was a particular way Sebastian was watching her. It was a different sort of piercing look. No, maybe it was a knowing look. One that said he understood things about her that she wished he didn't.

She'd kicked herself over and over for telling him about her past.

It had always been so easy to keep her past and present separate, other than her weekly calls to her mom.

But now that Sebastian knew, it felt as if her past was spilling into her present.

Yes, calling things off now rather than after the nuptials was probably the right plan.

She juggled the final drawer and went downstairs.

"That's the last of it?" Hank asked.

"It is. The new furniture's all there and set up. I don't know why I waited so long, Hank. I smile every time I walk into the apartment." The couch, lamps, bed and end table had been delivered yesterday, and she'd planned on sleeping there last night, but Sebastian convinced her to spend one more night at Hank's… with him.

He'd made a broad hint that she should invite him to try out her new bed in her new place since he'd helped shop for it, but she'd ignored it. She didn't want to make love to Sebastian in her new bed, in her apartment.

She wanted to keep those memories here and here alone. It seemed as if it would be easier to compartmentalize their relationship if she kept him separate from the rest of her life.

"Do you need any help?" Hank asked.

"No. I'll drop this off, and then, if you'll wait, I'll go with you over to the diner."

"I don't need a babysitter!" The normally affable Hank exploded in a burst of anger that reminded her of Sebastian. Well, Sebastian the way he'd been when he first returned to Valley Ridge. Something in him had settled since then. Maybe talking about his guilt had helped.

She'd like to think her confiding her past had helped him, but she knew better.

Right now, though, she needed to soothe Hank. "No, you don't need a babysitter. I was heading to the grocery store before my house calls. I need a couple things to tide me over until I can do a serious party-shop on Friday. You're still coming?"

The outburst was forgotten, and he smiled. "I wouldn't miss it."

"Give me a minute and we'll be on our way," she said as she left the drawer inside her apartment. She had to admit the space was beautiful. No longer cold and spare, the walls were bright, her furniture new and accented by a James Sabol print of the Brig *Niagara* that she'd bought years ago.

She'd dug around in her boxes and also found the hand-knotted glass fishing floats she'd purchased at an antiques store when she lived in Buffalo. On an end table was a small clear vase with the beach glass she'd collected.

A vintage area rug from MarVee's, featuring the same rich blue and brown tones but also a myriad of other colors, completed the room.

The apartment practically defined comfort and a real sense of home.

She should be over the moon with excitement.

She should be looking forward to climbing into her new bed, with its new linens, tonight.

Instead, she was lonely for Hank's house. Lonely for being so close to Hank and being able to look after him. And, in the interest of honesty, she missed knowing she could sneak across the hall tonight to Sebastian's room.

Now she was certain she shouldn't wait until after the wedding to call off the benefit part of her friendship with Sebastian.

A little part of her worried that it might already be too late.

Which was ridiculous.

Sebastian would be gone soon enough, and she'd get on with her life.

LILY SPENT THE REST of the week waiting to feel as if the very nicely renovated apartment was home. She was still waiting, tossing and turning at night. Yes, she definitely missed visiting Sebastian in his room and falling asleep in his arms.

She pushed away her worries. Today, she was celebrating her new home by inviting her friends over to dinner. It wasn't a huge party by any means—Sophie and Colton, Mattie and Finn, and Sebastian and Hank. But for someone who never had people to her house, much less had a party, it was exciting.

She'd bought a red-and-white-checkered cloth for the picnic table. She'd also bought a bright red silverware caddy and cute red lanterns at MarVee's. But her favorite was the mason jars she'd found at the Farm and House Supply store. She'd wrapped wires around the lips and strung them from the nearest tree to the porch roof. She'd put a tea light in each jar, and as the evening grew darker, she thought the makeshift lanterns looked beautiful.

"I get the feeling you're avoiding me," Sebastian said as he rounded the corner and came into the backyard.

"Would I invite you to my first official dinner party if I was avoiding you?" she asked.

"You—"

She was saved from whatever he was about to say as Hank arrived with Finn and Mattie. "Lily, it's lovely," Hank said. "We want the grand tour."

"Look at that table," Mattie remarked. "I'm sure that there's some rule about all your stuff having to match when you host a dinner party, right?"

"We're lucky if we can get the kids to eat off plates and not break them. I don't think there's a matched set of anything in the whole house. This is beautiful," Finn added gallantly.

Lily's nervousness disappeared at Mattie's teasing. "I guess that someone who doesn't know about the wonders of bridal showers couldn't be expected to understand necessary matching at dinner parties."

"But I do know about hostess gifts," Mattie proclaimed, revealing a small bag from behind her back.

Lily took the bag and was surprised at the heft of it. She put it on the picnic table and tore off the tissue paper. The gift was a stoneware crock, slightly larger than the ones they'd used as centerpieces at Sophie's shower. She took it out and there was a cobalt-blue rendition of Hank's house and her slightly worn glider. Underneath the hand-painted picture it read Lily's Home. Valley Ridge, New York.

Lily felt tears gather in her eyes, and a huge lump of emotion formed in her throat. She'd grown up at her parents' house, lived in dorms at college and even had an apartment in Buffalo, but she'd never really had anyplace that felt like home until now. Until here.

And it wasn't only the house—it was the people. As if on cue, Sophie and Colton rounded the corner. All of them. Hank, Sophie, Mattie and even the guys,

Finn and Colton. She brushed at her eyes and glanced at Sebastian and realized him most of all. They were *home* for her.

"Thanks," she managed to croak out.

"Oh, man. You cry at showers *and* at housewarming gifts? It was supposed to make you smile," Mattie groused.

"I'm smiling on the inside."

"Yeah, she is," Sebastian said. "It's a real smile. You can tell by the way her eyes crinkle. If she's faking, the wrinkles don't fall into the right places."

"Wait a minute, did you say I had wrinkles?" Lily asked, thankful to get past the emotional moment.

"I didn't mean old wrinkles like H—"

"Watch it, boy," Hank warned. "I might be old and I might have wrinkles, but I'm not so old I can't take you on."

"I was going to say Helen Rogers, the music teacher from school. Now, there was a wrinkled woman."

"I'm going to tell Miss Helen you said that," Lily warned.

Their teasing set the tone for the next hour. She gave her friends the grand tour, which took all of a couple minutes. Her apartment might be compact, but it was hers and it reflected her tastes. She was pleased with the results.

"I didn't do anything overly ambitious for our meal. I made salads, and there are burgers to grill and—"

Her cell phone rang. Part of her wanted very much to ignore it, but she couldn't. It could be one of her patients. She saw the caller ID. "Excuse me, everyone. I have to take this."

"I'll get more drinks," Sebastian offered.

She nodded and left her friends milling in her small living area. It wasn't until she walked toward the glider that she hit Talk.

If asked precisely what her mother said, Lily would be hard-pressed to come up with an answer; regardless, she knew what she had to do. She didn't have a choice.

This could be another boy-who-cried-wolf moment, and she could get there and find her mother had changed her mind, but she couldn't take that chance. "Mom, I'm getting in the car right now. Don't pack anything. Don't do anything to raise his suspicions. Just stay out of his way and stay safe. I'll be there as soon as I can. It's about an hour, maybe hour-and-a-half drive. I'll be there as quickly as I can. Please, Mom, please, this time come with me when I get there."

Lily hung up. She had to go apologize to her guests. She'd ask Sebastian to cook the burgers, and at least they could eat before they left.

What did she need? A purse. She needed a license and some money. Just a purse.

She sprinted toward the house and hardly spared a glance at her picnic table that had delighted her only seconds before. Sebastian appeared. The concern in his eyes was almost her undoing. "Lily, what's wrong? A patient?"

She wasn't surprised he knew something was wrong. "My mother."

"What's wrong?"

"She said she was ready to leave."

His expression told her he understood the import of what she was saying. "Where is she?"

"Franklin. Franklin, Pennsylvania. It's past Whedon, then Meadville. Off I-79."

"Your family's that close?" he asked.

"Distance isn't only measured in miles. My mother's been out of reach for most of my life. But now maybe she's close. I hope. I have to go right now. If he suspects, he'll—" She didn't finish the sentence. She'd seen what her father had done to her mother because the coffee wasn't hot enough, or because she didn't have his dinner ready, or…hell, simply because it was Monday. "I have to go."

"She's in danger," he stated, his tone serious.

She'd have never put it that way, but she knew it was true. "Yes."

"I know you're in a hurry, but let's tell everyone it's a family emergency and I'll come with you."

"I should argue. I should tell you I can do it myself, but thank you, Sebastian." He reached for her hand as they walked toward the house, but she pulled back. For an instant, there was a flash of anger on his face, then he gave the barest of nods and followed her into the apartment.

She glanced around at her friends and felt her own spurt of anger. She'd never had such friends, and she resented having to possibly hurt their feelings now. A remnant of the shame she once felt as a child, unable to bring anyone over to her house, hung over her.

But quickly she put that behind her. She had found people she trusted—a family. Yet her parents still messed it up.

She knew it wasn't fair.

She knew that this was what she'd spent years hoping for.

"I'm sorry. I'm about to do the rudest thing a host can do…. I'm about to leave. There are salads in the fridge, and the burgers are all ready to be grilled. Colton and Finn, if you'd do that, I'd be grateful. Stay, eat and accept my apologies. I have to go."

"Lily?" Mattie asked, a multitude of questions implied in her name.

"I owe you all an explanation, but it will have to keep. I've got to go and Sebastian's offered to go with me." She grabbed her purse and tossed her keys on the table. "You'll lock up?"

Mattie and Sophie both nodded, then came over and hugged her.

"Tell us whatever, whenever. We're here when you need us," Sophie promised.

"Yeah, you tell us where to pick up the body and we'll bury it for you," Mattie offered. And though it was a very morbid way to say she was the type of friend who'd do anything for a friend, Lily felt a warm glow.

"I'll call you tomorrow," she said and left, Sebastian right behind her.

"It'll be okay, Lil." He walked so close to her that she could feel the warmth of his body, but he didn't touch her again and she appreciated it. She was afraid she'd fall apart if he did.

At her car, he said, "Let me drive, Lily. You're all shaken up. Just let me help." And he steered her toward his car instead.

They rode in silence out of New York State, through North East and back to I-90, heading west. Sebastian didn't ask a question or say anything, and Lily stared silently out the window. The highway had twists and turns, but there were long stretches when she could see the lake. Normally, she enjoyed the view, but she didn't really see much of anything today.

"I've always wondered how no one ever reported my father. I'd sit on the swing and listen to the shouting—the neighbors had to have heard it. My father was so loud as he screamed. And my mother would be sporting a new bruise or walking with a limp the next day. How could they not know?"

"I'm sure they knew," Sebastian agreed. "But it's easier for some people if they don't acknowledge it."

"I know where there are women's shelters. I've offered to have her live with me." All those years, all the drinking, all the bruises. Lily confessed her secret worry. "I can't imagine what he's done to push her to the point of leaving."

"We'll be there soon, Lil," Sebastian vowed.

"I have exactly one good memory of my father," she mused, more to herself than to him. "Only one good memory. I was little. Maybe kindergarten. He put up a swing in the backyard off a silver-maple branch. I was so happy. Mom made a picnic, and we ate out in the backyard on a pink-and-yellow quilt, and my father pushed me on that swing. We laughed and we spent the afternoon together, like a real family doing what real families do. I sometimes think that having that one good day was worse than never having known one."

"Why?"

"Because in that memory I can see what we could have been. I can look back at that one day and see what other people had. When I went to school, I'd listen to all the girls talking about new clothes or boys they liked. They'd worry and whine. And I'd wonder what it was like to have your biggest worry be a fancy sweater your parents wouldn't buy you."

"I'm sorry, Lily."

"I told this guy I know that there's the world the way you wish it was or that you even need it to be—"

"And there's life the way it is. When you told me that, I thought you were being all Pollyanna."

"All sunshiny rainbows." She was smiling despite the tears.

"I wish I would have known. Understood. The fact you are who you are, it's a testament to your strength."

"I had to choose," she told him. "I could be bitter and lament my past, or—"

"You could be the incredible, warm, loving woman you are."

"Thank you. I don't think you're right, but thank you." No, she wasn't incredible or anything. If she was, she'd have found some way to get her mother out of there sooner. She tried to think of something more she could have done, but was at a loss.

"I've never told anyone about my parents before," she confessed.

"No one?"

"Not even Mattie and Sophie. I've thought about telling them for a long time, but I knew Sophie's heart would break for me, and she shouldn't suffer anything more than worrying about floral arrangements."

"Thanks for sharing."

"Thanks for listening. And thanks for coming."

SEBASTIAN TURNED SOUTH onto I-79. He glanced over at Lily, who was seemingly focused on the scenery. Trees. He'd forgotten there were so many trees in this part of the country. He hadn't been gone that long. He should have remembered. Along parts of the interstate, they were practically canopied beneath the leaves. They were a spring-fresh, new green. Later in the year, they'd shift to a more tired green, then to the brilliant fall foliage this region was known for.

He wanted to say something more. He wanted to offer her support. "Not all men are like your dad."

"I know. But he wasn't always like that, either. That day, when we had the picnic and he hung the swing, I got the merest glimpse of the man my mother fell in love with. The man she wanted to marry. Then he changed and she was stuck. I don't ever want to take a chance like that."

"You know what I always liked about you? Your sunshiny-rainbow optimism."

"I can't afford it in this case."

"Maybe you can't afford not to have it in this case. You've spent all this time trying to get your mom to safety. Has she ever called like this before?"

"She's almost left a couple times, but no, she's never asked me to come. I call her once a week, you heard, and I've worked to keep up a relationship with her. I've encouraged her to leave my dad as often as I could."

"And now she's called you. You never gave up and it's paying off." He was desperate for her to discover some optimism about her mother. It was so unlike Lily not to be optimistic.

"I have no idea what she'll do once we get her out of there. Like I said, perhaps a women's shelter? Or she can come home with me. I want her to come home with me." She leaned into him and ran her hand against his forearm. He wanted to reach across and hold her hand, but he didn't trust his weak hand to steer the car. He settled for welcoming her touch.

"Thank you. I've never had anyone to rely on. And now there's you, there's Hank, Mattie and Sophie."

"Don't forget Finn and Colton. And I know for a fact there are more. Miss Helen?"

She sighed in response. The car got quiet again. He understood that. Saying some things took everything a person had inside them. He knew he had his own emotional baggage he needed to air. And when he thought about people he could tell, he knew that once upon a time, he'd have told Hank, or Colton and Finn. Whereas now, the person he found himself wanting to tell was Lily.

He knew she still thought he was leaving, that he was "safe" because he wouldn't be sticking around and demanding a messy relationship with her. He didn't know exactly what his future would be, but he was positive that whatever it was, it was in Valley Ridge. Lily had taken over the diner's bookkeeping and she had her patients to care for. She couldn't keep an eye on Hank all day, every day.

He needed to tell her his plans, but he couldn't find the words. Hell, he might as well admit he was afraid she'd turn away from him.

If he waited long enough, perhaps he could sort of work up to it with her. After Colton's wedding, she'd realize he wasn't going anywhere when he didn't leave. By then he hoped she wouldn't mind. That she'd see what he was only beginning to realize. They belonged together.

He wasn't sure how he'd gotten this lucky. Okay, his arm might never rehabilitate fully and he might be clueless about what he was going to do with the rest of his life, but he was back in Valley Ridge, back with his friends and with Hank. Hank needed him, and he was able to stay.

Yes, he was lucky about all that.

But mainly, he was lucky to have found Lily.

She might deny it, but they were good for each other.

Later, he'd tell her. He'd open himself up the way she had to him. Maybe then she'd understand how much he trusted her, and maybe she would understand what they could have together.

They pulled off I-79 at the Franklin exit. Lily gave him directions through the town to a modest home on a quiet residential street.

Sebastian didn't think he'd ever been in Franklin before. "It reminds me of Valley Ridge," he said.

"It does. Maybe that's why I felt so at home there," Lily mused. "But I was able to be a part of Valley Ridge in a way I could never belong here. I could have friends and relationships."

"You couldn't here?" he asked.

"No. I kept my head down and I studied. I knew that an education was my only way out." She took a deep breath, got out of the car and approached the neat brick house.

Sebastian wasn't sure why, but he'd expected something run-down. Something that said, *An alcoholic lives here.*

But this was a fine home that would easily fit onto any one of Valley Ridge's streets.

Lily paused with her hand on the knob of the screen door. "You can wait here."

"You've trusted me with so much today—trust me to come in with you. I want to be certain your mom can leave with no trouble."

Lily smiled weakly and knocked on the front door. A woman answered. There was a ghost of Lily in her features. Dark hair that was sprinkled with streaks of gray. It might be curly like Lily's if she hadn't pulled it back into a severe bun. Her eyes were exactly the same color as her daughter's, but the crinkles at the sides of them were definitely not laugh lines. No, the lines on her face spoke of hard times and grief.

"Lily, you came."

"I said I would, Mom. I always told you that when you were ready I'd come."

"I know you said not to pack, but I have a bag with some clothes and another with my photo albums." She spotted Sebastian and looked startled.

"I'm Sebastian," he said quickly, extending his hand to shake hers. She drew back and immediately he felt sick. He recognized this behavior. But unlike Lily, her mother didn't force herself to step forward again. She kept out of reach.

"Sebastian, this is my mother, Vera. Mom, this is a good friend, Sebastian. He offered to drive me here today."

He could tell from the woman's face that she realized Lily must have told him what went on here. Horrified was how she looked.

He understood her embarrassment. He'd often hidden his arm and hand away, as if somehow no one would notice. He'd stopped doing it so gradually that he wasn't even sure when that had happened.

"Maybe I can carry your things out for you?" he offered.

She nodded and stepped farther back, giving him a

wide berth. "They're in the front closet. I didn't want your fa—anyone to see before you came."

Sebastian took the small suitcase and the light tote-bag. "Is there anything else you need, ma'am?"

Vera looked around the room, and Sebastian followed suit. It was a medium-size space with an open living-dining area. A narrow hall jutted off to the right. He assumed the bedrooms and bathroom were down that way.

"No. There's nothing else I want or need." Vera Paul straightened her shoulders, grabbed a purse off the hook by the door and crossed the threshold. In that one act, he saw Lily. He saw a hidden strength in Vera. One she probably didn't know she had. One he was hoping that Lily could see and foster.

Sebastian trailed after Vera, and Lily came last. He glanced back and saw her peering inside the house. He wondered what she was thinking. "Did you want to go out back?"

"No. He took that swing down when I was in high school. All that's left there is the trace of a memory."

"Of one happy day," he said.

"And what we could have been."

"There's the world the way you want it to be…"

"And the world the way it is." Lily squared her shoulders and gave a small nod. "And mom and I are going to have to find a way to deal with the way it is."

They went over to his car, where Lily's mom was waiting.

"So where are you going to take me?" she asked softly, seemingly resigned to having no say.

Here was a woman who hadn't had any say in anything for years.

"It's your choice, Mom. There are shelters. I have a

list. And I'll take you to any of them you want, or you can come home with me. I'd like it if you did, but this isn't about me. It's about you. About what you want. You're taking the first step, and you get to decide where you're stepping to."

"If you don't mind, I'd like to come home with you, Lily Claire, at least for a while, until I can decide what to do next. But I don't want to be a burden."

"Never that, Mom."

Lily gave him another small nod, and once inside the car, Sebastian started the engine and backed out of the driveway. "We're officially on our way, ladies."

They drove away from the house Lily had grown up in. The small, tidy jail her mother had lived in for years.

It seemed anticlimactic to Sebastian. He'd almost hoped that Lily's father would make a scene and try to stop them. But no one came. And they left.

Maybe anticlimax was part of the reason for his anger when he'd returned to Valley Ridge. He'd been a marine. He'd fought for his country. He'd always known he could be injured. But a freak two-second car accident? That seemed like an anticlimactic ending to the story. And his friends had kept on fighting without him. He'd let them down.

Sebastian snuck a quick look behind him. Lily was in the back and she sat resolutely, holding her mother's hand.

There was the world the way you wanted it, and the world the way it was. Sometimes, if you were really fortunate, the way you wanted it to be would match the way it was.

That was what was happening for Lily.

And maybe, if he was very careful, it could happen for him with her.

Sebastian headed through Franklin, then turned north on I-79. Back to Valley Ridge.

APPROACHING HANK'S HOUSE, Lily grew anxious that her mother was regretting leaving. Lily wanted to say something soothing. Something to prove to her mother that it would be all right. She might tell her mom that it was all right, but until she could feel it, Lily would be concerned for her.

After Lily showed her mother her renovated apartment, she hugged her. "I know it all feels surreal right now, Mom, but please give it some time. I'll help you however you'll let me. But for now, let's get you settled."

As she opened the bedroom door, her mother noticed the double bed and shook her head. "I won't take your bedroom, Lily Claire."

"Mom, I'll have to tell you about what we've done to the place. But know I've spent more time in the main house lately than in here."

"But, Lily..." Her mother stopped as if she wanted to argue but had forgotten how.

"Mom, please let me do this for you. It's a small enough thing. Take some time and figure out what you want to do."

"I can figure for a long time, but I don't think I'll come up with anything. I don't know how to do anything." Her mother seemed to shrink before her eyes, as if the enormity of what she'd done was pushing down on her.

"Mom, you took a first step. A big one. Try not to think too far ahead. Let's start with you'll stay here tonight, and tomorrow, you walk up the pathway to the kitchen door of the main house. Come on in. There will be coffee perking and breakfast. And after that—" She shrugged. "We'll work it out."

Her mother hesitated. "Okay."

"Did you want to talk about—" Her mother was already frowning before the question was even asked, so Lily let it go. She understood not wanting to talk about the past. So she settled for hugging her mother again. "Mom, I'm so happy you're here." And she was. The thought of her mother not being under her father's thumb soothed her.

"Your father's going to be so angry." Her mother's voice was a hoarse whisper, as if her father would somehow hear the words. "He doesn't like it when he comes home and I'm not there, especially after a boys' night—"

"But you're not there." Lily remembered boys' nights out. They were simply an excuse for her father to drink in the company of friends. And they never ended well for her mom when he came home. "You won't be there if he's mad."

That evoked a bit of a smile. "No, I won't."

"I know that the devil you know is sometimes easier to face than the one you don't, but please, Mom. Please give it a chance. I've got the name of someone you can talk to. You deserve to be happy."

Her mother didn't look convinced; still, she said, "I love you, Lily Claire. I know I didn't do right by you, but I've always loved you."

"And I've never doubted that, Mom. I love you, too." She looked at her mother's meager suitcase on the bed. "Do you need anything else?"

"No, dear."

"I'll be up for a few more hours if you want company, but it's fine if you want some alone time."

"Thank you, I do."

"Then I'll see you in the morning. If you need me, I can be here in a few seconds."

Once she was outside Lily thought about going into Hank's house, but instead, she sat on the glider. She rocked to and fro as twilight settled over the yard. She wished it were summer and fireflies were out. But she could hear insects whirring and chirping, and there was enough of a breeze that the leaves rustled. The old glider creaked softly. She closed her eyes and relished the sweet cacophony of the evening.

"Do you mind if I sit here?"

Lily wasn't surprised to see Sebastian standing next to the glider. "We have to stop meeting like this," she quipped, but she was afraid that it fell flat.

"You're worried," he stated as he sat down across from her.

"Yes. She took such a big step and she's afraid. She doesn't know what to do now."

"Why don't you see if she wants to help out at the diner? For now, at least," he suggested. "It would keep her busy and give her a purpose each day."

"That's nepotism. I don't want you to feel as if I'm taking advantage of you and Hank."

He was wishing he'd sat next to her.

"Lily, I was a jerk when I first came home."

"Only when you came home?" she teased.

"What I said, my suspicions about what you were doing and why, they were nothing." He leaned across the glider and gently caressed her cheek. "You stepped in and helped out my grandfather when I wasn't here, and you're still helping him, and you don't know how much you've helped me. I remember arriving back in Valley

Ridge and thinking I was numb. Everything seemed gray, nondescript, even meaningless. But slowly, I found my anger. Just that. Anger. Anger at a twist of fate that changed my future. Anger that I couldn't do the simplest tasks, like tying a shoe. But all of that was merely my way of hiding what I really felt. Guilt that a stupid accident was going to keep me from fighting next to my friends. And guilt that I couldn't—can't—save Hank. You took all that and smoothed it over. I still feel angry and guilty, but I understand it, and that has made all the difference."

He paused, then continued in a quiet voice, "After all you've done for me and Hank, how could we do any less for your mother?"

Lily wanted to deny what he'd said about her. Maybe she had helped, but he'd figured things out on his own. Not because of her, but because he was such an amazing man. He'd adapted and overcome so much, and looked to help others, his friends, neighbors, especially Hank.

"I hope my mother can find the strength to build a new life for herself," she admitted. "I've tried to get her to do this for years. I wanted her to see that she was worthy of being happy and safe. I don't want to mess up now."

"Your mom left on her own. This is up to her. We'll help, but it's on her, Lil." He moved to the seat next to her, and the glider tilted back at a severe angle.

"I know you're right."

He tucked her close to him and they sat together, rocking, watching the stars. They both sat up straight when they heard the sound of voices. It was Hank with Megan. Sebastian got out of the glider and called out, "Hi, guys."

"I went into the diner for a bit tonight, but I forgot it was Sunday and we close in the afternoon."

"I happened to see him," Megan said, "and we took a stroll back here."

"I'll walk you home," Sebastian said to the diner's part-time waitress.

"You guys know we live in Valley Ridge, not New York City, right?" Megan teased.

Sebastian gestured toward the path. "All right, come on, then, marine. Let's go."

Lily felt guilty. Her first move when they got back should have been to check on Hank, or send Sebastian into the house to check on him.

"You okay, Lily-girl?" Hank asked.

"Only tired." She stretched and took a deep breath. "My mom's come for a visit, Hank. I hope you don't mind that I gave her my place. I thought I'd move back into your house for the duration."

The older man leaned in and hugged her. "It's your home. Wherever I am, Lily, that's your home."

THE NEXT MORNING, Lily was the first one down to the kitchen. No surprise there. She was almost always up and about early. Those morning hours, where the only sounds were the birds chirping, an occasional car driving by and the newspaper thwapping against the front door, were usually her favorite.

She worried about her mother today. She worried about Hank.

She worried…

Lily reminded herself that all the worrying in the world wouldn't change anything as she began making the coffee and listened to the familiar chugging and hissing as it perked. Today was not going to be a day for quiet morning reflection, so rather than sitting and worrying, she decided to make muffins for breakfast. She found Mattie's recipe and made a batch. Lily had put them in the oven just as Hank arrived.

"'Morning, Hank," she called out.

He didn't smile or respond to her salutation, but sat down at his seat at the table. "Lily, before anyone else gets up, I want to talk to you as a nurse."

"Sure, Hank." She poured him a cup of coffee and sat down beside him.

"Thank you," he said, taking the cup and adding a teaspoon of sugar. "Now, Lily, I want you to make that appointment with the doctor. I seem to get confused a lot. Like this morning, I woke up and knew I should remember something you said last night, but I can't." He stirred his coffee with more force than was required.

"About last night—my mother's going to be in my apartment for a while, and unless you object, I'll live here with you and Sebastian."

"You're welcome to as long as you want," he told her. "It's your home."

That was the easy part. Lily gathered her courage and said, "And we already saw the doctor. You've got dementia, Hank. He put you on that new medicine?"

"Oh, right. But it won't cure me."

Her eyes welled up, but she refused to let the tears fall. Hank needed her to be strong. "No. Although it will help."

He thought for a moment, a serious look on his face. "I'll still get confused."

"Yes. And you have me to remind you," she promised. "I'll help as much as I can."

He reached out and patted her hand, trying to comfort her. Here he was losing himself to this horrible disease and he worried about her. "Do they have homes for this? Places I can go?"

"They do. But you're not there yet, Hank. You'll have good days and bad days. Right now it's mild and we can cope."

"But someday the medicine won't work and I'll get worse and worse." It was a simple statement, reflecting no fear.

"Yes," she said softly.

He nodded, stopped stirring his coffee and took a sip. "When the time comes, you'll find a home, right? Somewhere I'll be safe and won't put you to any trouble?"

"When the time comes, I will," she assured him, then repeated, "but you're not there yet."

"Can we keep this from Seb? I don't want him to stay for me."

"He's leaving after the wedding," she said, feeling a twinge of regret. She'd miss him. That hadn't happened before. Other than Justin, the other men she'd dated had been so casual and the relationship so short-lived that she'd never missed the guys when she broke things off. But that wouldn't happen with Sebastian. "I'm sure he'll visit as often as he can," she said as much for herself as for Hank.

"Well, okay, then. I can't do anything about it, so I'm not going to worry about it." He kissed her cheek. "Thank you for being honest with me."

"I'll never lie to you." Just like that, he put aside his concern. She wished she had that ability. The oven timer dinged. It was a relief to have something to do.

She set the muffin pan on a trivet and Hank said, "I

want to have you or Sebastian buy the rest of the diner from me. You two talk and let me know. I put the house in his name years ago, so that's already done."

She popped a muffin out of the tin and placed it on a plate, which she took to Hank. "I will. I'll talk to him." The soft tapping on the kitchen door interrupted them. "Now, if you'll wait right there, I want to introduce you to my mom."

Lily opened the door and her mother came in. "How did you sleep?" she asked as she studied her mother's appearance. Overall, her mom looked better than Lily expected. She waved her forward and shut the door.

"I slept wonderfully, Lily Claire. I want…" Her mom spied Hank and let her sentence fade.

Lily took her mom's hand and brought her toward the table. "Mom, I want you to meet one of my first friends here in Valley Ridge. Hank Bennington, this is my mother, Vera Paul."

Hank stood and motioned to a chair at the table. "It's a pleasure, ma'am. Now, I might forget you tomorrow, but you don't take offense, okay? Turns out I've got dementia."

"I'm so sorry," her mother said as she took the seat Hank had offered.

He sat as she did. "I'm lucky, the way I see it. I've got people like your daughter who will look after me."

Lily got her mother a cup of coffee and watched as Hank worked his magic. Some might think *magic* was too strong a word, but Lily wasn't sure. The ability to accept people, to embrace them as they are, was one of Hank's strongest gifts. She hadn't seen it when she'd met him, but she could now. He had a warmth and openness that invited trust and friendship.

Hank Bennington was the kind of man her mother needed in her life.

Lily mentioned a job for her mom at the diner, and Hank joined her in encouraging her mother to try it. "You'd be doing me a favor. Lily can't watch me all the time, and when I get worse, I'll need all the help I can get."

Sebastian came into the room, newspaper in hand. He got his coffee and a muffin before sitting down at the table. "Good morning, Mrs. Paul."

"Vera, please," she said timidly, as if unsure about questioning what he'd called her.

"Vera. Has Lily explained how mornings work around here? She gets the entertainment section of the paper. Hank gets the sports. Me, I'm national news, or I'm happy to switch if you prefer that over the local section?"

Lily could see her mother relax as she said, "Since your grandfather offered me a job at the diner, maybe I should start with the local section? I should learn what I can about my daughter's adopted hometown." Her mom paused, as if waiting to see if her wants were all right.

Sebastian reached under the table and patted Lily's knee. It was a small gesture that said he knew she was worried and that he was going to do what he could to be there for her.

Her entire life, Lily had felt alone. She knew her mother loved her, but prior to yesterday, not enough to leave her father. Lily had never had friends she could turn to. She'd never had someone to rely on.

But in that small gesture, Sebastian said she could rely on him. She could count on him and Hank.

Lily felt as if she let go of something she'd been holding on to. Resentment? Fear? She wasn't sure she could name it, but it had been broken, and if asked years from now, she'd say it was this morning, at this breakfast, that it had started to truly heal.

CHAPTER FOURTEEN

"LILY, YOUR MOM'LL be fine. Let's enjoy the night. The Stag and Drag will be fun. You deserve a little fun." Sebastian went to touch her, and she pulled away, giving him the look that said, *No one's supposed to know about us.*

He felt an old, familiar burst of anger, but he dismissed it. The past few weeks had taught him that and a lot more.

"It's a party, remember?" he prompted.

She raked her hand through her wild hair, setting her jumble of bracelets to clinking. "You're right. Of course, you're right."

"Red said he'd see to it they both got home after he closed the diner." Sebastian felt much more comfortable leaving his grandfather alone for the evening knowing Vera was in the house. She'd promised to check in on him.

Lily had found her mother a support group in nearby North East. Vera had gone to a meeting, though afterward, all she'd said was she would go again next week. Lily believed it was another big step.

The wedding party, along with a few other friends, gathered at the library and waited for their ride. Sebastian grinned as the party bus pulled into the parking lot.

"First stop, The Anchor Bar," announced Finn, who seemed to have taken on the role of cruise director.

The hour-plus trip to Buffalo sped by, filled with stories of the latest happenings around Valley Ridge and a lot of good-natured teasing of the bride and groom.

"The Anchor Bar," Finn called out, in case they'd missed that the bus had stopped in front of a giant neon anchor sign. They filed into the place and were shown to a large table at the back of the bar.

Sebastian reveled in an evening with old friends. Ray and Rich, Mattie's younger brothers, were both there. Dylan, in a very un-sherifflike capacity, was there. And Maeve Buchanan, who didn't look all that bookish.

He'd gone to sit by Lily, but she'd been dragged away by Mattie and Sophie. Instead, he sat next to Maeve. "So how are things with Valley Ridge's resident bad girl?"

"Probably about the same as with Valley Ridge's resident bad boy," she countered. "Changed."

"I thought maybe I'd see you at the diner."

She shook her head. "Most days I meet myself coming and going. I work all day in Ripley and spend most of my evenings at the library. A few book clubs are up and running. I'm too busy to eat most of the time, much less go out to eat."

"Yeah, I heard about the library. I know you always liked reading, but how did that happen?"

She laughed. "You know that I'm living at Mrs. Anderson's house?"

He hadn't. "The old librarian's place?"

She nodded again. "I looked across that empty parking lot at the quiet library, and really, there's nothing sadder than a library that's not being used. I talked to

Ray and he gave me permission to try to reopen it, and here we are."

The waitress came out with pitchers of beer and took their food orders.

When she left, he asked, "You volunteer your time, right? I mean, you've raised money but you've put it into books and stuff."

"Yes. Are you thinking about making a donation?"

"I might be. But you should be paid."

"I've got a job that pays well. Mrs. Anderson sold me the house at a ridiculously low price. I'm not rich, but I'm comfortable. If there's ever enough money to hire a librarian, then you bet, I'll apply. Until then, we'll get along with me volunteering. I'm thinking about asking the high school if there's a way we can have the older kids donate time for credit. A library-sciences elective or something, or maybe just for service hours. And computers. I'd like to have some available and..."

He smiled as he listened to Maeve wax enthusiastic over her hopes and plans for the library. If he accepted Ray's invitation and ran for town council, and if he won, he'd be in a position to help the library. He wasn't sure how. Maybe a grant?

"...the heart of a town should be its library," Maeve said. "Libraries are the great equalizer. They give everyone, rich or poor, the same opportunities. I can't stand to think of Valley Ridge without the library."

"If I can do anything, you'll let me know?" he asked.

The waitress placed a huge plate of wings in front of them, and Maeve picked one up, obviously not the least put off by the sauce that trickled down her hand. "I will," she replied, taking a large bite.

"After all those years of hanging out with you in the principal's office, I never really got you."

"How so?" she asked.

"I can't think of one bit of mischief that was ever attributed to you. You didn't hang with a bad crowd—"

"Neither did you. I mean, Finn and Colton were never really bad."

He chuckled. "No. I was dumb and got caught doing dumb stuff. The only thing I ever remember you doing was reading. And even though you occasionally got caught reading for pleasure rather than class work, that's not an offense you'd have to see the principal about."

"I am nothing if not a woman of mystery." She said it with a singsongy, bad-accented voice, and they both burst out laughing as Sebastian reached for a wing.

LILY SPIED SEBASTIAN laughing with Maeve Buchanan. She didn't know the town's volunteer librarian well, but she couldn't deny that she was attractive. Watching Maeve with Sebastian was unsettling. Why? He and Lily were both free agents. Just two people spending time with each other until he left. He was only a tryst.

Of course, she'd broken her own rule and spent nights in his bed. All night. She couldn't seem to help herself. She excused it away every time by reminding herself that he'd be gone soon.

"I guess I should stop trying to impress you, since it's obvious you're off the market."

"Huh?" Lily tore her gaze away from Sebastian and Maeve Buchanan and focused on Valley Ridge's law-enforcement officer, Dylan Long. "I'm sorry?"

"So am I," Dylan said with a dramatic sigh that didn't

quite match up to his huge grin. “I should have made a move before our local marine came home.”

She realized what he was saying. “Sebastian and I aren’t an item.”

He laughed. “Yeah, you can maybe sell that to a lot of people, but I’m a cop, remember? I was hired because of my keen insight, and I’m trained to look deeper than the surface. You are head over heels for him, and if the glares he’s been shooting at me are any indication, he feels the same.”

She glanced across the table at Sebastian and Maeve, and he wasn’t looking in Dylan’s direction. He was all googly-eyed about something Maeve was saying. “You’re nuts. He’s out of Valley Ridge as soon as the wedding’s over.”

“I don’t buy it. He came and talked to me about Hank’s condition.” Dylan shook his head. “He’s not the kind of guy who’d leave his grandfather.”

Caught off guard, Lily blurted, “Absolutely, he is. He told me as much.” She wasn’t sure who she wanted to persuade, Dylan or herself.

Dylan went from affable flirt to cop in a split second. “Just when did he tell you he was leaving?”

“When he arrived in town. He talked about needing to find out who he was. He wasn’t the Seb who left Valley Ridge to join up and he wasn’t Lieutenant Bennington anymore, either.”

“I suspect, since Hank’s diagnosis, that he’ll be figuring himself out here in Valley Ridge. Sebastian Bennington is a man of honor. He wouldn’t walk away and leave his grandfather alone.”

“Hank isn’t alone,” she protested. “He has me.”

“And he’ll have Sebastian, too.” Dylan took a long sip of his beer and eyed her.

The minute Dylan said the words, she knew he was right. How had she missed that? How had she let herself think that Sebastian would walk away from his grandfather when it was obvious that Hank was going to need him?

“This could be a good thing,” Dylan said quietly. “It’s obvious you both have feelings for each other.”

“Which only makes it worse.” If Mr. Insight was right about Sebastian staying—and she knew he was—then maybe he was right about her having feelings for him. More than friendly, trystlike feelings.

Lily felt a sense of panic and wanted to confront Sebastian this very second and tell him they were over.

She’d thought she would have until the wedding. She thought it would be easy. He’d leave town, and by the time he came back to visit, they’d both have put their brief affair behind them.

“Lily—” Dylan started to say, but Mattie and Sophie came and swept her up again. The guys had a big wing-off, seeing who could eat the most wings in three minutes.

Sebastian won. Seeing him there surrounded by friends, his barbecue-sauce-covered face grinning, she knew she’d been beyond stupid. Obviously he was staying. Not only for Hank—though she was sure that was the significant part—but for this. For his friends.

He’d come home damaged. It was more than physical; she knew that early on. He’d said he wasn’t the Seb who’d left Valley Ridge. And he wasn’t. He’d thought he’d need to go away to discover who he was now, but in truth, she didn't think he'd find himself anyplace other than his hometown.

"Lily, are you paying attention?" Sophie asked.

Lily forced a smile. "Sorry. I was lost in the moment. Have I mentioned before that I'm so happy for you?"

"There she is!" Mattie exclaimed. "Our little Miss Romance. The woman who insists that showers are pastel. And that traditions like 'Something old, something new, something borrowed, something blue' be adhered to."

"With a couple as perfect as Sophie and Colton, who'd want to mess with traditions?" Lily joked.

She glanced across the room at Sebastian, who was staring at her, questions in his eyes.

She did her best to smile and quickly took a mouthful of her beer.

She'd break up with him tomorrow, then worry about how to make that work. Great. She could add that to all her other worries. Her mom. Hank. Her booming business.

Still, she'd broken up with men before and managed to stay friendly.

She could do it again.

SEBASTIAN KNEW THAT something was wrong. After Lily had talked to Dylan, she'd started staring at him. Every time he caught her at it, she'd smile at him. But her smile didn't reach her eyes. Those now-familiar wrinkles didn't crinkle in the correct pattern. Sebastian could see it even from across the room. He doubted he'd get any answers from Lily, so he approached Dylan Long. "What were you and Lily talking about?" Sebastian asked as casually as he could manage.

"Just this and that," said Valley Ridge's cop.

"This and that my ass. I didn't need to be part of the conversation to know that my name was mentioned and now something's wrong with Lily. So do me a favor and give me a specific this or that."

"Maybe I said something about the two of you being a couple, and maybe she tried to make out that you weren't, and maybe she said something about you leaving, and maybe I said I didn't see that happening. You're not the sort of guy who'd let Hank deal with stuff on his own."

It was worse than he'd thought. "Maybe if you weren't a cop, I'd deck you right now."

"I knew the minute I said it that I shouldn't have. But honestly, how could she think you'd leave Hank?" Dylan looked well and truly perplexed.

"She needs to believe I'm going. It made me safe. But now that I'm not…" She was going to break up with him. Hell, he'd known it would happen the minute he'd seen her studying him like that. "I planned to let her figure it out for herself."

"I met her mom at the restaurant last week. She seems nice, but skittish. There's a shadow there. Jerry got a bit boisterous, goofing around with Eric and Mike from the pharmacy, and she looked ready to run. She didn't move exactly, but I saw it. It was a reflex—it was fear. Lily and her mom both had it bad, didn't they?"

Sebastian didn't feel as if he could betray Lily's confidence, even if Dylan had correctly guessed Vera's situation, so he said nothing.

That was all the confirmation Dylan needed. He nodded. "I don't need you to reveal anything confidential, but is there a chance Vera's husband will show up?"

"I don't think so, but yeah, I guess he could."

"If you see him, call me. I'll make sure he understands that we don't want him here. We take care of our own here. And they're both ours now."

Sebastian smacked the cop on the shoulder. "Thanks."

"And, Sebastian, really, I'm sorry. Like I said before, I don't know how she could think you'd leave Hank, but in actuality, I don't know how she could think you'd leave her. God, you, Colton and Finn. You've all got it bad this year."

"Finn?" Sebastian asked.

"You haven't noticed that he's in love with Mattie?"

"No. He's been around because of the kids...." The last word faded as he spotted his friend and Mattie. "Oh, hell."

"Yeah. With the three of you off the market, my life is going to suck. Single men in Valley Ridge are becoming more rare with each passing day. Me, Ray, Rich..." Dylan continued to rattle off more names, but Sebastian wasn't listening.

Sebastian was looking at Lily and wondering how he was going to handle things now. He thought he'd ease her into the idea of his staying.

And after that, he'd ease her into the idea that he loved her.

And if he was really lucky, after that, he could convince her that she loved him, too. His cell phone buzzed in his pocket, and when he went to send it to voice mail, he saw it was the diner. "Gotta take this, Dylan. Be right back."

He moved outside where he'd be able to hear. "Hey, Hank. What's up?"

"Sebastian, it's me, Vera. Hank's missing."

Sebastian froze. Not sure what to say, what to do. Lily's mother continued, "I don't know where to look. I don't know the town well enough. One minute he was here with me, Megan and Red, the next, he was gone. He knew that we were supposed to walk home together. Megan ran over to the house to see if he was there, but he's not. She's going to wait there in case he comes home, and I'm here at the diner. Megan said his car is missing. Red's calling in the rest of the employees and they'll start looking. I'm sure we'll find him. There must be a logical explanation. But Lily filled me in on his problems, and even though I've only been here a short time, I've noticed. I hate to cry wolf, but I'd hate even more not to do anything and then..."

She didn't voice exactly what "and then" was, but they both knew it wasn't good.

"I'll be home as soon as I can. Keep me posted."

"Do you need someone to come get you? I know you all drove down together."

"No. I'll hire a cab. It'll be faster. I'll call when I'm on my way."

Calm. Logic. Step by step, he told himself. First step was to get home. Sebastian went back into the bar and found Colton. "I hate to bail on you, but I've got to go."

"What happened?" the groom asked.

"It's Hank. He's missing. He must be around, and someone will find him in a minute and call me, but in case he's not..."

Colton nodded.

"I'll get a cab and call you when I find him."

"Like hell you will." Colton gave a shrill whistle he'd developed when they were kids, and the entire Stag and Drag party went silent and stared at him. "Hank's missing. Get on the party bus—we're heading home to look for him."

Pandemonium broke out. Finn found the server, paid the bill, and everyone else dashed back to the party bus.

"What happened?" Lily asked as she came up to him.

"Your mom called. Red was cooking, and she and Megan were serving customers. And they turned around and he was gone. Megan ran back to the house, but he wasn't there and neither was the car. Damn it, I should have taken away his keys."

"He never drives, Sebastian. Never. I don't think that car's moved from the garage since I moved in. There was no need."

"Obviously there was a need, or he wouldn't be gone now," he snapped. The frustration and anger that had until recently been his constant companions came back in a flash.

"You're right. I'm sorry. We'll find him."

The earlier happy mood had died an instant death.

We'll find him. That was what everybody told him on the party bus. Yet it only seemed to make him more nervous. As the driver sped back to Valley Ridge, they began to make plans. Colton drew out a grid of the town and assigned each of them a section.

Dylan called not only neighboring towns, in case Hank drove there, but also the New York and Pennsylvania State Police forces and gave them a heads-up, as well.

"I feel so helpless," Sebastian heard Dylan say to Colton.

He wanted to jump up and scream, *You think you feel helpless?* But he didn't. Partly because he'd been working at restraining his over-the-top responses, but mainly because Lily was sitting next to him, holding his hand, and she'd tightened hers at his friend's words, as if she knew what Sebastian was thinking.

"We'll find him," she whispered. "It sounds like half the town's out looking for him already. I'm sure someone will spot him soon."

Mattie came over and said that even though her mom was babysitting the kids, her father was going to drive up and down every street in town, looking for Hank's car.

"Don't forget the creek," Sebastian said as another in a long chain of horrible possibilities occurred to him. "The bridge over Park Street…there are pull offs on either side. He could have crashed into the water. Even flipped the car…" He let the sentence fade as the image of his grandfather drowning embedded itself in his mind.

"He's not that confused, Sebastian. He might get mixed up, especially at night, but he's not going to drive his car off the bridge," Lily said.

"What if he went down to one of the beaches?" Sebastian asked. There were docks and piers. Any number of ways a confused old man could end up in Lake Erie.

Sebastian had striven so hard to be all sunshiny rainbows like Pollyanna here, but all he could do for the remainder of the trip was think about the ways Hank could be injured or worse. Sebastian knew that even the most mundane moment could turn to tragedy in a heartbeat.

Everyone seemed to sense his need for quiet.

Lily continued to sit next to him and hold his hand for the entire ride.

And what little comfort he found was there in her grip.

LILY WISHED SHE COULD do more than hold Sebastian's hand on the bus. But she couldn't come up with anything. She speculated where Hank might have gone, but again, drew a blank.

She could practically feel the tension flowing from Sebastian, but he held himself in check. Once the party bus eventually dropped them off at the library, they all drove to the diner and hurried inside what had become command central.

Red greeted them. "Megan's still at your house, Sebastian. And..." He launched into who was where and what progress they had made.

Lily spotted her mother in the kitchen. "I'm sorry you had to deal with this, Mom."

"I'm the one who's sorry, Lily Claire. I've let you down again. I should have watched Hank closer."

"Mom, you weren't here to babysit. This is no one's fault. If I'd been here, I'd have been in the office, and he'd have still left."

"I wish I could do more." Her mother had coffee brewing in every pot and was busy putting out snacks for people who'd been out searching for Hank.

"You're doing a lot, Mom. I'm so glad you're here." She hugged her mom, and as her mother's arms enveloped her, Lily felt safe.

"I want to help. I'll do anything—"

"I know, Mom."

"I feel like I let you down again. All those years..." Her mom went silent.

In the midst of the chaos, Lily spotted Sebastian heading toward the door. She knew he was going out looking. If he hadn't taken off, she would have.

She followed him. "How about another pair of eyes?"

For a moment she thought he would say no, but he nodded and said nothing. He'd been pretty quiet ever since the bus, not that she blamed him.

His cell phone rang and he whipped it out of his pocket, hitting the speaker button. "Colton?"

"I stopped home to get a floodlight and found your grandfather's car parked behind my barn," Colton said. "I can't find him, but how far could he have gone on foot?"

"I'll be right out." Sebastian turned to Lily. "I'll take that pair of eyes."

"Let's take more than mine," she said, running back into the diner and giving everyone the news. "We're moving the search out to Colton's. He found Hank's car, but no Hank yet."

Sebastian was the first in a line of cars driving to the farm north of Five. Lily's eyes were glued to the road on her side of the car, just in case. "We'll find him," she repeated softly, as much because she needed to hear the words as Sebastian did.

They parked by Hank's car, and Colton came down from the house to meet them. "I've been all over the yard and buildings. No sign of him. Finn and Mattie should be here in a few minutes—they were on the far side of town when I called. And Dylan's on his way."

"Let's head to the woods," Sebastian said. "I can't help but worry about the creek. What if he falls in in the dark? There are a few sections that are deep."

Lily voiced her barely formed thought. "I was thinking of way back behind the barn. When we were out here for the picnic, Hank went in that direction with Mickey."

Colton nodded. “Mickey and the girls helped me put up a surprise for Sophie back there.”

“If Hank’s confused, I think he’d head somewhere he’d been recently rather than the woods,” she said.

“But what if he did?” Sebastian barked. “The creek’s not deep, but he’s an old, confused man. And the swimming hole is downstream. He could…”

Colton gave her a look that said, *I’ve got this.* “Seb, I don’t know that he’s ever gone in the woods, much less the swimming hole. If it were you or Finn who was missing out here, that’s where I’d look, but Lily’s right. Hank would go somewhere familiar to him, and other than my yard or house, the only place I know he’s ever been is with Mickey.”

“Fine,” Sebastian said. “We’ll start there and then we’ll move toward the woods.”

“I’ll stay here and whoever arrives first I’ll send to the creek. I’ll ring the bell if someone finds him.” Colton looked at Lily. “That bell can be heard for miles. It’s how we got called into dinner every night.”

With giantlike strides, Sebastian started for the area behind the barn.

“Slow up a bit,” Lily begged as she hurried to keep up.

“I don’t know why he’d go this way,” Sebastian grumbled.

“I don’t, either, but his car was parked by the barn, not back behind the house or closer to the woods. It makes as much sense as anything.” He’d slowed down, but she still had to sprint to match his pace. “What did Colton put back here?”

“Sophie wanted their wedding on his land. On the land where they’re planning to spend their future and raise a family. She'd chosen to have the ceremony under the trees, but he wanted something more, so he built an arbor and he's got viney, flowery stuff on it. It's supposed to bloom in mid-June. He wanted to surprise her."

"He is a perfect guy, isn't he? He knows her so well and would do anything for her. Sophie will love it."

He paused and then said, "I hope so."

"Perfect," she murmured.

Lily was so invested in Sophie and Colton's relationship because she needed a couple to believe in. She needed two people to marry and actually be happy. She thought of Finn and Mattie. She hadn't seen much of them together lately, but she suspected they might be on their way to a happily-ever-after, too.

She looked at the intense man walking next to her and suddenly wished things were different. She wished she could be Mattie or Sophie and build a life with a man. This man. But she knew how it would end. She remembered when she said she'd marry Justin. Panic had swept over her even though she'd pushed it aside and convinced herself she could ignore her past. "They're going to be happy, aren't they?"

"I think so. There will be good times and bad, but yes, I think they'll be happy." He stopped a moment, put his hands on her shoulders and made her face him. "He'd never hit her."

Lily almost laughed at the thought of Colton ever doing anything to hurt Sophie. "Well, obviously. I mean, if I thought he might, I'd never be in the wedding. I'd do whatever I could to stop Sophie, but he's not like that at all."

Sebastian nodded.

"I've seen all kinds of men at their worst, Sebastian.

When they're sick or injured. Joe's dad, for instance. He was in so much pain, and his wife had walked out on him and the kids, but even when he was grumpy with me, I knew he'd never hurt me. I really do know that all men aren't like my father. They don't drink and they don't prey on people who are weaker than they are."

She began walking toward the field again.

"Lily, I'll never hurt you," he said from behind her.

She didn't turn around. "I told you. I know that, too."

"You've trusted me, even when I was at my worst."

She wasn't sure why she'd trusted him at first, but he was right. She had. "I did. I do."

"So when I tell you that—"

She pointed at the gazebo that was visible in the moonlight. "There he is."

She ran toward the figure, or maybe she was running from whatever Sebastian's declaration was going to be. She didn't want to hear it. She didn't want to deal with it. "Hank?" she called.

Sebastian jogged close behind her. He still had a slight limp that was evident when he moved faster than a walk.

"Well, hi, you two," Hank said, as if nothing was wrong. As if they came to Colton's fields on a regular basis.

"Hank, what are you doing out here?" She spoke gently.

"I had a present for Sophie and Colton, but I didn't bring a ladder."

"A ladder?" Sebastian's concern sounded more like anger as he barked out the question.

"Betty and I got married on her father's back porch. All our guests were seated in chairs on the lawn. I know this isn't a porch but when Mickey showed it to me, I remembered. And hanging on the porch, there was a very small set of wind chimes. As Betty and I said our I-do's, they tinkled in the background. Betty told me afterward that it was the fairies blessing our wedding. She's always believed in things like fairies and happy endings, my Betty. I wanted to give that gift to…"

Hank hesitated.

"To Colton and Sophie?" Lily asked.

He sighed. "Yes."

"Hank, you should have let someone know where you were going." Again, Sebastian's worry seemed more like anger.

Lily watched Hank bristle. "I'm not a child," he proclaimed.

"No, you're not," she agreed. "But we love you and you worried us. No one knew where you were, and it's awfully late to be traipsing through fields."

Hank looked up as if he was surprised that it was dark. "What time is it?"

"After eleven."

"I didn't… I wasn't… I found the wind chimes at Quarters, and I thought I'd surprise Colton. I didn't realize it was so late. I only meant to be a minute." Hank was clearly rattled.

Lily hugged him. "It's okay, Hank. We found you and that's all that matters."

"I'd still like to put up the chimes." He reached into his pocket and pulled out a set of chimes that were smaller than her hand. He gave them a shake, and a soft tinkling sound filled the evening air. It seemed fitting among the chirps of crickets and other nighttime insects.

"I bet if we ask Mr. Lieutenant Marine here, he can take care of this."

Sebastian took the chimes and placed them easily on the frame.

"Thank you, Seb," Hank said.

Lily gave Sebastian's hand a small squeeze.

He sighed as if he were physically releasing all his anger. "You're welcome, Hank. Let's get you home."

Sebastian fell into step behind them. Lily could hear him making calls, letting everyone know that Hank was all right.

"He's mad," Hank whispered conspiratorially.

"Only because he was concerned for your safety." She took the older man's hand in her own. "It's okay, Hank. We'll just do our best. We'll get through this."

He nodded, but she didn't think he believed her.

They got back to Colton's house, and Sophie rushed out and hugged Hank, then Lily. "I'm so glad nothing bad happened, Hank."

"I'm fine. I wanted to give you a little surprise on your wedding day."

Sophie smiled. "First Colton's got a surprise for me, now you, Hank? I'm a lucky, lucky lady."

Dylan showed up with a group of folks, and as they all reassured themselves that Hank was indeed all right, they headed back to town.

Lily went to find Sebastian. "Why don't you take Hank home in his car? He has to be exhausted. I'll drive yours to the diner and make sure the place is closed up. I'm also going to make an executive decision—we're all taking the day off tomorrow. I'll post a sign and spread the word. I can't imagine we'd have much business anyway. Half the town was out tonight looking for Hank."

"Okay" was all Sebastian said.

"Listen, I know I don't have any rights and that nothing I say is going to make you feel better right now, but we'll make this work. I read about shoes that have GPS in them. I don't really think Hank's there yet, but we'll get him a pair. That should buy us both a measure of comfort. And we'll—"

She was silenced by Sebastian kissing her long and hard. "You do make me feel better. Just knowing I'm not in this alone makes me feel better. And telling you about..." He held up his left hand. "It's made a difference, too. Colton said something earlier about me wearing my dress blues to the wedding, and I didn't feel the guilt I've lived with since the accident."

The words came out rough, as if they were hard for him to say. Lily got that. There were suddenly things she wanted to say in return, but in the end, she couldn't. "I'll see you when I get home."

He nodded and turned to get Hank.

Lily watched him put his arm around his grandfather, wave goodbye to their friends and get in the car.

Sebastian had come back to Valley Ridge with visible scars. He definitely had more hurdles to overcome, and watching Hank decline would probably be the hardest thing he'd ever done, but she was sure he'd come out on the other side.

She wished she felt as if she would.

What she wanted to say was *I'll be here for you as long as you'll let me.* But the truth of the matter was she didn't know how to say those words. For years she'd told herself that she'd overcome her childhood. She lived life on her own terms and did a job that had meaning.

And yet, she couldn't tell a man who meant the world to her that…well, he meant the world to her.

She watched his car turn south onto the street and head back to Valley Ridge.

She found Sophie and Colton. "Sebastian and Hank are on their way home in his car. I'm taking Sebastian's, but before that, I wanted to tell you both how sorry I am that your party got interrupted."

Sophie hugged her. "Lily, I've been to countless parties in my life, and I can say this with a certain amount of expertise…. Parties are part of a day—they're only a couple of hours. Friends are for life. You, Sebastian and Hank mean more to me and Colton than any party. I know you want everything about my wedding to be perfect. And I love you for wanting that for us. But—" she leaned into her fiancé "—as long as this guy's waiting for me when I walk down the aisle, the wedding will be absolutely perfect."

Lily smiled. "I'll talk to you tomorrow."

She started to walk toward Sebastian's car when Sophie called to her. "Lily, you and Sebastian need to remember that you have friends and we're all here for you two and Hank."

The fact that Sophie paired her with Sebastian should have bothered her.

But it didn't.

She tried to decide how it felt, and despite Sebastian's insistence that she was Webster, the only word that came to mind was…*right.* It felt right being paired with Sebastian Bennington.

LILY PURPOSEFULLY TOOK her time closing the diner. She didn't want to face Sebastian tonight, now that she knew he wasn't leaving Valley Ridge. Maybe she'd always known. But until the words were actually spoken, she'd been able to convince herself otherwise. There was no more lying to herself. No more stalling. When she saw him again, she'd have to break things off and find a way to be friends.

She was almost at the front door of Hank's house when the glider creaked. She should have known. "You didn't have to wait up for me."

"We need to talk. Dylan told me that he told you I was staying."

He patted the seat next to him, but she stood beside the glider. If he touched her she might… Well, she wasn't sure what she might do, but what she might not do was end things between them, and the sooner that was done, the better. "Then I think it's time we called off our…"

"Love affair?"

"No. Tryst. That's a better description. A secret meeting. Only, now we're done meeting."

He got out of the glider. "No. It's not a secret. Half the town knows, and the rest will figure it out when we start dating in earnest."

Lily frowned. "That's not going to happen."

"It is. I'm going to court you, Lily. We can take things as slow as you need to, but we have something too precious to throw away because you're afraid."

"I'm not afraid of anything. I just know what a mess it will become. I tried it with Justin all those years ago. I can't—"

"I love you."

The words hung there and Lily felt that same sense

of panic. She couldn't even begin to formulate a logical answer. "No, you don't."

He reached for her, but she took a quick step back.

"I didn't want to say anything, Lily. Didn't want to push you, but life's too short, so you might as well adjust your reality to the fact that I love you. There's not a damned thing you can do about it."

"You'll get over it. Maybe you and Maeve?"

He laughed then, as if what she'd said was the best joke he'd ever heard. "Lily, haven't you learned anything? Benningtons aren't like that. We love once. And we love with our whole heart. My mother loved my father like that. When he left, he took her everything from her, and there was nothing left for me or for herself. Hank loved my grandmother like that. And I love you."

"So stop."

He started to reach for her again, but put his hands behind his back. "Might as well tell me to stop breathing. That would be easier. Listen, I was going to wait till after the wedding, let you realize I wasn't going."

"You could still go. You wanted to find yourself," she tried.

"I don't need to go anywhere to do that. I've found what I needed right here in Valley Ridge, with you and Hank. The boy I was is gone. The student, the marine…they're gone, too. Not really gone. Those facets are still part of the man I am now. I'm Sebastian Bennington. Loving grandson, diner owner, a possible town-council candidate. All those things define the new me. But number one, I'm the man who loves Lily Claire Paul."

"Don't. I already told you I can't."

"You can't love someone? That's crap, Lily. And kind of cowardly, too. You love. You love so many people.

It's why you're such a great nurse. Medical people speak about needing to distance themselves from patients, from difficult situations, but you couldn't manage it. That's one of the reasons you're here in Valley Ridge. You have patients you can care for long-term. You're the woman who will stay late and hold a baby so a new mom can sleep. You take meals to an injured single dad and his kids—"

"Stop! I'm the girl who never saved her mom. I sat out on a swing and let her be abused."

"You're the daughter who never gave up on her mother," he said softly. "You waited for her to realize she was brave enough to leave. You loved her enough to keep trying. You are so strong. Maybe that's the most important lesson I learned from you. How to be strong. How to take what life deals you and go on in spite of it." His voice dropped to a low whisper. "You can tell me not to love you, Lily, or that you don't love me. But I'm not going anywhere. I'm going to wait for you to realize that you love me, too. Be brave, Lily. Do it for you. You deserve to be happy. I make you happy, Lily, even if you can't see it yet."

He didn't reach for her, but merely leaned down and kissed her, then on he went into the house.

Now that he was no longer there, she slipped into the glider and stared at the door. "I told you not to fall in love with me."

Sebastian was wrong.

She wasn't strong. If she was, she'd chase after him and tell him…

She couldn't voice the words even to herself. Neither could she force herself to get up and go to him.

Instead, she sat on the swing. Alone.

CHAPTER FIFTEEN

THE DAY OF Sophie and Colton's wedding was notable for its blue sky and mild temperature. It was everything anyone could have wished for. Colton's fields were dotted with new corn shoots and lush grapevines, and the grass and trees were that vivid green that marked the beginning of their annual cycle of growth.

In the past two weeks, Lily had striven to put her relationship back on track with Sebastian. She moved into her apartment again and gave her mother the small bedroom while she took the couch. She still went to Hank's each morning for breakfast, and the four of them passed around the paper, sipped their coffee as they ate, while she pretended that Sebastian was a friend. Just some man she once had a brief fling with.

And she pretended it was working, even though she knew it wasn't.

That struck her as odd.

When she broke up with Justin, she'd felt regret. Not that she'd called off the engagement, but that she'd hurt him. He'd been a nice man who didn't deserve that.

She felt regret that she'd hurt Sebastian—but truth was, he didn't seem overly hurt. As a matter of fact, he gave her his piercing looks, and rather than pain, or even anger, she detected a hint of amusement mixed in with a bit of…smugness.

Today was about Colton and Sophie. For the first time since Hank's disappearance, she wasn't going to fret about Sebastian; she was simply going to concentrate on her friends.

"It's absolutely perfect," Lily reminded herself as she looked out Colton's bedroom window at his fields. She knew that soon, she, Sophie and Mattie would be walking over that ridge, where Colton was waiting with Finn and Sebastian at his side. She watched as guests parked along the long drive and took the now quite evident path to the wedding ceremony.

"Nothing's perfect, Lily," Sophie scolded. Though her giant grin belied her words.

"This is darned near close, though," Mattie said.

"Are people arriving?" Sophie asked.

"Most of Valley Ridge has come along your drive. Pretty soon they'll have to park on the road."

Lily turned away from the window and looked at Sophie. "You are beautiful."

"You're a good friend, so you're biased." Sophie checked her appearance in the mirror. "But I will confess I clean up pretty good."

Lily adjusted a few flowers in Sophie's hair. They both watched as Mattie tugged at her dress.

The three of them stood in front of the mirror.

"Soon we'll be helping Mattie put on her wedding dress," Sophie said in a mock whisper to Lily.

"Finn and I..." Mattie huffed a bit. "We're hardly dating, so we're not nearly ready to talk about something like that."

There in the mirror's reflection, Lily saw the truth of it. Mattie was totally in love with Finn. As much as Sophie was with Colton.

"Waltzing Mathilda has finished her wandering," Lily said, happy for both her friends. They both loved such wonderful men.

Sebastian was wonderful, too, a small voice in her head insisted.

Mattie and Sophie moved away from the mirror, but Lily continued to stand there, looking at herself. She tried to ignore what she saw. Just as she ignored the weird skip her heart gave every time Sebastian walked into a room. Just as she ignored the urge to tell him about…everything and anything. She hadn't realized how dependent she'd become on sharing with him. And hearing about his everything and anything in return.

She missed being in his bed, but more than that, she missed him. Period.

But every time she thought about telling him she missed him, she remembered the sense of panic she'd felt when she admitted she couldn't marry Justin. She could recall the exact moment vividly. And the further realization that she never wanted to marry anyone else, either.

But as she studied herself now, she didn't see panic or a woman who looked as if she wanted to hide. She saw in her own face what she'd seen in Mattie's and Sophie's. She saw a woman in love.

"I'll be back in a minute," she said and bolted from the room.

She ran outside, and from the porch, she scanned the crowd. Odds were Sebastian was already at the arbor with Finn and Colton. Then she spotted him by the barn.

As if he could read her mind, he looked toward the house and saw her. She waved to him, beckoning him.

And he didn't need any more of an invitation than that. He started to make his way toward her.

She didn't want to talk to him here, so she walked around the side of the house to Colton's old swing.

Only, it wasn't an old swing anymore. She didn't need to ask to know who'd fixed it.

SEBASTIAN SAW LILY wave at him from the farmhouse porch, then disappear from sight. He knew where she was going.

He left Hank with Lily's mom and followed Lily.

She stood next to the swing, smiling warmly. He thought he knew all her expressions, but he wasn't sure what this one was. "Are you okay?"

"Are you talking to me again?" she asked, still smiling.

"I never stopped talking to you," he said. "What's going on?"

"Sebastian, I..." She hesitated. "I want to be as brave as you. I need to be."

He scoffed, "I'm not brave."

She took his scarred hand in her own. "You are. You had your whole life planned out. You knew the awful risks, yet you went anyway. Joined the marines. Put yourself on the line to do what you thought was right. But that's not how things played out, and so you're here, building yourself a new life. You're helping your grandfather, the entire community. You faced something hard and here you are...doing so much good. Falling in love with me."

"Lily, I—"

"Let me finish," she said. "I need to take all these feelings and put them into words for my own sake as well as yours. I'm humbled by all of you—mom, Hank, you, Sebastian. When I realized I couldn't marry Justin, I assumed I couldn't marry because there was too much fear left from my childhood. But what I've now figured out is that with Justin it wasn't fear. What it was, or rather what it wasn't, was love. I didn't love him. Not like I should have. I loved the idea of him. I loved the idea of his family. But that's not the same thing.

"It's not that I haven't been afraid. It's that I haven't let my fear drive my life, not even in love—though I didn't know that before you."

He knew something of fear. It was what he felt whenever he thought of a life without Lily. But suddenly, he felt hope, not fear. "Are you saying what I think you're saying?"

"I'm saying I lied when I asked you not to fall in love with me. Do. Fall in love with me because..." She took a deep breath. "Because I love you. I'm not sure how it'll be, all of us together, and in Valley Ridge, but it'll be good, Sebastian. We can be good together."

That was all he needed. Sebastian took Lily into his arms and held her tight as he asked, "When did you figure it out? I thought I'd have to wait a lot longer."

"I was standing with Mattie and Sophie upstairs, in the house. I saw their expressions in the mirror...what it looked like to be in love. And when I looked at myself, I saw it there, too. Love. All my jumbled thoughts and emotions fell into place and I knew. But that's not the moment that I fell in love with you. I think it was when you told me what happened, about your injury. When I understood that you trusted me. And even though I wasn't ready to admit that I loved you, I obviously did, because I told you about my past. I told you things I've never told anyone. Because I do love you."

He kissed her then. It wasn't the first time they'd kissed. There had been kisses of greeting, of passion. There had been kisses for comfort.

But this one… This one was all about love.

"Fall in love with me," she repeated.

"It's too late for that," he assured her. "I've been in love with you for a long time."

They stood next to the swing, him in his dress blues, Lily in her blue bridesmaid's dress. They held each other and they didn't say anything because everything that needed to be said had been said. They loved each other.

Sebastian had truly found who he was now, and where he belonged. It wasn't in Valley Ridge, like he'd thought, but rather it was here in Lily's arms.

"Fall in love with me, okay?" she asked. "Just fall in love with me every day."

"That's exactly what I'll do," he promised.

EPILOGUE

SOPHIE ASKED, "Are you okay?" Lily had just returned to Colton's bedroom.

"What happened?" Mattie chimed in.

Lily wanted to tell them about her conversation with Sebastian—she wanted to tell the whole world that she was in love with the man, but this was Sophie's day, so all she said was, "It's a wedding and everything's beautifully decorated and ready. I'm so happy I—"

She was interrupted by a knock on the door.

Mattie's mother came into the room and said, "The minister's arrived, so it's time." She paused to look at each of them. "You girls are so gorgeous."

"They're gorgeous. I'm cleaned up a bit," Mattie teased.

"Gorgeous," her mother declared again as she kissed Mattie's cheek.

Mattie's mom went ahead of them to ask Randy, the guitarist, to begin the processional.

Lily and Mattie flanked Sophie as they walked up the path together.

"Are you nervous?" Mattie asked.

"No." Sophie practically glowed with happiness. "I've got my something old, something new, something borrowed and something blue. How could anything go wrong?" She gave them each a smile as they crested the rise.

Lily wanted to take in every detail. She wanted to remember everything about how the sun reflected on Colton's fields and the woods beyond. She'd worked so hard to help Sophie organize this perfect day.

Mismatched folding chairs holding half of Valley Ridge's population were disguised with Sophie's shades-of-white lace and ribbons. The light breeze sent the ends of the ribbons waving, as if even the chairs were applauding this marriage.

Farther down the aisle, she saw Colton's surprise for Sophie—the pristine arbor that had flowering vines along the sides and above the arch at the top. There were more white roses woven among them.

Lily glanced to her right and saw the guitarist playing. The guests were standing and turning to look back at them.

She spotted her mother and Hank and gave them a small wave.

In the blink of an eye, Lily forgot to take in the rest of the details. She barely registered the people who'd come to share Sophie and Colton's day. All she could do was gaze at Sebastian, waiting by the arbor.

Step.

Pause.

Step.

Pause.

Sebastian in his dress blues.

Sebastian smiling at her.

Sebastian, the man she loved.

She wanted nothing more than to run to his side, but she kept her steady pace.

Step.

Pause.

Step.

Pause.

At the arbor, to Sebastian, she mouthed the words *I love you.*

Lily watched as Mattie joined her and couldn't help but notice that her friend only had eyes for Finn.

Finally, it was Sophie's turn. Sophie's steps were faster than they should have been.

Step.

Step.

Step.

Split-second pause.

Step.

Step.

Step.

As Sophie reached Colton, he reached over and drew out a new, dressier-looking cowboy hat and plopped it on his head, which made Sophie laugh.

They joined hands and faced the minister. Hank's wind chimes sounded in the mild breeze. The blue June sky was brilliant. The faint scent of flowers perfumed the air.

The minister took a deep breath, ready to begin the service in earnest. "Dearly beloved…" A voice from among the beribboned chairs called out, "I object."

There was total silence, then the noise of everyone

turning to stare at a young, blue-haired girl at the back of the bride's side of the aisle. "You can't get married yet! Not when I've worked so hard to find you. No. It's not fair."

* * * * *

Don't miss the exciting conclusion to
A VALLEY RIDGE WEDDING
with Sophie and Colton's own story
coming next month
from Harlequin Superromance!
A WALK DOWN THE AISLE
will be available June 2013
wherever Harlequin books are sold.

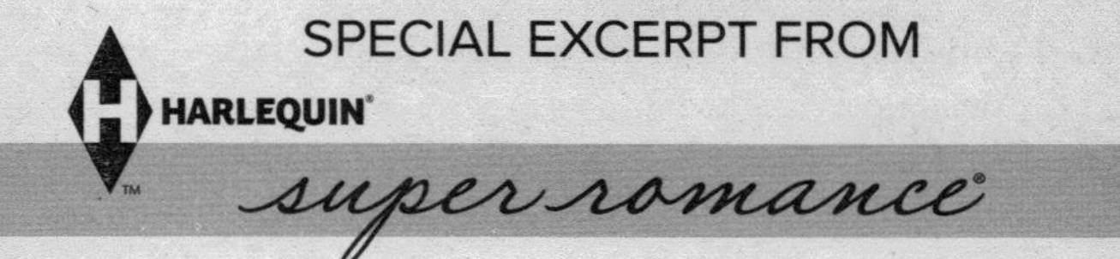

His Uptown Girl

By Liz Talley

It's time for Eleanor Theriot to get back into the dating scene. And now a friend has dared her to chat up the gorgeous guy who's standing across the street! How can she resist that dare? Read on for an exciting excerpt of the upcoming book

She could do this. Taking a deep breath, Eleanor Theriot stepped out of her shop onto Magazine Street. She shut the door behind her, gave it a little tug, then slapped a hand to her forehead and patted her pockets.

Damn, she was a good actress. Anyone watching would definitely think she'd locked herself out.

Hopefully that included Mr. Hunky Painter Dude, whom she intended to ask out. Like on a date.

She started toward him. The closer she got, the hotter—and younger—the guy looked.

This was stupid. He was out of her league.

Too hot for her.

Too young for her.

She needed to abandon this whole ruse. It was dumb to

pretend to be locked out simply to talk to the man. Then he lifted his head and caught her gaze.

Oh, dear Lord. Eyes the color of smoke swept over her. That look wasn't casual or dismissive. Oddly enough, his gaze felt…profound.

Or maybe she needed to drink less coffee. She had to be imagining a connection between them.

Now that she was standing in front of him, though, she had to see this ridiculous plan through. She licked her lips, wishing she'd put on the lip gloss. Not only did she feel stupid, but her lips were bare. Eleanor the Daring was appalled by Eleanor the Unprepared who had shown up in her stead.

"Hey, I'm Dez. Can I help you?" he asked.

You can if you toss me over your shoulder, and…

She didn't say that, of course.

"I'm looking for a screw." Eleanor cringed at what she did say. *So* much worse! "I mean, a *screwdriver.*" *Please let this nightmare end.* "I'm locked out."

Turns out Dez is *not* just a random guy and there's more than attraction pulling these two together! Find out what those connections are in HIS UPTOWN GIRL by Liz Talley, available June 2013 from Harlequin® Superromance®.

HSREXP0513